The Next Witness

KIRSTYN PETRAS

To Rosemarie, who saw the potential
&
Rhiannon, who ensured it was realized

April 2093

Alexander Covington leaned against the metal rail, a flask in his hand. He had left his car parked on the side of the bridge, not bothering with the hazards. At this time of day, who was going to disturb him?

Dawn light peaked over the horizon, casting a pinkish glow on Alexander's skin. He lifted the flask to his lips, the alcohol burning his throat. He wasn't aware of the taste, more so of the way it made his hand stop shaking. His hair had gone almost entirely gray these past months, his jacket hanging off his bones.

"I don't know why you wanted it to be here," he said, speaking towards the sky. "There were so many other places, so many other ways." No one answered him, the sound of a car driving past the only response.

"You know, I thought about writing you a letter," Alexander half-laughed, blinking away the tear forming in the corner of his eye, "like she does. But that seemed too…." He didn't know the word, and he let it go. "I started one, about five times, but anyway." He shook his head. "It would feel like I was saying what she did made sense." He looked down at his fingers clasped around the flask.

Another car whipped by, and he could feel the wind against the back of his neck. He was talking just to say something, and he cleared his throat. He still wasn't sure why he was doing this.

"I know we haven't, we were hard on each other, but," He ran a hand over his face, "You...I think...." He stopped again and took a breath.

"It's not like it matters." He looked over his left shoulder, at the small metal canister by his elbow. "And you had fucked up tastes in friends." He took a smaller swig, before tilting the flask upside down, and letting some of the contents fall into the water below the bridge.

"I'm glad, at least, I think I'm glad, I knew you," he said. "Though I'm still not sure if you deserved better, or if this is too generous."

Alexander opened the canister, to the pile of ashes inside. He stuck his finger in his mouth, and held it out, feeling for the wind. He held the canister out over the side and tilted it so the ashes tipped down towards the river.

He watched as some were carried away by the wind, lost to the currents they could not fight. Alexander tried to hold up the flask once more to the sunlight, but his arm did not want to lift; energy failing to move his limb. He shook his head, hunched his shoulders against the cool morning air, and turned back to his car, away from the water below.

June 2092: I

The music started softly; a guitar and bass playing a mellow tune. Melody paid it little attention, staring blankly out the window. It was open, trying to coax in a non–existent breeze. The summer air was stagnant around her, sticking to her skin, making her lungs feel heavy as they worked to inhale against the humidity.

The boy—she had already forgotten his name—straightened up from the speakers, wiping the remnants of white powder away from the bridge of his nose. He took a step, so he was standing behind her.

"What are you looking at?" he asked, craning his head down so it was all but resting on her shoulder, wrapping an arm around her waist.

"Nothing," Melody sighed, leaning her head against his chest.

"Good." He began kissing up her neck, and she closed her eyes.

The sirens blasted, covering the music. The boy pushed her against the wall as they kissed. She started unbuttoning his shirt, focusing on his lips, his chest, anything to block out the blaring sound outside.

The inhuman voice: *"Curfew is in effect. Curfew is in effect."*

Melody placed her hands on the boy's shoulders, steering him towards the bed. He fell back, and they broke apart as she removed her shirt. Her skin shone in the light of the window, a bead of sweat running between her breasts. He reached for her, his hands pulling her on top of him, her mouth trailing down to his chest. His lips hovered at her ear, whispering nonsense words of desire.

The siren burst through the night, serving a final warning shot. The boy flipped Melody over and started to remove his jeans. He looked into her face, a slightly vacant smile on his lips. He started to kiss her neck again. The noise outside was gone. All she could feel was the steady thrum of music, her breathing, his lips, and his teeth on her skin. She reveled in the near silence, wrapping one hand into his hair, the other digging its nails into his back. She relaxed into his arms, letting herself drift, until the sound of screaming pierced the air.

"No, no! I'm just going right there, I'm sorry!" The man outside screamed again, his pain audible to anyone on the block. Melody tensed underneath the boy's body, her eyes flickering open, looking towards the window.

"What's wrong?" He asked, leaning back to look at her.

Melody grimaced, but let her hand linger on his back. "Bit of a mood killer, don't you think?"

"Oh, yeah." He leaned over her towards the bedside table, picked up the remote, and aimed it at the speakers. The volume of the music rose, the bass increasing, and he tossed the remote aside. "There," and he leaned down towards her again. She closed her eyes and focused on him, her heartbeat, and the feel of him around her. She hardly even noticed when the screaming faded away.

———————

4

The clock was ticking on the wall, the second hand moving in time with the dull thud in the front of Melody's head. The clicking of Lucy's pen had joined about three minutes ago, every other 'tick' matching with the retracting or emerging pen tip. Melody stared at the document open on her computer, the words against the translucent glass screen blending into a cacophony of nonsense that made her brain feel too large for her skull. She couldn't even blame it on a hangover. It was just the morbidity of this assignment.

Her phone had rung almost the second curfew was lifted, a frantic Lucy on the other side already scrambling to sort out the budget proposal changes that their boss, Senator Arshem, was submitting to the Governmental Affairs committee.

"And we still have to get that speech ready for the amendment hearing and he sent it all to me at 2AM and asked why it wasn't done and—"

Melody had been leaning on her elbow in the boy's bed, one eye squinting to look out the window and see dawn light spilling into the room. She wasn't even sure what part of town she was in, and now she had to get her ass to Capitol Hill.

"Okay, okay," she'd said, her voice still groggy with sleep. She looked to make sure the boy was still sleeping, before lifting the covers off herself and beginning to pick up various articles of clothing. "I'm on my way."

"Thanks, Mel," Lucy sounded like she was about to cry, "Just, hurry, please?"

"Yeah," Melody had hung up the phone, grabbing her things as quickly and as quietly as she could. She hadn't wanted him waking up. Didn't want him asking where she was going or pretending to care. She'd slipped out of the bedroom and to the bathroom, looking around at the shower desperately in need of a clean. She'd found a towel on the back of the door, and some

5

soap on the edge of the tub. It was not ideal, she'd thought, giving the towel a questioning sniff, but going into work with last night's makeup under her eyes was also not an option. And that was that.

Now she was sitting at her desk with her long blonde hair in a still-damp braid, wearing yesterday's clothes, which, thankfully, had at least included a blazer as her jacket. Clearly not how she had envisioned the morning going.

Her original plan was to sneak off after curfew, though at a slightly more reasonable hour, go home, get ready, and meet Leo for breakfast. Leo's father, Greg, worked as a grocery store manager, and was able to sneak primo products away from time to time. Leo had been excited that the latest batch of Canadian maple syrup had cleared customs (i.e., hadn't all been taken by border patrol, or state patrols between the border and D.C.) and he was dead set on making a giant pancake breakfast for the family. And now she was going to have to show up hours late smelling like sandalwood and wrinkled clothes with bags under her eyes and a pounding headache that would not be solved by Leo entering overbearing-big-brother-mode and telling her she was a...

Well. He'd never actually *said* the word.

The speech was still staring at her, and she took a deep breath, trying to focus. A carved eagle above the clock stared down at her with beady eyes, cameras capturing every move in the office. If she was stuck like this, she'd at least move her mouse around occasionally, pretend to type, something to make it look like she was being productive.

But we have spent too many of our resources investigating Party children who wish to deviate from this pattern, who believe they deserve special training in order to switch branches. Too much time on those who demand special treatment for their own inadequacies and failures as American citizens.

We as a great nation ought not to be measured by the whining of those who do not understand how lucky they are to be separated from their counterparts by their inherited party status.

Redundant motherfucker, Melody thought, erasing some of the sentences. The speech was for the hearing for Senator Arshem's latest amendment on the Party Kids system. Officially known as the Government Professional Continuation Strategy, the current law ensured that any child born to a parent of Party status was automatically a Party member as well, and should that parent work in any government capacity, their child would attend training upon graduating high school to join the same branch of government as their parent in whatever capacity they chose. However, they could switch branches if they went through extra training and proved themselves capable. Arshem, as far as Melody knew, had never had a problem with the system prior to her hiring. But now that he was stuck with a Party Kid who had switched, well, he didn't want anyone questioning just how loyal he was to Our Dear Jameson and his country.

So Melody, on what was supposed to be her day off, was now editing a speech all about how much of a bitch she, and others like her, were, while waiting for Leo to berate her for fucking a stranger, and listening to Lucy's goddamn pen clicking on and on and...

"Lucy, please, stop," she hissed through gritted teeth at Lucy, head snapping to the side. Lucy jumped about a foot in the air, frantically glanced up at the eagle camera, and then back to Melody.

"Sorry," she mouthed, her big brown puppy dog eyes growing wide with apology, dropping the pen onto her desk.

Melody sighed, closing her eyes briefly. "It's fine," she whispered, and deleted a few more words on the document in front of her.

The sound of footsteps could be heard from the other side of the large oak doors, and Melody immediately stood up and moved to the wall, pressing herself against it as though she could disappear into the shadows.

"Well of course I'm not underestimating the problem, I'm saying that those are the numbers I can realistically attempt for." Arshem entered the office with two men trailing behind him. One looked to be a bit older than Melody, maybe late twenties, with shaggy brown hair, wearing a walnut-colored leather jacket with a policeman's badge hanging by a chain around his neck. The other looked about a decade older than that, with slicked back dark hair, a light gray suit, and shiny black tie.

"I understand that but—"

"I know, Detective, that you have been reviewing these budgeting concerns for quite some time, but I can't imagine what the Chief thinks I can do for you. We're strung up tight enough as is before you come in asking about what should be a state-level issue."

"But—" The detective tried again, but Arshem cut him off.

"Ah, Lucy," he said, turning to her desk, "Do you have the budgets ready?"

"Yes sir," she said quickly, pressing a button and immediately they could hear the printer whirring behind her.

"And... Karsh? What are you doing here?"

"Working on the speech for the amendment hearing, sir," Melody looked towards his chest, her head slightly bowed.

"I told Lucy to do that," Arshem said, frowning at her. "You weren't supposed to be in today."

"Lucy asked me for a hand, it's no trouble—"

"I didn't say it was trouble for you. Give it to Lucy when you're done. She needs to review it before I see it." Melody nodded, already tuning him out. If she gave Lucy everything Arshem asked her to, Lucy would have died from exhaustion months ago. She was barely hanging on as it was. Arshem gestured to the two men behind him. "Detective Covington, Officer Madden, these are my aides Lucy Moore and Melody Karsh." Melody barely acknowledged them, already sliding back towards her chair to sit down the second Arshem was out of the room.

"Karsh, since you're here, get some coffee for us," Arshem snapped at her. Melody nodded at no one in particular and left to get the pot. Down the hall, to the right, she entered the small station room aides used for exactly this task. Melody looked through the cabinets and found one of the nicer trays, silver carafe, white porcelain cups and saucers, and little spoons. While she waited for the coffee to brew, she set the little bowls of sugar and artificial creamer, before pouring the coffee into the carafe, and set some shortbread cookies on a plate. Tray set, she carefully walked back to Arshem's office, knocked lightly twice, and entered.

She made to walk in and out, setting the tray down as quickly as was safe. Covington and Arshem didn't pause their conversation, continuing on about rising crime rates or something similar, she couldn't quite tell. Officer Madden was already reaching for a cup as she straightened back up. He looked up at her, his green eyes meeting her blue ones, and raised the cup slightly towards her, a silent gesture of thanks. She gave him a quick nod and turned back around.

Melody closed the door to the office behind her and leaned against it, letting out a sigh, before returning to her chair.

Lucy inched her chair a few inches towards Melody, turning slightly. "Melody,"

Melody gave her a quick look.

"You okay?"

She nodded, her eyes back on the screen.

"Do you know them?" Lucy asked, head tilting back towards Arshem's door. Melody shook her head. "Seemed kind of…harsh, I guess." Lucy frowned. Melody nodded.

"Yeah, a little," The words on the screen were blurring again, and she shut her eyes tight, squeezing the lids together. She opened them, willing herself to focus, to get through the next however many pages, as quickly as possible.

Melody knocked on Leo's door, already picturing the exasperated look that would greet her on the other side. He opened the door after the third knock. His face, young for a twenty-one-year-old, had fallen from a bright smile into the scowl he reserved only for her. She could spot a few bits of egg in his short, untidy brown hair. He wasn't all that much taller than her, but in this instance, the few inches made her feel like he was towering over her. He raised his eyebrows, taking in messy, now quite frizzy, braid, her wrinkled clothes, the makeup free face.

"I'm—"

"Save it," he sighed. "Come in." He held open the door for her and she slid past him. The smell of pancakes greeted her, stacked up in a pan. The rest of the white and baby blue kitchen had been destroyed by his cooking. A stack of fried eggs sat on a plate. Dishes were piled everywhere: batter and eggshells littered the countertops. She reached up to his hair and pulled out the bits of food.

"You didn't finish cooking yet?"

"I didn't know how long you'd be," he shrugged, moving back to the stove where a couple pancakes sat bubbling in the pan, just waiting to be flipped. "Besides, it's been too hot, I've been

10

doing it in bursts."

"Sure," she sat down at the table. "Where are your parents? I thought they were joining us?"

"Dad had the afternoon shift, so I made him something earlier. But Mom has been working on campus all day too."

"Liz went in on a Saturday?" Liz was an art history professor at American University. If she was working during the weekend, it was grading papers in her armchair with a gallon of coffee by her side.

"Yeah, Mom wanted to switch some of her lesson plans around, so they have to approve it before Monday," he explained, "American added a course to her schedule two weeks before the semester started. They didn't approve the old instructor's syllabus and fired him. So, she's basically been building the class along week by week."

"That sucks."

"Oh yeah. We'll have wine ready for her when she comes home." Leo placed some pancakes and eggs on a plate and handed it to Melody, who was distracted from his story by the glass bottle of syrup sitting on the table.

"Oh wow, you actually did get it!"

Leo grinned, "Dad managed to sneak it out yesterday before it went on the shelves."

Melody took the bottle and poured a tiny amount onto the plate. She then picked up the plastic bottle of imitation syrup and poured a much larger amount. She cut a piece off of a pancake and combined the two together on the bite. She smiled at him, as he did the same.

He stared at her, hard for a moment. She was pretty sure if he could, he'd be sniffing her like a bomb sniffing dog. "Sean again?"

Melody shook her head. "Don't know his name. Ryan, maybe?"

"You know you're being stupid."

"I've made a note of it." They looked at each other across the table.

"Fine," he sighed, taking a large bite.

"Fine," she echoed, staring down at her plate. They'd had this talk before; the conversation was as repetitive and familiar as a game of catch, and if they let it continue, never ended in a pleasant manner. And she was really, really not in the mood for his moral righteousness.

Leo took a breath and cut another piece of pancake off. "So, how was work?"

Melody felt some of the tension in her shoulder release. "Sooner this fucking hearing is over, the better. Maybe then he'll stop trying to convince everyone he's not to blame for getting stuck with the devil's daughter."

Leo snorted. "Yeah, I was going to say, those horns are really protruding today."

Melody stuck her tongue out at him,

"Mature," he laughed.

"Extremely. Always." Melody took another bite of food, the sweetness of the syrup lingering on her tongue.

"I'm honestly surprised that Arshem is letting you in the room for that hearing, that's he's letting you touch any of it."

"Lucy made the point that if I'm in the room, if he can say I've been helping, it looks like I agree with it. It's pointless, the whole thing is going to take five minutes for the group of them to stroke themselves and say 'patriotism' as they turn an eagle whiter."

"I'm sorry, Mel. You'll stick around tonight, right? We'll watch a movie or something, snag some of Mom's wine. It'll be fun."

"Raincheck? I'm going out tonight."

"Again?" Leo asked, his eyebrows were creeping upwards once more. "Whatever. Be careful, okay?"

"Oh, come on, at least add a 'Have fun,' first."

"If I thought you did it for fun, I wouldn't be concerned."

Melody set her jaw, staring down at her plate, her fork picking at the food. Leo finished his meal in a similar silence, and Melody stood up to pick up her bag with half her pancakes untouched.

"Melody," He sounded exasperated, watching her shove her sunglasses back on. "I'm just saying you need to take a night off. What, I can't tell you what I think anymore?"

She cast him one last glance but said nothing, shutting the door a little too loudly behind her.

———————

"Thanks," said Melody, downing the whiskey in one. It burned her throat slightly, but it warmed her stomach in just the right way. Before she could ask, Rose, her favorite bartender at Black Thorn, grabbed the glass back and poured her another.

"You looked like you needed it." Rose grinned. "So, what's the plan? Staying up here and attempting to lure with your charm?"

"Am I not always charming?" Melody asked, and Rose laughed. She took a much smaller sip and looked around, taking in the crowd. The bar wasn't too busy yet, but it was Saturday evening and sure to fill up soon. She wasn't sure if she was in the mood for it tonight. Maybe she should've just stayed in for a glass of wine with Leo. "Actually, I'm meeting someone in a bit."

"Ah, okay. Let me know when you need more."

13

"Will do," Melody smiled and slid off the barstool, walking over to a table closer to the entrance to the bar. She did like this spot. It was close to home, and she'd been coming here so long that they never bothered to check her ID anymore.

She leaned against the leather of her seat and checked her phone. Sean was running late, as he often did. On cue, her phone started vibrating.

"Hello?"

"Hey, Sam, what's up?" Samantha, the name written on her fake ID. No one here had ever called her Melody.

"Nothing, just sitting at Black Thorn. I'm towards the front when you get here."

"Cool. Look, I know this probably isn't what you had in mind, but can a couple of my friends join us?" Sean's voice had lowered, and she suspected they were nearby, *"One of them, he's been having a really tough time at work, and I mean, you didn't want us, I mean, we're—"*

"No, I get it. Yeah, it'll be fine. But we can go a bit early then, yeah? Not really up for that much socializing, you know?"

"Yeah, all good. We'll just be another minute."

"Cool, see you in a bit." Melody sighed. It was true. She didn't exactly let these guys say that they were dating (mostly because she didn't consider it dating), and she didn't like others being brought into it. It tended to complicate matters. More people to lie to: fake names, fake pasts, all of it. She considered just getting up and leaving, but she didn't want to risk running into them on the way out. Besides, she did want his company tonight.

Sean came in, immediately spotted her, and smiled. As he waved to the people coming in behind him, Melody felt her chest constrict. There were very few times in her life where she'd thought to herself, so help me, Leo was right. But watching Officer

Madden walk into the bar next to Sean broke the top five, easy.

Madden brushed his hair out of his eyes, looking around the bar, as another guy Melody had never seen took the seat diagonal to her. Sean came around to her side of the table and gave her a quick kiss on the cheek.

Madden met Melody's eyes for the briefest of moments before saying, "Looks like she's already ahead of us. I need a beer. Derek, what about you?"

"Oh same," said the other boy. "Sean?"

"Yeah, oh, Sam, this is Logan, and Derek. Guys, this is Sam." Sean said, gesturing to Officer Madden and then the other boy. She focused her attention on Derek, and she forced herself to return his smile. Fear pulsed through her as she gave Logan a brief half glance of acknowledgment.

"I'll go get this round," Sean said, noticing nothing. "You need anything?" He asked Melody, who shook her head. Derek stood too, offering to help him carry. Melody opened her mouth to say something, but closed it again, instead focusing on her drink, and avoiding Logan's eyes.

"So, you're the Sam I've been hearing about?" Logan asked. She barely nodded.

"The 23-year-old accountant he met oh...three months ago?" he asked, and she nodded.

"I happen to know Arshem's assistants are 25 and 20." He said, tilting his head to the side. "So, I'm guessing you've got a damn good fake."

She knew she had to respond, but it felt like the words were stuck in the back of her throat.

"Are you going to speak?" she thought she heard laughter in his voice. She managed to look up at him.

15

"If you're going to arrest me, you might want to do it now, before he wastes his money," she said quietly.

The officer frowned, scratching a spot on his chin. "Why Sam?"

She shrugged.

"That's not an answer." His voice was colder, and she looked away again, checking that Sean and Derek were still waiting at the bar.

"I didn't choose it," she said.

"Let me see it," he demanded.

She reached into her purse and pulled out her wallet. She opened the zipper pocket, pulled out the fake ID, and passed it to him. He raised an eyebrow.

"I've never seen one this good." He murmured. He made no gesture to hand it back. She hadn't expected him to.

"I'm not telling you where it came from," she said, shoving her wallet back into her bag. She wasn't sure what he was doing, why he wasn't immediately taking her in.

"I won't ask you to." He stared at her. "Though I am curious why, as a Party member, you'd risk this. You know it's an offense to lie about Party status. If anyone else found that, investigation for espionage and treason would be the least of your concerns."

"Anyone else?" She couldn't keep the hope out of her voice. More questions were forming in her mind, but hearing the others come back silenced them. Sean handed Logan his drink.

"Thanks," Logan said, as though nothing odd had just happened. "Appreciate it."

"Yeah, well, after the week you've had." Sean sighed.

"Yeah, what's been happening? All I heard was Covington's been on your ass," Derek said.

"Well, that's pretty much all there is to it. He's still pissed he's got some 'junior' to take care of when he's just made Detective. Wants to deal with big cases, to cut his teeth. But they stuck him with training me." Logan sighed. "And he's basically just been given research assignments and begging Congress for more money since he was promoted. Judicial branch bitch work, essentially, most of which he keeps trying to filter down to me."

Derek sighed, "You knew this could happen when you went for Judicial, though."

"Logan's a Party Kid," Sean explained, in response to Melody's quizzical look.

"Yeah, his parents were in Executive." Derek said, "But he went for Judicial instead."

"Ah," she said before taking another sip. She wasn't sure how people outside of the Party system normally reacted to that information. She didn't want to risk too strong or weak of a reaction. Drinking more seemed easiest.

"You had a meeting on the Hill today, didn't you?" Sean asked. "How'd that go?"

Logan let out a snort. "Yeah, so Senator Arshem, the guy we were meeting with today, is on the Governmental Affairs and Crime and Terrorism committees. He said that if Covington helped him to do some 'research' for this bill he's proposing, he'd lobby Crime and Terrorism for D.C. getting some more money from the federal budget. I sincerely doubt he's going to do it, but our captain told Covington to agree and that's the end of it." He met Melody's gaze out of the corner of his eye and continued, "Arshem's bill would take out the option for Party Kids to switch branches. One of his assistants switched. Her dad was in Judicial. Arshem fucking hates her." He let out a half laugh and took a large sip of his drink.

17

"Wait, wait," Derek looked confused, "Is he having you 'research' his assistant?"

Melody chose not to look at Logan, instead casting Sean a quick glance as his hand rested on her thigh.

"No, not yet, anyway." Logan said, "He's just having Covington get him whatever stats he can about Party Kids who switch. He's afraid if his assistant is arrested, it'll look bad on him for not catching her himself. So, we're leaving her alone."

Melody didn't dare let out of the sigh of relief she desperately wanted to, instead taking a long sip of whiskey.

"You know, I do need another," she said. "I'll be right back." She stood up from the table, and walked quickly over to the bar, catching Rose's eye. In far too little time, she was making her way back to sit beside Sean and was more than a little annoyed to hear they were still talking about the amendment hearing. She'd had more than enough of it today. She looked up at Sean and leaned in closer to his ear. A few whispered words, and his fingers were trailing towards her inner thigh.

"Soon," he said quietly. "Very soon."

She gave him a smile, trying to tune out Derek, who for goodness knew what reason, was still talking.

"What's even the point of that bill?" Derek frowned, "If it's already such a bitch to switch branches, there can't be too many people who'd even want to try. Why take away the option?"

"Derek—"

"No, I'm serious! Why be such an asshole about it? Does he really think that's how the government is being infected? Kids trying to do *more* work?"

"Derek!" Sean hissed, but Derek wasn't listening. Melody's nerves were already on edge, and they couldn't risk any more

18

attention being brought to their table. She caught the gaze of one man looking directly at them. He looked away when she made eye contact, but she knew he was still listening.

"This fucking system, getting all these Party Kids to sell their souls before they're even born—"

But Logan kicked Derek under the table, finally silencing him. Sean scowled, staring daggers at Derek. Melody cleared her throat and tried to tilt her head towards the man listening.

Derek's face grew slightly red. He spoke quickly and a bit more loudly. "I'm sure it's all in the best interest. President Jamison is a visionary in that sense—"

"Damn it if that isn't true!" said a different man at the next table, raising his glass.

Logan copied him, and began to yell, "TO THE PRESIDENT, TO THE STARS AND STRIPES."

Everyone began to stand, and shout along with him, "TO THE EAGLE, AND THE LAND!" And everyone drank as one.

Melody relaxed a bit as the other man settled comfortably back into his seat. She looked over at Derek who was gulping down his drink. Logan was pointedly avoiding her gaze as well. Sean still glared at Derek, and Melody excused herself to the bathroom to escape the awkwardness of the table.

———

"You good?" Sean asked her as she lay back against his pillows staring at the ceiling. He was leaning against the window, rolling himself a cigarette.

"What was up with Derek?" She asked.

"Nothing," he said bluntly.

"Yes, Logan started the toast out of sheer patriotism, not to help cover his friend's ass."

Sean snorted at her sarcastic tone but wouldn't meet her gaze. "He's got…"

"Got what?"

"Look, we don't really talk about it, but we don't shut him down either unless…" There was something on the tip of his tongue, and she knew she could probably pry it out of him if she tried. She felt he liked her enough to tell her his thoughts, but she didn't like to think where the conversation could lead, if she could stay in character, or how she'd start digging into it. Melody decided to let the silence hang in case he felt like saying anything else. Eventually, he continued, "His grandfather was alive, when, you know, the War happened."

He fumbled with the cigarette, the cream of the paper contrasting with the darkness of his skin. She stared at his fingers as they tried to roll the paper and not lose the tobacco. She held out her hand to him and he placed it in her palm. His eyes focused on her tongue as it traced along the edge of the paper before she motioned for him to continue speaking.

"I guess, well, he didn't really talk to Derek—he was smart enough not to. But, it seems he let things slip out here and there, and it got into Derek's kid brain. Derek's usually smart enough to not talk about it in front of people. And sometimes…" Sean paled, and she could see fear flit across his eyes. She handed him back the cigarette, but he didn't immediately light it. He held it up to his mouth and shook his head. He placed the cigarette in the ashtray on the windowsill and sat back on the bed beside her. His arm wrapped around her shoulder, his thumb rubbing a circle on her skin. "I don't know, the guy's an idiot. Besides, I can think of something I'd much rather be doing than talking about him." He bent down to kiss her, and she closed her eyes and let him.

The buzzer sounding in the morning was nothing short of a foghorn in her ears. Melody picked herself up from the couch, knocking over a bottle in the process. The sound of it smashing did nothing to help her head. "Oh, fuck off," she muttered as the buzzer screeched through the apartment again. She stumbled to the phone and grabbed it in a frantic attempt to stop the noise. "What?" She hissed.

"Melody, open the damn door." It was Leo.

"No."

"Open it or I will just keep pressing the buzzer."

"I hope you die," she said as she pressed the button to let him in. She unlocked the apartment door and then collapsed onto the sofa again.

Leo shut the door gently behind him when he came in, bringing the lovely smell of coffee with him. He crept to the couch and placed the cup on the coffee table in front of her, letting the scent waft to her nose.

"You going to tell me what happened?" He asked. She made an incoherent grunting sound.

"You know I shouldn't be nice to you. You're supposed to text me after you go out that you're alive. I had to call your office, and Lucy told me that you'd called out today."

"Yeah well, they took my Saturday."

"You never call out sick. What's going on?"

"I couldn't go back to the office yet."

"Why?"

"It's complicated." She pulled a pillow over her head and rolled over.

"You know I'm just going to stay here until you talk."

21

"Unfortunately, yeah, I do."

"How bad?" He asked. Melody shrugged, though the gesture lost most of its effect, hidden by the cushion.

"That doesn't answer the question." He pulled the pillow away and glared down at her.

"A detective and his junior came into the office Saturday to meet with Arshem. Was introduced to them. Turned out the officer is friends with Sean. The officer and this other guy, another friend, tagged along for drinks. He knew my name wasn't Sam—took my ID. He didn't out me, but he knows something's up. Him and his boss are working with Arshem doing research on the Party Kids amendment; Arshem had told them to leave me alone, but who knows if they listened to him, or if Arshem will change his mind. So yes, I've been hiding. Happy?"

"No, you idiot, I am not happy." Leo grabbed her arm and pulled her upright. "So instead of calling me so we could sort this out, you spent the entire night drinking? You know that affects me too? Not to mention my mom and dad. What were you thinking?"

"I did not spend the entire night drinking." She wrenched her arm away from him, "I didn't get any sleep. I cleared out the apartment of all booze, hid Mom's letters, then was trying to take a nap when you called. I've been trying not to contact anyone. I don't want to be dragging anyone else into this mess in case they had someone watching the place."

"Oh," he said, deflating. He looked down at the ground, at the broken bottle on the floor. "What's this then?" He pointed an accusatory finger at the ground.

"It was juice, you asshole." She practically jumped off the couch and stalked into the kitchen, digging under the sink for a pan to sweep it into.

"Ah. Okay. Look, Mel—"

"Just go," she snapped.

"No, look—"

"No, you 'look.' I am not dealing with you accusing me or yelling at me about this or any of it right now, okay? I was going to check in in a few days, after they'd had plenty of time to decide whether or not to go pounding down my door. So, if all you're going to do is condescend to me about things I already know, you can just fuck right off, Leo." She knelt down and started to sweep the pieces of glass into the pan.

He didn't move for a few moments, but then spoke again. "Melody, listen—"

She glared up at him, her look making him stop mid-sentence.

"Go," she said again, and turned her gaze back to the floor. He waited another moment, but when it became clear she had nothing more to say, he started for the door.

She dropped the dustpan and sat down on the couch. She pulled her legs to her chest and pressed her head to her knees. She closed her eyes, forcing herself to breathe. She felt herself calm down, her heart rate slow, and her breathing return to normal. She let herself linger there—safe for the moment—before returning to the mess.

It was true, that she had gotten rid of all the booze bottles during the night. She'd left Sean's apartment as soon as curfew had ended, and she'd come back to pace around the apartment. She tried to pour herself a drink, but her hands shook so badly the bottle had fallen and smashed. She'd stared into the sink, watching her blood swirl in with the brown liquid down the drain. After wrapping up the cut, she'd thrown everything away. Surely, if the cops came for her, any evidence against her found in the house

23

would just make it worse. Underage drinking wasn't a major crime, but it wouldn't exactly help her case.

The real problem was the letters. Letters that would get her charged with treason and who knew what else, but that she couldn't bring herself to destroy. Letters that had now been carefully hidden in files, in manuals, under floorboards, in suitcases, anywhere someone might miss them until she could move them to Liz's library.

Melody threw out the pieces of the juice bottle and sank onto the sofa. She'd forgotten about the coffee Leo had brought and saw the bag sitting beside it. She peeked inside and saw a chocolate muffin. The gesture made her want to laugh and cry at the same time. She took a long sip of the coffee, before setting it back on the table and picking up the remote. She flicked through the channels listlessly, settling on a cooking show. Her eyelids began to droop.

The buzzer ringing wasn't quite as painful the second time around. Melody woke up to a near pitch-black apartment and looked around blearily, trying to sort out what was happening. The buzzer sounded again, and she stumbled off the couch and towards the door.

"Hello?" she asked.

"Melody, it's me. Let me in, please." She heard Liz's voice through the intercom. She immediately pushed the button to give her access and turned on the lights. She frowned, looking at the now cold coffee on the table, and was throwing it down the sink when she heard Liz knocking. She tossed the cup into the trashcan and opened the door.

"Hi," Melody said, standing to the side to let her in.

"You look terrible," Liz said bluntly, turning on the air conditioning unit. Melody let out a small sigh of relief as the cool air blasted through the sweltering apartment.

"Yeah, I'd assume so," Melody said, sitting back on the couch.

"Leo told me what happened."

"Yeah," Melody looked guiltily down at the floor.

"Melody, give the boy a break. He's an idiot. I know that better than anyone. I tried to raise him to be smarter than that, but what can I say? He's as tactless as his father."

"I know. I'll call him later."

"Good. Anyway, I mostly came to give you this. Leo said you'd need a new one," she reached into her purse and pulled out a card. She handed it to Melody, who took it and looked it over.

"Catrina Allen?"

"We weren't going to give you the same name, were we?"

"Thanks, Liz."

"Don't mention it. Keep it safe." She planted herself firmly on a chair. Her short brown hair fell over her right shoulder, and she set her too–thin arms on the armrests, giving Melody a piercing look. "Now, what do you think the situation is?"

Melody ran her fingers through her hair. "Honestly, I'm not too sure." She told Liz the story and everything it seemed Logan had been trying to tell her. "It was that last guy, though, Derek. I could see it; Logan and Sean were both trying to protect him. He didn't seem exactly…"

"Happy?"

"Exactly. Derek seemed like he was going to talk more, and not favorably, about the Party system. He clearly felt bad that Logan was taking shit for not going into the same branch as his parents. But—"

"Were you overheard?" Liz looked concerned.

"Kind of. When he started really going for it this one guy at the next table started listening in, and we all tried to shut him up. Derek finally caught on and changed tact, saying Jamison was a visionary, and Logan started the toast."

"Good call." Liz nodded. "So then what happened?"

"Well, I asked Sean about it that night, and all he said was that Derek has ideas, and then he tried to stop the conversation. But I think there's more to it than that."

"What makes you say that?"

"Logan's a cop, and Sean's had family arrested and killed before. It can't just be that Derek is only one of them who doesn't like what's going on. Otherwise, Logan would have arrested me straight away, especially if he thought it would get his boss off his back."

"You sure about that? It wasn't just that he didn't want to arrest you in front of Sean? It sounds like Sean is getting pretty attached."

Melody scrunched her nose. "I've made it clear to Sean that there's a firm limit to what I want from him. So, I would hope not. I don't understand why he let those guys tag along yesterday anyway."

"Maybe he was trying to find an excuse for you to meet his friends?"

"Don't tell me that."

Liz smiled softly at her as Melody lay her head on the side of the couch, then said seriously. "I think you should make contact again."

"What?"

"With Logan. Get his story. See what he wants, if he wants

anything. We need to make sure we're safe."

"You think that'll be safe within itself?"

"Not particularly, but they haven't torn down your door yet. And, just in case, you know the plan."

"Yeah, I do, and speaking of, I have some things for your library."

Liz nodded, "Yeah, Leo mentioned that as well." She waited patiently while Melody collected all the letters from their hiding spaces, wrapped them in brown paper, and stuck them in the bottom of a grocery bag. She opened the fridge and frowned at the bare contents before placing an expired carton of milk and a bag of lettuce on top of them.

"Good." Liz said, taking the bag, "I'll see you tomorrow for dinner."

"I wasn't planning on—"

"I'll see you tomorrow for dinner!" She waved over her shoulder, and Melody managed to crack a smile.

"Of course."

Liz closed the door behind her, and Melody looked back at the card. Her picture was there, the same one from a year ago, the one that had been taken almost as soon as she'd gotten back from Quantico. She knew Liz's contacts worked fast, but she was still surprised. She suspected that Liz had always had more than one, just in case. Almost unconsciously, she turned back to the TV, changing it over to the news.

"And today, President Jamison, in a meeting with his Cabinet, discussed the distribution of funds to the reconstruction projects of Chicago and Boston," the reporter began, and Melody changed it to a show she'd seen before, a mindless sitcom. She let the colors blur before her eyes, lying sideways on the sofa, seeing

27

no reason to move. The sirens blasted, filling the air with pulsing, mind-numbing noise. She closed her eyes, taking a deep breath in, and out.

———

Melody was waiting, sitting on a park bench. She was attempting to read a magazine, but she kept looking over the top of it, impatient for his arrival. She'd gotten Logan's number from Sean's phone, and it hadn't been that difficult to convince him to meet with her. The park was fairly empty. A mother was helping her daughter feed a few ducks crumbs alongside the murky pond, a few people were walking through quickly, and others were scattered, leaning against the old and withered trees, or else occupying the remaining benches. The sky was a gloomy gray, but the humidity weighed on Melody, sweat clinging to her skin. The lack of people made her more nervous. There was less of a crowd to be lost in.

"You look awfully conspicuous, you know," a voice said. She jumped. He'd suddenly sat down right beside her.

"Well, you are late," she grumbled, starting to put the magazine away.

"You'd make a terrible spy," he said, looking to his right, "Keep pretending to read."

"I'm not trying to be a spy."

"So, texting me from a blocked number, telling me to meet you in a park a fair distance away from where either of us works, and trying to be nonchalant are signs of…what, exactly?"

"Being careful."

"Right." Logan stole a glance at her and grinned. She was staring resolutely at a spot on the page. "So, what did you want?"

"Why didn't you arrest me?"

"Who says I'm not going to?"

28

"It's been a week. You're not going to."

"Maybe we're gathering evidence."

"Maybe you're terrible at bullshitting."

"Or I knew you wouldn't believe me."

"If you wanted to arrest me, why would you need an excuse?"

He didn't answer her but looked around the park; carefully examining the others there, making sure no one else was listening.

"You're right. I wouldn't need anything. A Party member with that ID, especially a Party Kid with your history, we'd have everything we'd need to take you in. You could be plotting against them, or planning to run away, wanting to cross state borders unknown to anyone."

"So, I repeat the question. Why didn't you?"

"Isn't it obvious?" He asked.

"Clearly not."

He sighed. "I felt sorry for you."

That had not been the answer she expected. She had to fight to keep her eyes on the article she'd been pretending to read, and, to give herself time to form words, flipped over the page.

"What?" She managed.

"Well, yeah. I saw Arshem's expression when we went to the office. You heard my story that night, you know, with Covington and all. I don't think you're plotting anything; we all need to blow off steam. Be able to go relax, meet guys like Sean without that hanging over you. Not have people on guard every second they're around you." He snorted. "Not to mention, it wouldn't make my life easier with Covington if I did what Arshem told us not to. You can calm down."

"But you still took the ID."

29

"Couldn't let you off that easily," he said, flashing her a skeptical glance. "But arresting a Party Kid for anything close to treason would give the rest of us even more shit to deal with. You with me?"

She started to nod, and then realized he wasn't looking at her and said, "Yeah, I'm with you." She paused for a moment then went on, "So what's the story with Derek?"

Logan considered for a second and then said, "He works at a news station. Hears a lot of stuff he doesn't want to and doesn't know when to keep his mouth shut. End of." He said it with such finality that she didn't dare ask any more about it. "What's your story, then, Karsh?" He asked.

"What do you mean?"

"Just that. Your dad's in Judicial, a federal judge no less, and then you go and do the fast track program and go for Legislative. You're smart, but you got caught by a junior detective. So, what's the deal?"

"There is no deal." She shrugged. "I wanted to be on my own as quickly as possible, I was still living with Dad the summer before training. I didn't want to stay at Quantico longer than I had to, even though I knew it'd be rough going into Legislative. Because I'd passed through the fast track, I was given slightly better treatment than I would have otherwise. Then, I had a salary, so I got my own apartment. I wanted Legislative over Judicial because I'd rather make the laws than enforce them. If I were anybody else's kid, it wouldn't matter. If you were anybody else's kid, it wouldn't matter."

"Well, not 'anybody' else's."

"Oh, don't do semantics," she snapped. "It's annoying. And you know what I mean."

"So, you're going to try to change the laws?"

"I'm not suicidal," she said quietly.

"Fair enough."

"What's your story, then?" She demanded.

"I don't know. Same as you, I guess. Nothing my parents were doing seemed interesting enough to me. So, I figured I'd try to make something work in a different branch, and deal with what came with that." His voice was almost emotionless.

"And here we are."

"Here we are." He agreed. They sat in silence for a minute.

"I hope you understand that this doesn't change anything." His voice was cold, and he was staring determinedly at the trees across from them.

"In what sense?"

"I'm still a cop. I covered for you once, but—"

"I'm a Party member too, as we've just been discussing." She looked at him, to make sure that he understood her. Covert decorum be damned.

"Well, you've got your people to think about. Whoever made that ID, for one."

"And you've got Derek. What would they say if a cop didn't turn in someone with, oh, what would they call it? 'Revolutionary ideas?' Just because they were friends?" They didn't look at each other, but she could sense his smile. She stood up, folding the magazine under her arm, making a show of looking at her phone. "Well, thank you, Logan. I do appreciate your...understanding." She smiled at finding the right word.

"Maybe I'll see you around," he said.

"Yeah. Hope not." She turned away from him and walked quickly out of the park.

"What do we see when we look at a Party member?" Arshem asked the committee room at large. "We see loyalty. Integrity. We see a person vetted by this country to protect it and its interests. We see someone raised by the very best this country has to offer, and they, in turn, offer their services to our nation.

"Now, we have been lenient, to a point. We assume that children will follow in their parents' footsteps. Children that have grown in a house that understands the intricacies of our judicial system are the best suited to join the Judicial branch of our government when they come of age. We trust that which we know.

"But we have spent too many of our resources investigating Party children who wish to deviate from this pattern, who believe they deserve special treatment and special training in order to switch branches.

"I put it to you, members of this esteemed committee, that we cannot trust these individuals. That we must be strict in our enforcement of Party rules. We must tread carefully during these treacherous times. We are on the path to ensuring the Greatness of this Nation once more. I, for one, will not risk our progress and our future based on the foolish whims of youth. I hope you are all wise enough to do the same." Arshem leaned back in his seat, looking very satisfied with himself. Various members of the Governmental Affairs committee looked moderately convinced, others skeptical.

"You make a good case, Senator, but I would point out that the talent of our Party members should not be restricted to one specific group or another. Why, you would be out one aide if the rules regarding branches were to be tightened." Senator Lewis leaned forward, speaking into his own microphone, "By all means, I agree with you that we trust those we know, those who we have seen since birth grow under Party leadership, expertise, and parental guidance. But I would argue that you are risking losing talent and unique skills by forcing children to follow in their parents' footsteps so specifically. We should be opening these doors more, not less."

Arshem scowled at the mention of Melody but otherwise remained calm.

"Well, to be fair, Senator," a different man, Senator Dewson, began, "There are many honorable Legislative Party members whose children would relish the opportunity to work alongside those in this committee, but have instead been relegated to other positions, as every seat has been filled."

Melody forced herself to continue to sit up straight in her seat. She was sitting behind Arshem with Lucy, waiting to give him notes and cues if necessary.

"And, Senator, why stop there? Why not just open the doors to all citizens to be Party members? Think of all the *talent*—" Arshem spoke the word with a mocking reverence, and many across the room began snickering, "that we may be missing. We are here today to revisit the structuring of the Party family system, to bolster the security of our ranks, and you would see us falter, you would see us damaged from the inside. Entitled children do not set examples for the rest to follow."

"So, what would you see done to those who have achieved positions outside of their family's line, Senator Arshem?" Lewis asked. "What would happen to those who have gone through the process of proving their loyalty? What about those who wish to join the military? Surely, you wouldn't doubt those who wish to serve their country to the highest possible degree?"

"Those already in positions would stay in their current positions. Those in training would start the process over. Military exceptions would remain unaffected," Arshem replied. Lewis scowled. He knew these points would win over wavering members of the committee. It wasn't an issue that demanded their attention or care. If Arshem's argument was at all convincing, they'd vote yes to make their tee time and be done with it.

"Senator Lewis, do you have a rebuttal?" The committee chair, Senator Potter, asked with a tilt of his head. Lewis took a look around the room, scanning each face carefully.

"No, I yield my remaining time," Lewis said with a scowl.

Potter nodded and began to call for a vote, his secretary tallying every 'Aye' from the gathered senators. Melody chewed her lip, burying her head in the numbers and words on the papers in front of her, trying to block out the roaring in her ears.

Arshem smiled as his motion passed. The bill would be taken to the Senate floor, where they would vote on whether President Jamison would review it for final implementation.

But, Melody knew, that was a formality. The Senate floor never questioned the committee's decision. If anything were to change at this point, it would be from Jamison's end, which was exceedingly rare.

She waited until the senators had filed out before beginning to pick up the files and clear away debris from Arshem's seat, Lucy having walked out with Arshem. She was so lost in thought that she jumped when she heard a voice calling to her from the doorway.

"Ms. Karsh?"

"Oh, Senator Lewis. Can I help you with something?" Melody asked.

"No, I just wanted to tell you that I was sorry about the

34

result today. I wish it had gone differently." His eyes met hers, and she knew he was apologizing for more than just the result.

"The committee did what it felt was best for the security of our nation," she replied smoothly, with no hint of emotion in her face or tone.

"I know. But, even so." He inclined his head to her, and she did the same. She let out a slow exhale when he left the room again, clutching the papers to her chest.

––––––––––

"I don't like it," Leo said. He was glaring at the TV, though, for the time being, it had been muted while Melody concluded the story.

"I know you don't like it," she said, picking up her book, "But it doesn't sound as though Logan's going to be reporting on me, does it?"

"Not at the moment," He admitted.

"So, we just have to avoid him, and it'll be fine." She wanted to let the matter drop.

"You're not seeing Sean, anymore? Cause you might bump into him if Sean's around."

"I feel if I just abruptly stop seeing him, after all that crap the other night, it'll look bad. Besides, we don't know that Liz's suspicion wasn't true, that he wasn't lenient on me because of Sean. I'll see Sean at least once more, and then I'll call it off."

"You don't actually like him, do you?" Melody looked over her shoulder to give Leo a scathing look. "Okay, okay. Sorry."

"Whether I like him or not is irrelevant." She said, twisting back around.

"He's the only one who would still call you Sam."

"Yes." She settled back against Leo's legs. They were sitting in his basement, him unsuccessfully watching TV, her unsuccessfully reading one of the books from Liz's library she'd been trying to get through for the past month. They sat quietly for a while; Leo having turned the volume back up before he spoke again.

"Just, how do you know—"

"I don't, Leo." She slammed her book shut, her temper flaring up, "I don't know if Logan's not being a narcissistic ass who will report the whole thing to his boss. But, if he did, wouldn't they have come marching into my place by now? They don't exactly wait around with things like this. If he wanted to act, I'd be in a cell right now. So, no, I don't know if he's going to say anything, but I don't *think* he will. Liz agrees with me."

"You would drag in Mom."

"She usually makes you change your mind."

"She usually annoys the hell out of me, is what she does." He grumbled, and Melody smiled.

"So long as you trust me. Besides, if all goes to hell, we have the plan."

"Don't talk to me about the plan. Hiding in the trunk of a car for hours isn't a plan."

"It's better than nothing."

"But you could say that about a lot of things. Tap dancing in front of the guards, punching a judge in the nose, trying to—"

"Those aren't legitimate plans!" Melody laughed.

"Yeah, but by your logic, they're 'better than nothing.'"

She hit him with a couch cushion. He grabbed it from her and asked, "What did you grab, anyways?" She held up the book.

"Same one as last time, that one on the Cold War."

"So, you're trying to torture yourself?" He rolled his eyes.

"At this point, it's more determination to finish the damn thing." She shrugged, "But yeah. Annoying, frustrating, same as pretty much all the ones she has."

"Yet, you do this to yourself anyway."

"Well, you could do with torturing yourself a little more, you never read anymore."

"I watch this shit, don't I?" He gestured to the TV.

"That's not the same thing. Everyone watches that crap."

"What do you think is going to happen with the reconstruction funds?" She knew he was trying to change the subject, but she leaned back and said,

"Oh, I don't know. Whether or not they cut the funding, Jamison will spin it as a part of rebuilding the Great American Nation, or something like that." Melody shrugged. Leo grunted in response.

They settled back into silence for a while before they heard Liz's footsteps coming downstairs.

"Hey, Leo, it's getting late, did you already have dinner?" She called down, sticking her head around the landing.

"Yeah, we ate." He called back.

"We? Oh, Melody, sorry didn't see you."

"No problem, I should be getting home," she stood up and stretched, marking her place in the book.

Melody could still remember the time five years ago when she'd come to Liz with tears streaming down her face, telling her that she wasn't going to write letters anymore, that it was pointless. It was then that Liz had grabbed a flashlight, and said they were going "to the library." A very confused Melody had followed her and watched as Liz lifted the top of the coffee table in the living room. Beneath several blankets were piles of books, old magazines, and newspaper clippings. By now, they'd started to crumble with no way to preserve them. They'd been taken from actual libraries, snuck away from the old book burnings, or had been owned by Liz's family and been hidden since the very first arrests.

Melody had tried to convince Liz that she needed a better hiding spot for the collection, but Liz had always said that any guests she wanted to have wouldn't look too closely, and if she was ever in a position where the house was being searched, she was damned regardless, so why waste the effort in pulling up floorboards.

Melody put the book back in its place, put the blankets back on top, and shut the coffee table lid before grabbing her bag.

"You sure you don't want to stay here? Will you make it back in time? I already saw officers starting to line up." Liz frowned at Melody.

"Why? Curfew's not for another two hours,"

"I don't know, did they say anything about it beginning early tonight?"

"Turn up the news," Melody said, poking Leo. He rolled his eyes at her but did so. The newscaster was talking about the economy, and the newsreel at the bottom was continuing the coverage of the reconstruction funds, and spouting local news headlines, nothing about the curfew. "They wouldn't start it early and not say." Melody said with a shrug.

"I don't know," Liz sounded worried, "You've got your badge, right? Maybe put it on?"

"No, that'll look suspicious if I'm coming from your place, make it look like I was investigating you as a Party member or something. If it starts to look bad, I'll keep it out once I get a bit further away. If I stay here tonight, I'll never get into work tomorrow with the morning buses."

"True. Okay, let me know when you get back," Liz said.

"Will do. See you, Leo,"

"Be careful," he said, turning to look at her as she climbed the steps to the first floor.

She hurried out of the house, walking quickly to the nearby bus stop. Liz had been right; the police officers were already taking their places. There weren't as many as there would be if it was indeed curfew, but their presence on the side streets made Melody's hair stand on end. She waited impatiently for the bus, and when it finally arrived, she all but jumped on, showing her Party badge to the driver for her free fare. As they drove along back towards Capitol Hill, she watched as more and more officers appear. She could not fathom why tonight they were out so early.

She was the only one to get off the bus at Seward Square. The place was teeming with police. A couple were leaning against some of the trees marked with giant crosses, the chalk faded in places because they'd been marked for removal so long ago.

"Hey!" One of them said, "What are you doing out here?"

Melody held her badge tightly. "I'm just going home." She said, as politely as possible.

"Likely." The officer snorted, taking a step towards her. "What's your name?"

"Melody Karsh. I'm a Party member," she said, holding out the badge to him. "Sir, I'm just on my way home. It's on 4th Street, it's five minutes away."

"Where'd you get that thing, then?" He said, trying to take the badge away from her, "It looks like a pretty pathetic fake to me."

"Sir, if you take away a Party member's badge—"

"Are you threatening me?" He whispered, taking a step closer to her.

"No." She tried to stay calm, but felt panic creeping into her voice. "I'm just saying that taking away a Party member's badge is an imprisonable offense." She couldn't understand why this was happening. She had the badge. If he'd bothered to check, she had her Party issued gun, and her ID badge for the Senate building. All things she was required to carry at all times. Instead, his face was shining with glee, and sweat. His thinning hair was sticking to his scalp, and his crooked teeth that showed as his smile grew wider made him look every part of the uneducated idiot he surely was.

"Don't go citing the law to me," He spat at her, and he slammed the badge out of her hand, "Let's see how long it takes for the plastic to smash, shall we?" He raised his foot above it.

"Hey!" A voice called over.

"Madden, you're just in time!" The officer laughed, "Want to get the cuffs ready?" Melody snapped around. For once, she was unbelievably grateful for coincidence.

"What are you doing Lee?" Logan snapped.

"This bitch tried to claim she was a Party member; can you believe it?" Officer Lee was still laughing.

"She is, you prick! She's a senator's aide!" Logan shoved Melody to the side, scooped the badge up from beneath Lee's offending foot, and held it up to his face. "Did you even bother to check it?" Lee sighed and pulled out a scanner.

The Party badges were a simple design, the head of an eagle, but with red jewels for eyes. Behind the jewels was a very small electronic ID. When he scanned it, he could see Melody's name and Party ID number.

Melody could see the color leave Lee's face as he handed the badge back to her. "Right. Well," he began to splutter, "Well, it doesn't explain why she's out here, anyway."

"We are not collecting Party members in our sweeps, you fucking moron." Logan hissed through gritted teeth. "I'll take her home. You're lucky you didn't destroy that thing." He glared at Lee, who glared back. Lee turned away and headed deeper into the Square, other officers coming out to meet him, as Logan pushed Melody down the street. She could hear Lee behind them as they began to walk, ranting about the 'almost' detective pulling rank, no doubt just to take care of his stuck–up bitch.

"Come on," Logan muttered, clearly trying to ignore him as much as she was, "You've got to get out of here."

"Logan, what the hell is going on?"

"Not here. Where's your place?" Melody told him, and he began walking quickly, making her almost jog to keep up with him. She waited until they were almost to her apartment before trying to speak, but he silenced her again. Once she was outside the building she stopped and said,

"Well, you're either explaining now, or you're coming up."

"Up." His matter-of-factness made her stare in disbelief. "Go. Quickly."

She fumbled with the keys for a moment out of nerves before leading him inside and up the stairs. She held the door to the unit open for him and watched as he took the place in, from the mess on the coffee table, to the Party-approved books on the shelves above the TV, to the neatly organized kitchen.

"Sit, if you want," she said, gesturing to the couch.

"No, it's fine. I'll need to get back in a minute." His eyes snapped back to her.

"Okay. What's going on? Why couldn't we talk outside?"

"Because they are everywhere tonight."

"And you didn't want to be overheard."

"Exactly."

"So why was tonight a curfew before curfew?"

"Well, we got word that there's a planned protest of sorts happening the first week of July, so it was decided if we made a few arrests, publicized them…"

"You'd scare people, and there'd be no protest. But there are always rumors that there's going to be a protest the first week of July. There never is."

"Yeah, I don't know why, but that's what I was told when I first came on to the force, and maybe it's just because I'm a higher rank now that I'm under Covington, so I see more of it. But it's different this time. They're taking whatever threats, whatever reports, more seriously."

"Lucy was telling me about this, it's always 'different.' I had to help with Arshem's latest plan about terrorism and patriotism just in case there was police action. She says we do it every year."

"Well, maybe you'll have to use it this time. I can't tell you any more details, Covington is not exactly the type to answer questions. But these things just bring out guys like Lee, who are a bit… overenthusiastic. Clutching the few scraps of power they can get and taking the only moment they can to watch the ants dance. I almost wish he had crushed the badge, so I could arrest him myself."

"Don't say that," Melody said sharply.

Logan looked at her for a second, his green eyes cloudy with an emotion she couldn't figure out. "No, you're right. I don't. Anyway, I should get back. Look," He seemed to be debating with himself for a moment then said quietly. "You might want to tell your, well, your friends," he looked meaningfully at her. "That this is going to go on for a few days. Play it safe for a while. Go home early, all that. Hear me?"

"I hear you," she said. He hurried out the door and it slammed shut behind him. She knew it was an accident, but it still made her wince. She messaged Liz and Leo to let them know she was alright, and then went to the window and peered through the blinds. She couldn't see them, but she could feel them hiding in the dark, the hairs prickling on the back of her neck.

She dropped the blinds and walked towards her bedroom, wishing she had a drink. Instead, she pulled on pajamas, and retrieved a notebook, tearing out a sheet of paper.

"Dear Mom,

I had to hide all the letters in the library. I know you won't care, but it's annoying, not being able to have them all here with me. I guess it's a selfish complaint. I know it's safer to just destroy them, but I can't bear to do that.

I saw that Logan guy again today; do you remember me talking about him? He said that the police are worried that there's going to be a protest in the first week of July. Because, Independence Day. Except he doesn't know that, because of course, they aren't going to tell the cops there used to be this national holiday the first week of July. Although, from what Liz told me all her grandparents said about it was that it involved fireworks and eating lots of meat. So, not exactly 'protest day' material, but I guess the name is there? Maybe it's a, you-had-to-be-there, type of thing.

I'm getting off track here. There are so many officers outside right now, it's kind of scaring me, Mom. I almost wish I'd stayed at Liz's. I don't know how that would've made it better, but then I wouldn't have been alone, at least.

An officer tried to take my badge, actually. I wanted to scream at him, to just let him keep it. But that just sounds stupid. It protects me, and it's killing me. He was going to crush it, and I just wanted him to do it. I can't, but he could. He could and then it wouldn't be my fault—it wouldn't be my choice. I know it wouldn't mean anything, wouldn't do anything, but it would

43

sure make me feel better.

Leo's still good. Annoyed at me for planning to see Sean again, but then again, I'm annoyed at him for a fair number of things too.

I wish you were here. I know I say that every time. But it's true.

Love,

Melody"

July 2092

"Just the magazine?" The old man asked, smiling at her.

"Yeah, thanks," Melody said distractedly, already skimming through it. It had been a long day, running back and forth between Arshem's office, where he had back-to-back meetings with other senators and security officials, running through any changes the bill might need, and a back room where Lucy and several other aides were crammed together frantically trying to edit the bill to reflect such changes.

"That'll be $6.00, miss." He gave her an apologetic smile.

Melody scowled. She was not in the mood to deal with this shit. She was hungry and tired, and her neck and back ached. She pulled back her jacket, revealing the Party badge in a wordless exchange.

"Ah, yes, of course, miss, have a nice day." He paled under her expression and turned to the next customer in line. Melody stood to the side of the newsstand, continuing to pore over the magazine. There was nothing on the bill yet, not that there would be. Not until it came to a full Senate vote. Just some fluff piece about Jamison's recent visit to the UK. The wind blew gently through her hair as she skimmed through the latest stories on the

45

supposed economic upswing, the falling unemployment rates, the renewed trade talks with East Asia.

"What on earth is she doing?" She heard a man next to her exclaim.

She turned around and saw that a crowd had begun to gather around a cluster of buildings across the street. Some were calling out, screaming and pointing, but before Melody could pick out the actual problem, she heard someone cry, "She's going to jump!"

Melody jerked her head towards the sky to see a woman standing on a windowsill about seven stories up. But the woman wasn't looking at the ground. She was clinging to the window frame behind her, looking petrified with fear. She opened her mouth and closed it again several times.

"She's insane! Absolutely insane," the old man running the newsstand muttered, before leaning back in his chair and turning his attention to the book lying on his lap.

Melody looked back up at the woman, overwhelmed by morbid curiosity. The woman just stood on the windowsill, eyes closed, head lifted towards the sky. The crowd began to grow, people started shouting for the police, other people poked their heads out of windows in the same building, begging or screaming at her to get back inside. Melody hadn't noticed how big the crowd was until she decided she'd seen enough and started struggling to move away.

"Oh, say can you see, by the dawn's early light," The woman's singing pierced the air, and the crowd fell silent for the briefest moment before they began shouting at her to get down again.

"What so proudly we hailed at the twilight's last gleaming? Whose broad stripes and bright stars through the perilous fight, over the ramparts we watched were so gallantly streaming?" She kept losing the tune, her voice

wavering, unsure of what she was singing, or how the song was really supposed to go.

A dozen or so officers had arrived, adding to the confusion. Over the screaming of the crowd, they were heard through a megaphone, "Cease and desist! Return inside immediately!"

"And the rocket's red glare, the bombs bursting in air, gave proof through the night, that our flag was still there." She kept singing, still with her eyes closed, still clinging to the windowsill for dear life, as if the entire world depended on her being able to keep singing. Her voice kept cracking. It sounded like she was sobbing, in fear, or some other emotion, Melody couldn't tell.

Melody watched in horrified fascination as others began to join the woman. A man a floor above her appeared in his windowsill, another woman below her, a few on the same floor. The officers were in disarray, trying to consult with each other, frantically making calls. The crowd fought against itself, some trying to leave while more tried to enter, or come closer, to see and hear what was happening.

"Oh say does that Star-Spangled Banner yet wave, O'er the land of the free and the home of the brave!"

"Cease and desist immediately! We have been authorized to—" But the cop with the megaphone had it wrestled away from him by another officer.

"We will shoot you if you don't return inside now! Go back inside and you will not be harmed!" he ordered. The officers began to fight each other, yelling at each other, unsure of what to do. But the singers didn't stop. They didn't even look down. Another woman came out to the window, holding a small child in her arms, as though singing to the baby instead of the public below.

"Everyone, leave now and you will not be harmed!" An

officer yelled, but it was no good. The area was so full, people pushing in all directions. Melody tried to force her way out but kept being shoved back into the newsstand by the throng.

The singing voices kept building, and Melody tried desperately to claw away from the mass of bodies. She knew what this must be—the protest Logan had been talking about—but it didn't make sense. The date was wrong. She couldn't dwell on that now; she had to get out, and get out now, fight against a mass that neither wanted to move nor stay in place. She had just spotted an opening she could try to slip through when she heard a voice behind her then made her stomach drop.

The old man working at the newsstand had managed to climb onto the table supporting the register, and, with his hand over his heart, began to sing too.

She looked around, and saw, to her horror, Officer Lee running towards her.

Without thinking, she clambered up onto the newsstand alongside the old man and punched him full in the face. Her fist felt raw, but she punched again, and he fell, toppling off the stand to the ground below.

Police were still coming towards the stand, and Melody tried desperately to get down, to get to her badge and show she was not a singer, but it was too late. Lee grabbed her around the stomach and pulled her to the ground, her head banging painfully off the pavement, just as the sound of gunshots rang through the air. The screaming was deafening as the officer yanked her arms behind her and cuffed her. He forced her to stand as blood dripped from her head to the ground. More gunshots, and Melody blinked through the blood, and saw the woman fall from the window down to the sidewalk below.

"State your name, occupation, and the current date."

"Melody Karsh. I'm the junior aide to Senator Arshem. It's July 6th."

"And why are you here today?" Melody blinked up at Officer Lee, blood still dripping into her eye. She couldn't reach her face to put pressure on the cut above her brow, her hands were cuffed to the table.

"I was caught at the riot, I was on my way home, I was trying to get out, to get away from it, but it was too crowded. I saw that old man near me join in, and I—"

"Why do you say it was a riot?" Lee glared down at her.

"What else would you call it?"

"Do you know anyone involved?"

"No."

"What was the name of the song?"

"I have no idea."

"Yes, you do."

"You're going to be asking everyone who you caught there this question. I don't know. I've never heard it before. I have no idea what those people were doing. I stopped to get a magazine and was reading it when that woman started singing. I tried to leave but it was too packed, everything was chaos. You saw me try to help you, I stopped that man, I was trying to get my badge up before you tackled me."

"No, you know what I saw, you little piece of shit? I saw a girl with a little power think she doesn't have to play by the rules. I think I saw you join the riot, that you started singing too. I think I saw—" But Lee stopped, and Melody could guess why. Outside the door of the interrogation room, they could hear a shouting voice, and it was coming closer.

"I want to know what room she's in!"

"Mr. Karsh, please, they're in the middle of—"

"She is a Party member, and as such, that requires—"

"I know, Mr. Karsh, but she was found at the scene right next to one of the rioters."

"It was across the street from the Senate building you idiot! Now tell me where she is!"

The door slammed open, and the silhouette of a tall, slim man filled the frame.

"What the hell did you do to my daughter?"

"Who are you and why are you interrupting this interrogation?" Lee stood up, doing his best to look intimidating.

"I am Thomas Karsh, and what the hell is my daughter doing handcuffed in a cell?"

"I am conducting an interrogation, Karsh, you have no authority to be here." Lee looked wary of the man, and Karsh seemed to expand.

"I have every right to be here. As a federal judge, it is my duty to intervene if and when these matters get out of hand. Now, tell me, what has she done?"

"If I may, Karsh, you may be a bit biased in this case. You don't have the authority to—"

"You're Officer Lee?" He interrupted.

"Yes," Lee said, perhaps a bit too proudly.

"So, you're the one who almost destroyed her badge because you didn't think she was a Party member in the first place? You're the one that arrested her after she was found to have helped you take one of those traitors down?"

"How did you—?"

"Don't question my loyalties, and I won't question yours, you insignificant piece of shit. Now, tell me, what has she done?"

Lee's face was flushed. Thomas raised an eyebrow.

"It doesn't explain what she was doing there in the first place."

"I told you, it's on my way home from work!" Melody tried to defend herself, but her father held up a hand.

"Was she found to be singing herself?"

Lee hesitated. "No."

"Did she follow police instructions? Did she cooperate following her arrest? Has she acted as a loyal and faithful Party member should and does?"

"Yes." Lee's voice was small, but bitter.

"Then get the cuffs off her and let her leave." Thomas's voice was so low and dangerous that Lee didn't dare disobey. But, as he undid the cuffs, he let his hand dig painfully into her arm, and she took it as the warning he meant it to be.

"And someone get a damn bandage for her head," Thomas yelled down the hall.

————————

They said nothing to each other as they walked out of the building five minutes later, the cut on Melody's head cleaned and sealed.

"Thanks," she finally said.

"It was on your way home." It was more of a statement than a question.

"I'm on 4th now." She assured him, "So yeah."

"I'm going to be hearing about this for weeks." His tone was icy.

"I'm sorry," she didn't look at him.

"I don't know how you'll recover from this one." He sighed. "Your mother, Legislative, now this…. they're already calling it the Anthem Riot."

She didn't ask why. He would expect her to, but she didn't want to provoke him any further.

"I should come see your place, at some point, I suppose," he said.

"I guess." She shrugged. "It's nice." It was an empty invitation. The words they were supposed to say. He would never come, and she didn't want him to.

"I'm sure." He looked down at her. "Is Arshem treating you well?"

"Not really. But did you expect him to?"

"No." He looked out to the sky, where the sun was almost fully set. "I should be getting home. Cases in the morning."

"Right."

"I expect they'll be searching your house, so you might want to call a friend and stay there tonight."

"What?"

"They're searching everyone who was at the riot, anyone who was arrested. I could get you out of there," he jerked his head back towards the station, "But my reach is only so far."

"Right," she said again.

"Stay out of trouble." He said and started to walk down the street. He took a few strides and then turned around again. "Melody," He began, awkwardly.

"Yeah?"

"You have a place to go?"

"Yeah."

"Okay. Good." He nodded and turned around again. She

waited until he was far enough away, and then walked quickly in the opposite direction, all but breaking out into a run.

What was in the apartment? Was there anything there? The bottles had been cleared away weeks ago, so that was fine. The ID had been in her purse, but it had been stuck behind her actual one and they hadn't moved that. She had checked when she'd gotten it back, so that was okay. The letters were all in the library now...

Except one. That last one. The one she'd written the night Logan had been in the house. It talked about the library, Liz; it mentioned Leo, Logan, and Sean explicitly. She'd hidden it in the lining of a book, waiting until she could transfer it to the library. She just hadn't had a chance to get over to their house. She hadn't thought about it in any urgent sense. And it was hidden, right? In a Party-approved book, they wouldn't check the lining, would they?

Still. Maybe she could go in and grab it, say she just wanted to grab a few things for the night...

She hurried down the rows of houses and apartments, before seeing something that made her slow down. She could see a line of cars, their lights on, crowding around the building.

Was that for her? She couldn't tell at this distance, and if it was, then she was dead if she walked by. She ducked behind a tree. She needed to call Liz, see what she thought was best to do.

Her fingers were shaking so badly she couldn't turn her phone on. She dropped it in the grass beneath her, and when she stooped to pick it up, she saw figures move outside her front door.

Logan was walking out of the building, a piece of paper in his hands. His eyes darted back and forth across the page. He looked beyond the paper into the street, head turning like a radar dish, as if scanning for any threats in the distance. He stopped turning for a moment, tilted his head to the side. Melody thought he'd spotted her, and she stood, frozen to the spot. Maybe she was imagining it, but she thought she could see his hand holding the page lift up, just slightly, and his eyes widening. Trying to tell her something.

Covington burst from the door behind, and started screaming at Logan, snatching the paper from his hands. His face was red, and the voice Melody heard was almost too violent to come from a normal human. "What the fuck are you doing, Madden?" he shouted. "That's evidence. Don't fucking take it outside!"

For a moment, Melody couldn't breathe. All her body's routine functions had become impossible. She fell to her knees on the grass, her back pressed to the tree, trying to remember how to get oxygen into her body.

They'd found it.

She was dead. Or as good as.

She managed to return to her feet on legs that did not want to support her, and leaned against the tree.

There was only one thing for it.

She reached into her bag and pulled out the Party badge. She gave it one last look of purest loathing, and flung it as far away from her as she possibly could.

From the case file of Melody Karsh: July 2092-April 2093
May 2090

Dear Mom,

Finally got the rest of my stuff packed, leaving for Quantico on Monday. Dropping some of the important stuff with Leo and Liz, but most of it is going to a storage unit until I can get back and sort out a place. Taking all bets on if Dad bothers to say goodbye. I haven't told him I'm switching to Legislative yet. My guess is he'll hear about it while I'm gone and can't talk to him anyway. There will probably be a letter that makes its way through with him disowning me or something.

Leo's been really quiet the last couple days. He wasn't even there the last time I came by with boxes. I saw his course catalog for his first semester on his desk, and I couldn't help but go through it. I wish I was going with him, that we were choosing courses together, walking to the campus, getting a dorm room. I guess I'll sort of have one for the next year, but…it's not the same.

Liz wants to have tea tomorrow, and I think I know what she's going to say. She wants to tell me that one year isn't a big deal, that I can make it through with my head intact, and to write letters to her instead of you if I need to. To destroy them after, but so that I don't lose the outlet. And in a year, she'll still be here. The library will still be there. Leo will be there. And they'll help me get back to who I was. But that's the thing—they will have a year, more, if I can't get through fast track—to move on with their lives. Leo will get through a year at American, Liz will keep working. They will go to work, school, buy groceries, come home, watch the news, read and continue with whatever is it they're doing. And I'll be separated from them, unaware of anything outside of the Party's indoctrination. And who's to say whether or not I'll want to go back. I think that's what scares me the most—that I'll start to actually believe what they tell me. That I'll want to come back and report them both.

I had a nightmare last night; my eyes were blank, and white. I had a gun in my hand, pointed between Leo's eyes. And he was pleading with me, telling me who he was, and I didn't hear him. I didn't know him.

What do you think happens when all the Party Kids go? Do they start to fear us, the ones we went to school with for years? That we grew up with? Had our first dates with? Do they think we'll come back and no longer know them, or care to know them? That we will move on, live the lives they can never have without a thought if they resent us or miss us—because we don't have to care.

Did you ever feel that way about Dad? Did he become someone different before your eyes? Is that why you left?

Love,
Melody

October 2092: II

Alexander groaned and rolled over, his wife panting beside him, sharing an ecstasy so rarely felt these days. He waited for a few moments, savoring the silence, before saying,

"I think we're going to check Philadelphia next."

Jordan said nothing. She reached over to the floor beside the bed and grabbed her robe. She sat up on the bed, pulling it on.

"What?" he asked.

"Nothing."

"Don't do that, what do you want to say," he demanded, leaning up on an elbow.

"Just, I have to wonder when you're getting off if it's because you're actually with me or because you're picturing her in handcuffs." She stood, not looking at him, tying the robe closed.

He tried to grin, sliding along the bed closer to her, "Well I'd much rather—"

"Don't even." She was across the room in two quick strides and slammed the bathroom door in his face. He sat on the edge of the bed, pinching the skin above his nose, trying to keep control as the usual anger rose within him. He finally punched the mattress, which did nothing to calm his fury, grabbed a pillow and one of the throw blankets, and reluctantly headed to the couch downstairs.

Alexander was on his fourth cup of coffee by the time Logan walked into the office. He raised an eyebrow as Logan ran a hand awkwardly against the back of his head, his eyes going wide at the sight of Covington.

"I thought I was early."

"I didn't sleep," Alex said simply. "What have you got for me?"

"The Philadelphia police are on board, they've agreed to do extra sweeps, and searches on new arrivals fitting her description, and we've told them she might be using the name Samantha Trillow."

"Still not sure about that alias," Alex muttered, draining his mug.

"I don't think Sean was lying," Logan replied.

"Whatever. We can't ask him again now." He set the mug aside and dug through his desk for the file.

"I thought you were taking a break from those?"

"I was." He pulled out a few of the letters, scanning the original words against his notes, highlights, and arrows. "I still find the whole concept morbid."

"We all do. Apparently, she found it comforting."

"'I wish I was with you. I wish I was anywhere else. This place is a suffocating hellish pit filled with disgusting, pathetic excuses for people.' You call that comforting?"

"Isn't that one of the older ones?"

"Yeah, I think so."

"So, she'd be around, what fifteen, sixteen?"

"Writing to your dead mother is more excusable when you're fifteen? Saying you'd rather be buried than alive with your father is alright because you're a teenager?"

"I never said it was alright," Logan said, calm in the face of Alexander's mounting anger. Alex grunted and continued to scan through the pages. "What are you looking for, anyway?" Logan asked, "You've been through those things a thousand times."

"Still might've missed something; a note, a clue, anything about where they might've gone. She just mentions 'the plan,' a few times, but there's got to be some detail about the plan somewhere. A mention of a city she wanted to go to."

"I'm going to call Virginia and Maryland, see if they've turned up anything."

"You do that," Alex said to Logan's back as he strode out of the office.

He embraced the silence that followed for a glorious minute before footsteps and then a cheerful "Alexander!" cut through the room.

"What's up, Lieu?" He asked. Normally, he liked Parker. Parker was about ten years older than him and had progressed to being the unit's lieutenant. He'd been a great mentor to Alex, and they had double dates with their wives at least once a month. That said, Parker at eight-thirty in the morning after he'd had no sleep could go fuck right off.

"Bad night?"

"Wouldn't want to repeat it. What've you got for me?"

"Nothing too important."

"Then why are you here?" Alex glowered at him.

"Come on, we're getting out of the office for a bit."

"I've got work to do, Parker."

59

"Your wife just called me."

"Oh."

"Get up. Let's go." Parker tapped the desk. Alex sighed. He got up and shoved his jacket on.

Parker led the way outside and out onto the sidewalk. They passed the new construction sites, the few shops around the station, and were nearing a more residential neighborhood before either spoke again.

"Where the hell are we going?"

"We're not going anywhere. We're just walking." Parker didn't look back at him or break his stride.

"We'll be missed if we're gone too long."

"You're in charge of the Karsh case. You can do whatever the hell you want."

"No, I can't. And what about you?"

"I'll be fine." Parker shrugged. They went on a bit further, before Parker asked, "So, you want to tell me what happened?"

Alex sighed, "I don't know,"

"Oh, come on. Jordan had to have a reason to call me and ask if you were here. I guess she woke up and you were already gone?"

"Yeah, something like that."

"What happened?"

"You already know. It's what's been happening. She's feeling threatened by this brat."

"Be more specific."

Alex sighed again. "It was my fault. We'd finally, you know," Parker nodded, and Alex continued, "And she rolls over and I said we were going to start checking Philadelphia."

"You are an idiot."

60

"I know. I don't know why I wanted to tell her then, it was…
it wasn't as though I was thinking about it during, but, as soon as it
was done all the thoughts just came crashing down again."

"Have you talked to her about the case?"

"No, you know that's not—"

"Oh, cut the shit. No details, but the general concept. Does
she know what it'll mean for you if Karsh isn't caught?"

"She probably has a guess."

"Alex, take the day off. Go home. Be honest about what's
at stake here. Might even help you if you talk."

"I don't need to—"

"I don't care what you need, think about her. You're one
step away from calling Jordan Melody, and she deserves to know it's
not because you've got a hard-on for some nameless petty criminal."

Alex didn't say anything, just aimlessly looked around. The
sidewalks around him were all but clear of people. Children were
in school. Parents were at work or at home. The sun was weakly
shining down on them, the last of the summer heat finally starting
to dissipate. By all accounts, a peaceful day.

"Yeah, yeah you're right." He said. "I'll head back now."

"Good," Parker said, clapping him on the back. The two
men began to quickly walk back in the other direction.

"So, tell me," Parker said after a few minutes, "How's it
been going with Logan?"

"Why'd you stick me with that kid?" Alex seethed.

"One, because it's my job, and two, because he's not a bad
kid." Parker didn't look the least bit perturbed. "Now, tell me."

"He's fine. He had a decent excuse for being in Karsh's
letter. He's still on desk duty for the time being."

"Look, Alex, Logan didn't do anything wrong. He saved a Party member from an overzealous officer. That's all any of them knew at the time. He was doing his job. Lee's been screaming 'I told you so' at him for the last three months, so the least you can do, as his supposed mentor, is to lay off a bit."

"Parker," Alex stopped and turned to face his friend. "Look at the last Party Kid who went off the track. When we all said, 'It's okay, trust them.' When we said, 'What could they do?' We have to keep an eye on these guys. We can't—"

"Logan's not Melody," Parker stated.

"How do you know?"

"Because we searched his place from top to bottom. Because he was the one who originally found the letter. Because we questioned him. Because he's passed every single test. Because he's put up with you for almost two years and has not had a single blemish on his record. That Karsh girl, she was friends with the Myers family. You know we had our eyes on them. Then we found the library. We found her other letters. Her mother...well," Parker shrugged. "Look, I don't want to say this stuff runs in the blood, but. You've met her father. It couldn't have come from there."

"And that has what to do with Logan?"

"Logan's not like that. Logan's got it alright up here," Parker pointed to his head. "His parents are good people. His family have been Party members since its founding. By all means, keep a collar on him, but give him some room to move, you know?"

"Do you have to make him sound like a pet I'm stuck with?"

"I couldn't think of a better metaphor off the top of my head." Parker chuckled, stuck his hands in his pockets, and started walking again.

———

Alex hesitantly walked through the door to find Jordan standing over the small stove, breaking dry spaghetti to get the noodles to fit into the pot.

"Why are you home?" She asked.

"I took the afternoon off."

"You can't do that," she said warily.

"I…" He didn't know how to start. He sat down at the table and shrugged out of his jacket. She just kept stirring.

"Parker sent you home?" She asked.

"Kind of."

"He knows you too well."

"He's known me too long," he said, leaning his head on his fist.

They waited in silence for a minute.

"Were you going to actually talk or just stare at me?" She asked.

"I like staring at you."

"Do you think being cute is going to work right now?" She asked, wiping some of the steam off her face.

"It's worth a try."

"Alex," she said, turning to face him, "I know you can't talk about it. Okay? You can never talk about it. But you give me these fucking details like I'm supposed to care when I don't know this girl. I don't know what she's done. I don't know why it's so important that you're tracking her from here when the Pennsylvania or Maryland or whatever police could be taking care of it when she's gone there. And I don't know why you come home at three in the morning looking like you've seen a ghost and tell me you just wish you could call your mother, and then go slumping off to bed. How is that supposed to…. I don't…I don't know anymore, Alex.

But I didn't…" She turned back to the stove, leaning over the pot. He stood up, wanting to hug her, but she held up a hand. "Don't. Just don't right now."

"I want to tell you," he said gently.

"But you're not allowed to." She said, trying to keep her voice steady.

"No, I–I'm going to." He took the pot, moved it to a different burner, and turned off the heat. Then, he reached for her hand and led her to a seat at the table. She slowly sat down, looking at him guardedly.

"It's not a trick." He told her. "I trust you. This isn't going to work if you're suspicious of me."

"You're a detective." She almost laughed.

"Well," he shrugged. "Listen." He didn't know where to begin. "You remember the Anthem Riot, back in July?"

"Yeah?"

"Well, this girl, Melody Karsh, we found her there. It turned out that she had no connection to it, but still, anyone caught there was arrested and interrogated. Her father was a very prominent judge and came to get her out. Since this all happened, he's been demoted, that doesn't matter, anyway, by the time he came her apartment was already being searched."

"And you found something?" She asked eagerly. He gave her a look and she said, "Sorry. Keep going."

"Yeah. We found something. We found a letter written to her mother. It mentioned a few people, Logan included, and some…" He cast around for a phrase he could use that didn't reveal too much, "anti-government tendencies, and a library.

"Well, we guessed where that library might be, and we found it, along with years and years' worth of letters. The letters are all...I don't know how to describe just how heinous they are. Just vicious, slanderous, disgusting lies." His hand had curled into a fist without his realizing, and she put her hand on top of it, running her thumb against his knuckles. "There were books too, all from the banned list from years ago, and newspapers and magazines. There may have been more, we couldn't really tell if any had been cleared out. There was enough space there. But the letters...

"Jordan, her mother's been dead since she was two. There was a group attempting to flee to the UK, and the ship was neutralized. No survivors. Caused a lot of problems for Karsh's dad then too. It was when he was gaining traction, just starting as a lawyer, but he was able to avoid a demotion because he'd filed for a divorce and custody of their daughter. But can you imagine? Writing about shit like that to the mother who abandoned you? How twisted do you have to...?" He took a breath, trying to calm himself. "So, we think she knew we'd find the letters, and that's why she ran. Got a decent head start on us. We have no idea where she went. She must have had some sort of ID to cross the D.C. border and from there...who knows where she went. That's why we're lost. We've been checking surrounding states, but with the delays in rebuilding and lapses in state security outside the D.C. area, you know, it's so bad, especially out West, and up around New York... she could just blend into a crowd, and we'd never see her again."

"But you haven't been publicizing her missing at all," Jordan said.

"Of course we have! Almost every police station on the East Coast knows! I've been pushing for more resources, asking for help, but they're not—"

"That's not what I'm talking about," Jordan shook her head, cutting him off. "You haven't been publicizing it to the people."

He looked at her in disbelief.

"Jordan, we would never publicize a threat to the Party. Any instance of a Party member breaking ranks. And besides, now it's too late. It's been too long. We somehow have let a terrorist go missing for three months."

"So?" She asked, "Don't tell them it's been three months. If I weren't living with you, I wouldn't know you'd been working on this case for more than a day."

"But they won't—"

"Why would you ask?" She raised her eyebrows. "If you catch her, they won't blame you for whatever tactics you use to get there. And if you don't find her, well it will be the same end either way, won't it? That's what you're trying to tell me?"

He looked at her in wonder.

"So... you're suggesting get everyone to look for her?"

"Exactly. Why take it all on yourself?" She said, "Like with missing kids, or other criminals, let the mob catch the bitch. You take the credit."

He ran a hand over his face, "Maybe, I don't know, insinuating a weakness in the Party.... people have been killed for much less."

"But you're dead either way." Jordan's voice didn't break, but it was close, "That's what you're telling me. You find her, or you're dead. So why not use every method you can?"

He gave her a small smile. "You're an incredible woman, you know that?"

"Whatever's happening between us, I need you next to me," She squeezed his hand with hers.

"Are we okay then?" He asked, meeting her eyes, looking for the comfort only they could provide.

66

"We will be," she said. She gestured at him to come closer, and she pulled him into a kiss.

————

"This is ridiculous," Derek grumbled, changing the camera angle for the sixth time.

"You know how she gets," Morgan shrugged. "She's having a bad hair day."

"Oh, please let me zoom in on the one strand that's not perfectly in place," Derek hissed, "Because people care so fucking much."

"Hmm," Morgan hummed indulgently. "Well, she knows the interview is important."

"The interview is important because of Covington. Not because of Denise."

"Look, we're going on in five minutes. Just keep her happy for five minutes so we can get this done," Morgan pleaded, giving him her patented puppy dog eyes. He looked away.

"Fine. But I'm doing it for you, not for that bitch." He went back to the camera. She patted him on the shoulder and crossed the room towards the detective, making sure everything was ready. Denise was examining her reflection on the various monitors and seemed satisfied. Finally.

Derek looked over at the detective. He looked tired despite the work the makeup team had tried to do. Derek had to admit, even with the shadows under his eyes, with the prominent cheekbones and strong chin, crisp black suit and Party badge sticking out of his breast pocket, Covington looked more than a little intimidating.

Morgan and Derek had been placing bets all morning about what the interview was about. Derek had tried to message Logan asking why, but had received no response. All they had been

67

told was that Covington had an announcement, and that they were to ask no follow up questions. With no context and no authority to say otherwise, the crew could only shrug and work as they otherwise would. "Derek, you with us?" He heard Morgan's voice. He jumped and focused on the camera, zooming in so the picture was only on Denise's face.

"Ready!" He called.

"Right, we're live, in 10, 9, 8," Morgan started counting down, putting down her fingers, but the detective said,

"Wait!" He reached into his jacket pocket and pulled out a portable drive. "These need to be used when I speak. You'll know when." A confused Morgan took the drive and gave it to an assistant who ran the drive up to the mixing booth above the stage.

Morgan looked at the detective, who nodded, and she began the countdown again. "10, 9, 8, 7, 6, 5, 4," she mouthed the last three numbers, and pointed to Denise.

"Good morning, Nation!" Denise said brightly, managing to show every single one of her bright teeth with her smile. She began with the morning headlines, her tone bright in the right places, somber in others. She spoke on the trade deal with China, excitedly proclaiming the sharing of technological progress was within reach, gave a brief commentary on the President's desire to reclaim the Virgin Islands, and spoke of the recent developments in the reconstruction of New York. Finally, she turned towards Derek's camera.

"And now, this morning we welcome Detective Alexander Covington for a public service announcement." Derek zoomed out the camera to encompass Covington in the frame. "Now, Detective, you've said you had a matter of great importance to share with us today."

"Indeed." Covington, Derek thought as he zoomed in, could not have looked less at home in front of a camera. "We have received information regarding a small terrorist organization residing within our country, and we would like to urge the public to be vigilant and help in the aid and capture of these individuals. Our primary target is twenty-year-old Melody Karsh," Covington said, "I believe we have a picture?"

"Yes, it should be right in the top corner of the screen," Denise said, and Derek could see her looking up towards the techs, rather than into the camera.

"Right." Covington shifted in his seat, "We have uncovered information that leads us to believe this group is plotting against the government. We were able to detain an accomplice of Karsh, and it was revealed that she was operating under an alias, Samantha, or Sam, Trillow. The accomplice denied any contact with her other affiliates, Elizabeth, Gregory, and Leon Myers. We have to assume, however, that they could be using aliases as well."

Derek's hand tightened on the camera stand. Her name was Sam? And Sean had…no. It was too big of a coincidence. Even so…he wanted to see that picture.

"They should also be aware," Covington continued, "That these people are skilled at distributing anti-government propaganda and are determined to escape justice. I will not get into the specifics of the propaganda for obvious reasons, but those who commit treason must be held accountable. The public must be cautious and alert and report any sightings of Karsh or the Myers family."

"How long ago did they disappear?" Denise asked.

Everyone froze. Morgan started frantically looking around as if searching for a black hole to jump into.

"The moment it was determined we had lost trace of her we began our investigation. We are positive she and the others will be found quickly, but the public should remain vigilant and help our investigation during this time." Covington's face did not show a trace of rage, but the room could feel it emanating from him in waves.

"Commercial!" Morgan frantically mouthed, "Go to commercial!"

"Well, we thank you very much, Detective Covington, for your time and encourage the public to cooperate fully. And now, a word from our sponsors."

"Clear!" Morgan called, and Covington stood up. He ripped the microphone off his blazer, and, without a word, strode out of the studio. Morgan started screaming the second he was out of earshot.

"Do you want us shut down?! Do you have any idea what you've done?!"

"Morgan, what is he going to do?" Denise asked, leaning back. "Look, he didn't want me to ask a question, and I did anyway. They never actually announce stories like this. I wanted to know why – how far she could have gotten – the fact he didn't answer doesn't make that look good, does it?"

Morgan gaped at her, before returning to the mixing booth. Derek followed her and peeked over her shoulder to watch the playback.

There, on the screen, were the pictures of the so-called terrorists. And there was her picture. She'd been at the bar, waiting for Sean, however long ago. He'd seen her picture, the background of Sean's phone, heard Sean talk about her, mope about her, drink himself stupid over her.

"We have a problem." He muttered to Morgan.

"What?" Morgan jumped, not having seen him following her. "Why?"

"Because I'm pretty sure that girl's been gone a hell of a lot longer than you think."

———

Derek ignored the girl at the desk and strode past the men and women who reeked of sweat, unconscious of his distinct presence. He sidled through the equipment, around the exercise bikes, the racks of weights, and finally saw him, doing a chest press, staring determinedly at the ceiling.

"Logan."

"I think you're wearing the wrong clothes." Logan said, not looking at Derek.

"Didn't intend to stay."

"So why are you here?"

"Don't act stupid, Logan, it's beneath you."

"Fine. Then stop trying to play detective and following me."

"You're the one who put me out of a job."

"You can blame Denise for that."

"She get the same as Sean? Or was she too pretty for that?"

Logan flinched.

"Don't talk about that stuff here."

"Well apparently, here is the only place we can talk about it. I'm sick of this shit, Logan. If this is the reason Sean disappeared - if it's got something to do with that Kar—"

Logan slammed the weights down and sat bolt upright, glaring at Derek.

"Shut. Up."

"Are you going to talk to me then?"

"Fine. But not here. Meet me at my place in an hour."

"You promise?"

"Not if you keep asking if I promise. It's annoying."

"Fine. See you later." Derek said, walking back out of the gym.

True to his word, Logan appeared in front of his apartment building an hour later, to Derek's slight surprise. He said nothing, but let Logan open the door and walked in behind him.

Logan's place was a sparse studio, a couple of chairs, a sofa bed, and a TV, but it wasn't lacking comforts, Derek thought, as Logan handed him a glass of whiskey and they sat down on opposite chairs.

"You know you can't just start saying that shit out in the open. We've talked about that," Logan said, after taking a sip.

"My show was cancelled after Denise ran her mouth asking a question Covington didn't want to answer. Sean was taken in because he dated a girl who used a fake name. You killed him, don't even fucking try to deny it."

Logan put his glass on the end table, running a finger around the rim of it, before answering.

"Denise isn't dead yet," he said. "But you are right, Sean is."

"Of course." Derek drained half his glass before continuing, "I'm not going to apologize if it disrupts your world if I go to you demanding answers, alright?"

"Why do you get answers and no one else does?" Logan asked.

"Sean was my friend. He was yours too, or did you forget that?"

"Of course I didn't forget that. But Denise is someone's friend too, and so were countless of other people, and what fucking answers do they get?" Logan stood up.

"I'm not saying it's fair. But I know you, and I'm going to use you. Why was Sean arrested? Why do they actually want that Karsh girl arrested? Why are they really considering her a terrorist?" Derek demanded. Logan sighed, running his hand through his light brown hair so it stood up on end.

"Look, I can't tell you much, okay? We're guessing she was using a fake ID, and that's how she was able to fool Sean. We know she was dating other guys too, hell, you and I heard Sean complaining about that, but we don't have any way to track them down. Sean was mentioned in a letter we found in her apartment. What was written in the letter is why she was arrested and why it was decided to interrogate Sean."

"But how did they know it was our Sean? You didn't—"

"No. I didn't." Logan's face darkened, "I knew Sean had no idea, and I knew what would happen if they found him. No, a couple days after she disappeared, he sent her flowers."

"Dumbass." Derek leaned his face into his hand.

"Yeah, well, he told them right away he had no idea what was going on. That he'd been dating a girl named Samantha Trillow who worked as an accountant. That he hadn't heard from her in a while, they had never once discussed anything political. He said he'd never, ever heard of Melody Karsh."

"Did they buy it?"

Logan raised an eyebrow. "Eventually, they admitted he was probably just a guy who'd been tricked, but what do you do at that point? You can't just let him go." He went to pour himself another drink, and Derek sank further into his chair.

"So, why now? Why are they trying to get the story of her disappearing out there?"

"Covington made that decision without anyone knowing. My guess is, he knows he's fucked. She's probably buried deep in some city, with a new ID and you know how those things go. How many people do you see every day without actually looking at them? Covington must have decided that making some semblance of a public plea would be best."

"So, this girl gets to leave, go off somewhere, and Sean gets tortured and dies 'cause he fucked a terrorist?" Derek slammed his glass down.

"Derek," Logan snapped. "We both know she's not a terrorist."

Derek took several deep breaths. "What was in the letter?"

"Derek—"

"I have a right to know!" Derek's voice was rising, and he couldn't stop it, "I have a right to know what made them think she was such a traitor they went after him. What made them kill him. I deserve to fucking know." He could feel his eyes burning, and he stood up, turning away from Logan, glaring at the floor, beginning to pace around the room. "It's not right. You know, I know, everyone fucking knows it. I want to know what was written in that damn letter."

Logan looked at Derek, watching him as he wandered like a lost child. "I never said this was right." He crossed the room to the bookshelf. He pulled a file, stuffed between some of the volumes, and fished out a piece of paper.

"You have to understand something first. There's a lot at stake here." he said calmly. "Sit down, okay. Look at me." Derek took another moment, then sat back down.

"What?" he asked.

"Karsh was a Party member. On top of that, her mother

was killed eighteen years ago fleeing the country, and trying to help others flee the country. You have to know how they would look at a case like this. What they would assume based on who she is, and it would raise questions into how deep into the Party this goes."

"This is what made them go after Sean? If there is some deep dark plot what does that have to do with him?"

Logan eyed him warily but handed over the letter. Derek read it through.

"What the fuck is this?" He asked, waving it around.

"That's the letter."

"This? This is what made them go after Sean?"

"Well, it's what made us track down that library, and from there, we found a massive collection of letters like that."

"But why would you even need to go hunting for them? Why would this make you want to go after that girl? She's just ranting, saying she's scared of the police, being dramatic about being a Party member, that's it. That's fucking it."

"Yeah, I know."

"So, you killed Sean because some girl was bitching to her mother?"

"Dead mother, technically," Logan muttered, running a hand over his jaw.

Derek wanted to punch him.

"Do you really think that matters? She was upset. That's all. She's not saying let's blow up the president, she was just—"

"Well, there's the Independence Day thing—"

"Like that matters."

"Well, with the banned books—"

"So, kill her ex because she liked to read?!" Derek was practically shouting now.

"Be quiet," Logan hissed, "I get it. You're upset. But you've got to think. Yes, she liked to read. But what was she reading? You had a member of the Party capable of spreading these ideas. You know how they would've looked at that. You know what they would've thought that meant."

"But was she doing any of that? Did they talk to the people working with her? Or who she was working for? No, they talked to a guy who had nothing to do with it."

"You don't know that."

"Am I wrong?"

Logan sighed. "Anyone who worked with her said they had no idea about anything, the fake name, anything about what the letters said. Nothing. Arshem immediately had to cover his own ass, saying he 'suspected', so they did base a lot on that, but—"

"Arshem...you worked with him, didn't you? Had an axe to grind with her because she didn't follow her dad, she deviated like you?" Derek barely gave Logan enough time to nod before storming ahead, "Sure, only listen to the guy that already hated her. That's it. So, you fuckers went after Sean, and for what?"

"So, what are you going to do?" Logan shot back, "Start shouting in the streets that it was unfair that he died? No one will care; no one gives a damn about Sean. I'm sorry. I hate it too. But all you're going to do is get yourself killed."

Derek looked down at the letter for a moment, looking at the words, the way her pen had flitted across the paper.

"But—"

"No, now you listen. You want to give people something to think about, something to scream about, sure, fine, whatever. You want them to be as angry as you. Am I right?" Logan guessed. Derek nodded.

"But Sean is the wrong person. Don't argue. You know it's true. People will ask why he was more important than their kids and friends that died the same way, if they even bother to ask. Or they'll list him as another statistic, just another young black man who crossed the wrong side of the law. And anyone who actually pays attention? All it will do is lead them back to his friends, you and me."

"You really want me to just sit back and swallow this."

"No. I'm saying look at the bigger picture. You have to know what that letter would mean to people, if they were to see it. Who was associated with Sean's death that, eventually, you'll be able to use to highlight this? Call attention to all this crap? Who was the first terrorist in who knows how long to be on the national news *before* they were caught? If someone were to start something, something that could matter, who would unite people? Who would the public organize around?"

Derek looked blankly up at Logan.

"But I hate her."

"You don't have to like her to use her."

"Didn't...didn't you blame her?" Derek asked.

"Nah. I just thought she was careless, and desperate. But malicious?" Logan shrugged, splitting the rest of the bottle between their glasses. "No more than the rest of us."

Derek reread the letter, aware of Logan watching him closely. "What?"

"You didn't get this from me. If anyone realizes you have it, you will go down, and you will be killed. They will question who gave it to you. I'm not dying for you, Derek, and I'm not dying for someone who is already dead."

They said nothing, finishing their drinks in silence.

December 2092

Covington stood in the hallway waiting for Parker. He never liked coming down here, but he also wasn't in a position to argue after Parker's continued support, even after his former lieutenant had been moved to the Prevention Unit in November. Parker claimed it was a promotion, but Covington knew it was punishment for allowing him to act without supervision. So, he stood, trying to block out the screams as he scratched his neck, pretending the whole scenario was something he did every day.

Parker came out, shedding a pair of gloves and locking the door behind him.

"Sorry, Alexander. I didn't expect this to take so long," he said. "We've tried pretty much everything and we're having to get creative."

"This is for...?" Covington asked.

"The information I have for you, come on, let's talk upstairs." Parker said, walking swiftly down the hall. "I had to track down a couple leads to figure it out, which is why I didn't come to you sooner, but I think you'll be appreciative."

"Is this about the vandalism?"

"Are you using that tame of a word?"

"It's what we're saying to suppress how far it's spread." Covington grumbled.

"How far *has* it spread?"

"We reckon Maryland, if not farther."

"Surprised to see you're still breathing. Not bad, surprised, mind you."

"Yeah, turns out putting my face on TV, associated with her, means if I'm taken off the case the public might suspect issues with the investigation. No one wants to touch this mess, it's easier for higher ups if everything is traced back to me. We've finally got another team giving us help—I don't have time to deal with this shit and the Karsh case. I've been begging for more backup, for more help of any kind. They gave me four men when I asked for at least ten. I know it's my fault."

"Yeah, well, I think I can help stabilize this fiasco." Parker said.

"What've you found?"

"You'll see." Parker led him up the stairs and opened the door to his office.

"It's the file there," he pointed, and Covington picked it up. He skimmed past the pictures of graffiti, the portraits drawn in spray paint along rooftops, the words across windows and bricks. He felt his stomach churn every time he saw them. He instead flipped over to the report.

"How did you find this?" He asked, his eyes wide.

"A kid we picked up after curfew," Parker said, grinning proudly, "He claimed to know people in the 'Free Melody' movement. We tracked down his leads and found one guy with a list of locations hidden in his apartment. The first place on the list was Garfield Heights. We staked it out for a week, and the thugs did show up but there weren't enough of us. They escaped. Those are all the pictures from that night. So, we have to assume that everything else on that list is legitimate, it's just a matter of getting him to give us the dates and times. That's who I was in session with just now."

Covington stared at the list.

"The Navy Yard? What the hell do they want to do there?"

"More of the same, I'm assuming. We've got to have a larger unit ready to catch them. Stop them before they can do any more damage."

"Yes, but," Covington said slowly, "I've got an idea."

"What's that?" Parker pulled the file away from Alexander, "You want to catch these fuckers, right?"

Covington raised an eyebrow. "Obviously, I do. But it's more than that. Even if we catch the ones that are at the Yard, there's no guarantee that'll be all of them, or that they'll give up everyone involved. What we've got to do is ensure that none of those pieces of shit tries this again."

"Ah." Parker smiled. "I got you. What do you need me to do?"

———————

"Derek, come on, don't be greedy!" Lena laughed, reaching out her hand. He grinned, handing over the bottle. She took a swig, and he went back to the spray paint.

"FREE MELODY" covered the bricks in spiky, red writing. They'd already done all the other houses on the street, filled the mailboxes with copies of the letter. Benji was standing at the side of the house, painting another portrait of Melody with Fred. Morgan was finishing up the slogan on the previous house. The work had gotten sloppier as they'd gone through the supply of beer, but it was still recognizable. They'd done it enough times by now they could practically do it asleep. Derek took a step back to admire the paint and pulled out a plastic bag from his pocket. He made a fist and poured some of the white powder between his forefinger and thumb, pressed his nose to his skin, and snorted it.

"Jackie won't be happy that you took more of that," Morgan looked over at him, frowning.

"Is Jackie going to find out?" Lena narrowed her eyes at Morgan as Derek passed her the bag.

"How many more do you think we should do?" Benji asked. Derek waited for Lena to give him the bag back and took another hit before answering.

"I think we're alright for tonight."

"Good," Morgan said, sitting on the ground next to Lena and stealing her bottle.

"Hey!"

"There's a couple more, don't worry," Derek passed the six pack beside him towards her and she, Benji, and Fred each took one.

"We should probably pack it in though," Fred suggested, "It's already almost two."

"Yeah, good shout." Derek nodded, and then began to put the cans of spray paint into the bag. Benji, whether confused by darkness or inebriation, accidentally tossed his empty bottle as well, and the sound of the glass shattering echoed across the pavement.

"You idiot!" Morgan hissed at him. Derek froze, looking around. A porch light turned on, and he pointed the group in the opposite direction of the house.

They began to backtrack, heading along the sidewalk towards a grassy area where they could hide amongst the trees. Every noise seemed to echo in Derek's ears. As they approached the end of the next row of houses, he could swear he heard extra footsteps. He held up a hand to stop his friends behind him.

"They had to have gone this way," the voice was faint, but distinct, "They wouldn't have been stupid enough to go towards that noisy bitch."

Morgan's eyes went wide, looking at Derek. The others started to back up in the opposite direction of the voices. But, in his haste to move, Fred tripped over Lena, and they both fell to the ground. Lena's shriek pierced the sky, and before they could say anything else they saw the beams of flashlights pointed in their direction. Without thinking, Derek grabbed Fred's collar, and pulled him up, Benji doing the same with Lena, and they took off running. He tried to block out all sounds, the shouts of the officers behind him, the panting of the others, someone's muffled moans, and just concentrated on putting as much distance between himself and the lights as possible. They rounded a corner and found themselves in front of a community garden. Derek ducked behind a tree, gasping for breath.

He looked around and saw everyone behind him and breathed a sigh of relief. He peeked his head out to carefully check outside the garden.

"Dammit."

"They didn't go far,"

"Check in here?"

"Yes, sir."

He frantically motioned to the others, and crouched down low against a bush, waiting for the officers to enter the garden. As they did, he sneaked back out the garden entrance to the sidewalk as quietly as he could, hoping against hope that he wouldn't be seen. He kept his quiet pace up along the sidewalk, leading the others, when he heard a twig snap.

There was no helping it. He took one moment to see the stricken looks of Morgan and Benji, who were right behind him, and then started sprinting again. He had no idea where they were going, just that they had to get away from the officers behind them.

Except that fifty feet in front of them was another set of flashlights, and footsteps closing in. Derek tore to the side, almost slamming into the side of a building in his desperate attempt to get away. He found himself in an alleyway, looking around frantically. He saw the ladder to a fire escape and jumped up, trying to reach the bottom rung. He managed to grab it, lifting himself up, and climbed to the first landing.

"Derek!" He heard Morgan's cries beneath him. He turned around and lowered a hand to her as Benji followed his path, already climbing up the ladder, Fred waiting beneath him with the officers on their heels. He pulled Morgan up and then kept climbing, trying not to think about where Lena had gone.

He reached the top, and pulled himself onto the roof, helping Morgan after him. Only then did he look down to decide where to go next, and what he saw made his blood run cold.

An officer was pulling Benji's legs, trying to force him to come down, but Benji wasn't giving up; his grip on the ladder so strong it was making his knuckles turn white.

"Lucas, move!" The other called, aiming a gun up at the pair of them. Benji, not looking down, didn't see why he was now free to move, but took the opportunity to frantically climb, and the bullet, instead of hitting his back, hit him on his thigh. He screamed in agony, his leg sliding, and he slipped down the ladder. The officer named Lucas grabbed him, and forced him, still standing, leg bleeding, into cuffs.

Derek, beside Morgan, could feel her start to move, and

pulled her back.

"No, we have to—"

He said nothing, but grabbed her arm tightly, and pulled her towards the door into the building.

"We can't!"

"They're coming for us too," He whispered, refusing to look behind him.

"But Benji, Fred, Lena—"

Derek didn't reply, but forced the door open and dragged her inside, trying to ignore the cries of pain echoing below him.

———

Alexander stood beside Parker at the podium, feeling particularly smug. The reporters were gathered around, waiting for their speeches, the three prisoners waiting on the platform. The cameras were all pointing at him and Parker for the time being, but that would soon change. Sure, they had extracted very little from the prisoners. They still did not have a name of the leader of their organization, or whatever it was. They did not know how it was being planned, or what the goal was, if there was one, other than that they didn't think it was fair that Karsh was being charged with treason.

"A silly thing to die for, really," he'd told Parker and Jordan over dinner as they celebrated the capture.

And yes, they had only captured three of the supposed five idiots that were in the Navy Yard neighborhood that night, and the attacks had not stopped yet. But, after this, no one would dare to try again.

"Thank you all for coming today," Parker began, "Detective Covington and I are very grateful that you are here to witness the events today. Thanks to the investigative work by my unit, and the team established by Detective Covington, we have been able to detain and interrogate terrorists operating within our city and the Washington metropolitan area. We are here today to witness these criminals be brought to justice. Detective Covington?"

Alexander took the podium as Parker stood aside. Facing the reporters with pride he stated, "As you well know, individuals have been spreading vicious slander and vandalizing our city for the past two months. We have, with the help of Lieutenant Parker, been able to detain these individuals. They are operating under the delusion that this country will allow terrorists to go free. That those who spread lies and propaganda about our Great Nation are not treacherous. They believe that Melody Karsh is not guilty of any wrongdoing. She is a traitor to this government as are those who stand beside her, and their actions will be met with the full consequences of the law. We are here to show what those consequences are." He gestured to the prisoners. Blindfolded, hands bound, they stood on the platform beneath individual nooses.

"They have been sentenced to execution today and will provide an example of what happens to traitors. We are a strong, united nation, under the leadership of Our Dear Jamison. Thank you." He stood back, facing the prisoners.

———

Lena, Fred, and Benji stood on the platform, Lena shaking, Fred's blindfold soaked with tears. The nooses were fitted around their necks. In the audience, though Covington had no way of knowing, Derek stood at the back looking on without really seeing, his brain struggling to process what was unfolding before his eyes. Benji's leg had been haphazardly wrapped with gauze. Dried blood and dirt caked the clumsy bandaging, and it would not support his weight. His face shone with sweat at the effort of staying upright.

No last words.

No pleas.

A pull of a lever and they fell.

Nearly 700 miles away, Melody watched as the legs twitched, and moved no more.

From the case file of Melody Karsh: July 2092-April 2093 July 2091

Dear Mom,

So, I thought living with Dad was hell, but fuck, Arshem is giving him a run for his money. I heard about my assignment right before I got back, and I'd heard things about him, looked up his record, the bills he's passed, the committees he's on. Governmental Affairs—what could be a better place to start? I think I actually felt excited for a second.

Lucy was nice, she took me around the building, showed me where everything I would need is, and warned me that Arshem was 'temperamental.' That's an understatement. Mom, he came in, scoffed at me, and stormed into his office after hissing Lucy's name. She told me not to worry, but it's clear. He does not like being stuck with me.

Who can blame him, though? Anyone who got stuck with me would have their reputation tarnished, to work with someone who deviated off the track. Arshem's kids are still too young, but you know full well that if they tried, he'd disown them. Ship them to a reconstruction city. Hide them in some way.

He won't let me touch his speeches, won't let me do anything except get him coffee and sit at my desk. Silently. Lucy is grateful to have the extra help. She had me work on one of his speeches, and I told her to take credit for it when all was said and done. He said he loved it, that it read perfectly. And then complained that the coffee I made for him was too hot.

You'll never guess what research I've been doing this past week. We're trying to petition for better intelligence sharing with the UK again. Arshem is against it, saying we can't trust the whims of a parliament for something as vital as the sharing of critical intelligence. Meanwhile, I'm just sitting in the corner trying not to laugh. Remember when I wanted to join Executive for the chance to get over there?

I shouldn't have had so much wine tonight. I don't want to think about that.

Leo's been getting on my case lately about that. Saying I go out too much, that I need to calm down. Fuck him. He gets to go to school, go to classes, for free because Liz teaches there. What right does he have to bitch about my life? He has no fucking idea. He doesn't even bother to read the stuff in the library anymore. He says it makes him too depressed. I remember, it was a few years ago now, Dad took me to one of his conferences, and he took me to some of the reconstruction cities out that way. He had a really nice rental car, and we drove around. And he told me how lucky I was to have been born into the Party, that I'd never have to live like this.

He was so proud of himself too, saying that one day, when I was done with my training, I'd get the chance to help people like that. Now, I've read enough of the clippings from that time to realize what that all means. It's a testament, isn't it? To what was fought for, what was lost. And we're going to hide or destroy every last memory of that fight, no matter how many people that kills. And I'm now working for one of the senators that supplies funding for this shit.

But Leo thinks it's cool to say I need to back off the booze. You know I love him, Mom, but seriously. He needs to shut up.

Love,
Melody

III

Melody sat on the fire escape, a bottle wrapped in a paper bag stuck between her knees. Her eyes were closed, and her forehead leaned against the bars of the railing, feeling the light breeze on her skin. She'd been sitting in the same spot since she'd seen the report, watching the sky fade from an early morning sun to twilight. The noises around her had faded into a distant thumping in the back of her skull.

People had died. People were dying. For her. In her name.

She had to suppress the urge to throw up again.

She clutched the bottle tightly and took another great swig. It burned the back of her throat, but she kept drinking until she heard a voice below her.

"Erin!"

She looked down.

"Hey Dale." She tried to make her voice sound normal. Dale, the neighbor below her, looked up at her from his own fire escape.

"Didn't see you at the site today."

"No, I, I didn't feel too well." She clutched the bottle between her knees, not sure if she cared whether or not he saw.

"Don't worry. Your brother covered for you. He's a good kid."

"Yeah. He is." She tried to smile.

"Here, toss me a bit of that." He reached up and she passed the bottle down to him.

"Tastes like shit." He grimaced.

"What do you expect?"

He made a noncommittal grunt and took another swig.

"You'll be back tomorrow?"

"Sure."

He looked out into the distance for a moment, the Manhattan skyline across the river, the mass construction zone stretching out right in front of them along the Brooklyn coast.

"I like this time of night." He sighed. "It's peaceful."

"Mm." She took the bottle he handed back to her, and he stared at her, studying her face.

"You sure you're okay?"

"Yeah." She nodded.

"You came from Chicago, yeah?"

"What?" The change of subject caught her off guard. "Oh, oh yeah, when the funds dried up, we started making our way up here."

"Yeah. I keep thinking, I might want to head out of here someday, but then..." He gestured out to the water, to the sky, to the buildings in the distance, magically preserved in isolation.

"Mm," she said again, "It's nicer here." She took another drink, and they let the silence hang.

A knock on the side of the windowsill made her jump, and Leo appeared, a cigarette resting behind his ear. His hair, now black and shaggy, hung around his head, the setting sun throwing

94

his gaunt cheekbones into a sharper focus.

"Trade you," he said quietly, reaching for the bottle. She handed it to him wordlessly, and he handed her the cigarette. He looked down and nodded to Dale.

"Hey John." Dale grinned up at him.

"Hey,"

"I was just about to turn in, you keep an eye on her, alright?"

"I'm good, Dale, promise." Melody tried to reassure him, but it was Leo's nod that made him wave a hand in wordless goodbye. He turned around, heading back inside, shutting his door behind him. Leo handed a lighter to Melody, taking a drink from the bottle.

"Fuck, what is this?"

"Vodka, from the bodega a couple blocks down."

"Fuck." He repeated.

"It was cheap." She shrugged, lighting the cigarette, breathing deeply. She pointed it at the bottle. "Thought you didn't approve?"

He shrugged, sitting across from her, staring at a point just above her head. The sky around them continued to darken, and they listlessly traded the vodka back and forth.

"Melody," He said, quietly, when the sky was lit with streetlamps, "I know what you must be thinking," He ignored her mutinous expression and continued, "I know that right now all you're thinking about is going back. You don't have to. It's not your fault."

"They're dying, Leo." She whispered.

"It's not your responsibility."

She glared at him.

"You didn't ask them to do any of this. You left."

She couldn't look at him. Couldn't look at anything. Couldn't sit still, but couldn't move. Couldn't deal with the mountainous pile of guilt threatening to overwhelm her, pull her over a dangerous edge.

"I have to stop this, Leo."

"How?"

"I don't know. I'll find Logan. He's the one who all but told me to run. He's on the force. He'll know something."

"How are you going to do that?"

"I don't know. He's not answering my messages. I've been texting, tried calling, but he's not answering. I think I've got to find him, in person. I can't—people can't be fucking dying because of me, Leo. I can't let it happen. I can't sit here and keep pretending we can rebuild Brooklyn while that's happening."

She was shaking so badly she almost dropped the bottle. He came across the platform and took it from her, placing it to the side. He didn't try to hold her, just put a hand on her knee.

It was enough to steady her as they sat in silence. Darkness enveloped them, and he took her frozen hands, puffing hot air on them, rubbing them between his own, trying to bring feeling back into the fingers.

"Dale still hasn't put it together?"

"Hm?" It was an effort to bring her attention back to him.

"Dale still thinks you're Erin, not Melody."

"Oh, yeah, seems to, anyway."

Leo nodded, more to himself than to her.

"Has anyone figured it out, do you think?"

She looked up at him. Her blue eyes were covered in brown colored contacts and her hair, chopped short and dyed a dark brown as soon as possible after they'd left D.C., sat straight around her face. Her frame, much like his, was leaner and tougher from the months in Brooklyn. The chances of someone just glancing at her and thinking she was the girl on the news were very slim.

"I'm not sure. A few, maybe? I think I see it in their faces. I haven't heard any announcements about police presence being increased up here though, so if anyone knows, they haven't said anything."

"And Dale really thinks we went to Chicago first?"

"Or he's willing to go along with the lie. Whether he actually believes it or not I honestly can't tell."

Leo looked over her head out towards the neighboring buildings, lost in thought. She leaned her head against his shoulder. She felt him shiver, and took a deep breath, resigned.

"Come on."

"Come on where?"

"We're going back inside." She stood up, and held out a hand to him. He took it and stood. She climbed back into the window, and threw a blanket around her shoulders.

They crowded around the radiator, Leo pulling another blanket from her bed. The temperature was not that much different outside than inside, but at least there were more available layers.

Those working to rebuild the outer boroughs of New York were automatically given housing in exchange for their work, in addition to two meals a day. Single rooms were given to those in construction and utilities, suites to those in lower management, consulting, lower public service positions, and married couples with children under 18. Full apartments were given to those in higher tier positions. Leo and Melody had been placed in the same building, with Greg and Liz two blocks over. The high mobility of workers between various construction cities like Chicago and Houston, and the overall dreary, exhausted atmosphere meant that the four had been able to slip in without much suspicion from

Brooklyn law enforcement or New York state border patrol. The tiny room, with its twin bed, thin blankets, bare white walls, and tiny dresser with TV, was as bleak and plain as it was when Melody had first arrived. Greg and Liz had attempted to add some homey touches to theirs—adding an extra blanket, a vase of flowers— little nods to staying in one place for a while. Melody, however, had never felt the urge to make the room feel like home. It had always been temporary. She'd known that.

Leo didn't say anything for a while, but stole glances at her from time to time. She'd turned on the TV, waiting for any other news, hair on the back of her neck standing on end.

"We're safe here." He said finally. He knew better than to hug her, than to comfort her, but was still attempting to reassure her.

"It's not going to be 'safe' anywhere." She murmured. "Eventually they'll bring the search far enough up North, the police up here will get their shit together, the reward will be enough for people to turn me in, even if they wouldn't before. We could get along here for a while longer but eventually we'd have to leave. And that's not the point. They're dying, Leo. You want me to stay because Dale's nice about me missing work? I'm going. I'm leaving. I'm going to stop it." She didn't look at him, kept staring at her hands, running them back and forth across the fabric of her pants, feeling her palms sweat even though her fingers were still frozen cold.

Leo seemed to hesitate on the verge of speech for a moment, clearly weighing out his words.

"Are you sure you're leaving to stop it?"

Her eyes snapped up to meet his.

"What?"

"Are you this upset because you need it to stop, or because you weren't there to start it?" Her gaze left him quaking.

"Start what, exactly? A doomed attempt at resistance? A creative form of mass suicide? Am I sad I'm not there with a noose around my neck? I can't say that I am."

"But you're saying you want to go back. You're saying you want to stop them. You could just let it die out, if it's that hopeless, they don't need you to end it. You could stay here, and the result would be the same."

Melody stood up, letting the blanket fall off her. She moved to the dresser and began emptying out drawers of her few possessions.

"I could stay here, and they would die, or I could go, and they could die. I could have stayed, turned myself in, and none of this would have happened. Instead, they had time to do…whatever the fuck this is."

"Exactly. They had time to do something you couldn't. Something you would have never let yourself consider. And maybe, now that it's happening, you want to be a part of that."

She reached under the bed for her backpack and began shoving things into it indiscriminately. "You can come with, or not, I don't give a shit. But I'm going."

He watched her movement and smiled, somewhat sadly. "You do to care what I do. Where you go, I go. But you know, if you do go back, you'll die. You'll never get out again. You've… you've got to know that, before you…" He let the sentence hang. They stared at each other, and he understood in the silence that she was not changing her mind.

"So, when do we leave?"

———

"I hate driving." Leo groaned.

"Why are you complaining? You're not driving."

"But I'm still in the car. It's essentially the same."

"No, it's not." Melody rolled her eyes, and Leo grunted.

"Hey, any word from Logan yet?"

"Nope." Melody had been waiting for the phone to buzz since she'd sent the latest text three hours ago, and it didn't help that Leo kept asking every ten minutes if there had been a response.

"You sure he—"

"I will specifically crash your side of the car."

"It's just a question."

"It was 'just a question' the first fifty times."

"Fine." He sighed, leaning back into the seat.

The phone buzzed. They glanced at each other.

"It's not like I can look at it." She said pointedly. He reached for the cup holder and grabbed the phone.

"He says, 'You're fucking insane. You were here the whole time?'"

"Tell him 'No, of course not. Do you know who it is?'"

Leo typed for a moment. They sat in silence for a few seconds.

"'Go to Channel 7. Ask for D.'"

"D?" Melody asked, but before Leo could reply to the text, the phone vibrated again.

"'And don't text me again.'"

They looked at each other.

"Well, it's the best we've got." Melody shrugged.

"So…you're just going to walk into a news station?"

"We'll see how the checkpoint goes." She said, trying to sound more confident than she felt.

When they finally reached the checkpoint into D.C., she passed over their IDs with a respectful smile to the guard on duty and explained they were coming into town for the holidays to visit relatives. He merely nodded in a bored sort of way after running the IDs through the scanner. After they passed the inspection, they were waved through the gate without another look. Erin and John Thackeray had entered the city without any problems.

Yet, Melody stayed tense as they drove through familiar streets, passing by old landmarks, the paused construction of new, cheap apartment buildings, the brown, dead grass, the people scurrying along the streets. The city was tense, even more so than before.

They approached downtown and parked the car in a garage. Melody shoved sunglasses on, though it wasn't that bright, for the added protection. They walked back outside and quickly darted along the streets, following directions from Leo's phone.

They climbed up the steps of the building, a skyscraper with a full courtyard in the front. A neat little row of bushes and flowers circled the national and Party flags, waving high in the sky, dancing against the sun. Inside, there weren't many people wandering around, but through the glass of the front door they could see a guard at the security desk. They looked at each other.

"So, we ask for D?" Leo looked skeptical.

"I guess…" Melody looked around. "I guess, there's got to be someone who comes down a lot, right? We just have to check the sign in."

"You're going to get us killed," Leo seethed.

"At least I'm trying to think of something!" Melody shot back at him. Someone else was speaking to the security guard, and Melody stole her chance. She hurried into the building and walked determinedly up to the desk. She looked down at the log in book. For the ones for Channel 7, a fair few were signed in as a "Meeting with Des." That was probably it, she reasoned. She waited until the

101

woman had finished up with her conversation, and then moved to stand in front of the security guard.

"Good afternoon," He said, "How can I help you?"

"Hi," she said, trying not to sound nervous. "I need to get to Channel 7; I'm here for a meeting with Des."

He blinked at her.

"You're a...friend?" he asked doubtfully.

"Yeah." She nodded, trying to appear more confident than she felt.

"Because he never comes in before 6 or 7; he works the night shift." He raised his eyebrows.

"Oh." She felt her stomach drop, and for a split second her face betrayed her disappointment. It was a trap. Logan had to have tricked her. She was going to be caught and arrested and—

"He didn't tell you?" He was looking more and more confused.

"No, I must have made a mistake, I'm very sorry." She turned to leave, but decided to try once more before giving up. "Listen. I don't have a way to contact him, but we were supposed to talk today. I can't come back tonight. Do you have a way to help?"

The guard looked at her. He seemed to be sizing her up. He gestured to her to lean closer. When she did, he said quietly, "The holiday the first week of July?"

Her stomach twisted. He was looking at her nervously, expectantly. If he *was* a part of the movement, he was putting an awful lot on the line too. She could be a cop. This could be their code; to see who was on their side. She had to try. She'd come here, and couldn't walk away.

"Independence Day." She breathed in little more than a whisper.

102

He didn't acknowledge the answer, but instead, wrote something down on the corner of a piece of paper, and tore it off for her. And with that, he sat back in his chair and turned his face to look at the security screens. She looked down at the piece of paper as she walked out the door. It was a phone number. She crushed it in her hand.

How all of these idiots hadn't died already was nothing short of a miracle.

The phone rang twice.

"Hello?"

"Is this Des?"

"Who is this?"

"We need to meet."

"Who is this?" The voice sounded almost panicked.

Melody weighed the words carefully.

"I'm a...sort of a friend of Logan's."

"What's your name?"

"Erin Thackeray." The words had stopped sounding unnatural some time ago.

"You couldn't just come to the station?"

"That's how I got your number. Logan didn't tell me to come at night. He leaves out details sometimes." Melody smiled to herself.

"Yeah. He didn't tell me about you." He still sounded suspicious.

"Like I said. We're only sort of friends."

"So, what do you want?"

"We need to meet. Now."

"Look, I don't know you, I don't—"

"You need to meet with me." Melody cut him off. "Trust me. You want to hear what I have to say. I passed your guard's test. I know Logan. You can trust me."

Silence.

"Okay. Come to mine."

He gave her the address, and she hung up without another word.

She didn't want Leo to come, but he insisted. She knew it was no use arguing with him, so in another twenty minutes, they were in front of the building, buzzing to be let in. It was a shabby looking shade of grey, with the customary flag fluttering in the breeze above them.

"Hello?"

"It's Erin."

"There are two of you." He must have had a camera.

"It's my brother."

"Fine."

He hit the button to let them in, and they hurried inside.

She knocked twice, and he opened the door a crack, made sure it was just the two of them, and let them in.

They didn't say anything for a second.

"You're Logan's friend?" Derek asked.

"Not exactly." Leo leaned against the wall with his arms crossed.

"Why are you here? Who are you?"

Melody looked him up and down. He was not what she had expected. Not that she'd known what to expect. But this guy... she remembered him, vaguely. She'd met him. The same night she'd met Logan. The realization of who it was hit her and she fought to keep her reaction internal. Why Logan hadn't hinted at

that, just said it was the same person they'd already talked about...
but whatever. There were more pressing matters.

"I'm Melody," she said. For all the drama that sentence
presented, it sounded very lame. "You've been using me to start
your fucking revolution and it's gotten people killed. You can't use
me anymore. I'm back, and I'm not going to let you." She knew
that it was just going from bad to worse, but that was what she'd
wanted to say, even if it sounded ridiculous.

He blinked.

"You're not Melody." He snorted. "Get out of here."

"Yeah, she is." Leo said defensively.

"Oh yeah?" Derek smirked, "And who the fuck are you?
That dude who went with her?"

"Yeah, that's Leo." She said, quietly, but determinedly.

Derek stared from one to the other.

"You're insane. The pair of you. You got it into your heads
that you wanted to be heroes, to stop this from infringing on
your precious lives, or whatever, but you're idiots. You don't look
anything like Karsh. Her picture is all over the place."

"Okay," Melody said, "So ask me something to prove
myself. You must remember something about me from when we
met all those months ago. But I was Sam, back then."

Derek gaped at her. "Fuck. How the fuck did you... Did
Logan tell you I was...did he tell you he showed me the letter?"

It felt like her stomach had dropped beneath the
floorboards. Logan had given him the letter? The news clips had
said they were 'spreading propaganda'—was this it?

"Logan shared the letter with you?"

Derek looked angry with himself.

"Tell me something about the letters," He said, eyes narrowing in suspicion, "Something only you would know. I need to know you're not a cop."

Melody rolled her eyes. "If this is how you monitor someone for your organization, you're doing a piss poor job of monitoring your organization. Anything only I would know, you wouldn't. But, okay. Fine. I started writing letters to my dead mother from the time I could hold a pen." Melody said. "There were more in a hidden library in Leo's house, those were all written from the time I was 16, from the time I found out that she wasn't actually in the UK, that her ship had been sunk by ICE, and that my father had been lying to me my entire life."

Derek blinked.

"I wrote the letter Logan gave you. I suppose you've been spreading it, and I guess using it as a code to figure out who's actually on board with your damn revolution. Though I've got to say, you need something a hell of a lot more subtle than 'Independence Day.' Independence Day? Are you kidding me? After the Anthem Riot and everything? You make that your fucking code word?"

"Hang on a minute—"

"And if you are spreading the letters then everyone knows that Independence Day is a thing you absolute moron. Could you have picked anything more obvious? Are you trying to get all your people killed?"

She was breathing heavily, all the anger and resentment she'd felt for months coming out and landing on this man. He was still looking at her like some sort of mythological creature.

"How did you...where...where have you been?" He asked weakly.

"Hiding." She shrugged. They'd already decided not to say anywhere specific, to protect Liz and Greg.

"But how did you get back?"

She raised an eyebrow. "You're the one basing a campaign around me, and you didn't believe me when I said who I was. You think a guy sitting at a checkpoint all day is going to give a damn?"

He opened and closed his mouth a few times, then turned to the kitchen.

"Where are you going?" She snapped at him.

"I need a drink," he called back to them. Leo gave her a look.

She sat down on one of the chairs in the living room, and Derek came back with a beer.

"You've got to let me get my head around this," he said. "How did you leave? Why did you come back? What's the deal with you and Logan?"

She could feel Leo's eyes on her but didn't look at him again.

"How we left, where we went, doesn't matter. I came back because you decided to make me a martyr and, amazingly, I'm not 100% on board with that shit. Logan and I met the same day I met you. I was the girl in the senator's office he was talking about. The one Arshem was pissed at. I doubt you remember. Anyway, he recognized me. Recognized that Sean was calling me by a fake name. Confiscated my fake ID. We, well, we didn't become friends, but..."

"He protected you. Kind of."

"Kind of." She nodded. "I saw the execution. When we were on our way back to D.C., I sent him a message asking if he knew anything. Didn't say it was from me, but he knew. Said not to text him again, but to go to Channel 7 and ask for D."

Derek scowled. "He probably forgot that the code name is 'Des'."

"Well, that's the story. Now it's your turn. Why did you start this? Why the fuck did you start this? What did you say to Logan that got him to show you that letter?" Melody fumed.

Derek didn't say anything for a while. He took a few sips of beer and pulled his phone out of his pocket. He spent a little while looking through it, and then passed it to her. She read through the messages quickly, trying to control her nausea. It was such unbridled honesty, his emotions fumbled and nonsensical. She'd known, at some level, that Sean didn't view their arrangement as casually as she did, but she didn't know it had been this bad.

"Why are you showing me this?" she asked, handing the phone back, not looking at him.

"He's dead," he said coldly. She felt the color leave her face.

"Why? I didn't... He didn't have any connection to... How would they have even known how to find him? Logan didn't...?"

"No. He wouldn't," Derek's eyes flashed. "The poor bastard tried to send you flowers."

Leo groaned behind her.

"I told you," he said. "I told you not to go out with those guys; I told you that it was only going to end badly."

"Are you seriously trying to make me feel worse?" Melody snapped around to look at him, "Are you really going to bring up all that shit now?" Leo shrank back against the wall at her look.

"How many others were there? Other guys like Sean?" Derek raised his eyebrows.

"Really? We're going to pick apart my sex life?" Melody snapped at him.

"Well, who knows how many other people you're responsible for." He shot back.

"You want to talk about people we're responsible for? What

about the people who were just hanged? Whose fault is that?" She could see him going red but kept pushing, "All you're doing is letting innocent people die, and one of them is going to crack and lead the police straight to you. And then what will you do?"

Derek stood up and leaned over her, pushing her back farther into the chair.

"You only care about saving your own skin. That's why you're here. Stop pretending you care about the people that died on that platform. I was their friend. I was there with them when they were caught."

"Of course you were. Did you have a plan to escape if something went wrong or did you figure, eh, screw it, it'll be fine?"

Derek's face was bright red with fury. He looked like a balloon ready to pop. "You're gonna fucking stand there and lecture me? You had a chance to do something, and you ran. You just let Sean die. You could've fought, you could've stood up to people like Covington, you and Logan, and instead you yell at me when I try to actually—"

"Try to do what?" She stood up too, pushing the chair back so she could face him head on. "What's the plan? Tell me. Do you have a plan? Or is it just to spread a name around and hope it does some abstract 'thing'?"

"I..." he tried to form words and couldn't. He turned away from her, running a hand through his hair.

She took a moment to breathe, and then spoke more calmly.

"You think for a moment I haven't wanted to do what you've been doing? Stand against the Party? Say this isn't fair? When I was there, working for Arshem, it was hell. And you have no idea what it was like at Quantico before that. But you know what happened during the War. We don't have anything left to fight for. This is what we're left with. You've got to stop this, Derek. We've got to make the most of what's left and try to keep ourselves sane and safe."

He didn't answer her. He drank some more, looking around at the books on the shelves.

"You know what happened during the War?" His tone sounded off to Melody, and she didn't say anything. He continued, "You've read about it? You know what happened? You know why it started and what actually went down?"

"Sort of," she said cautiously. His voice had her on edge, and she didn't quite know why. "It's not like Liz's library was complete. She heard the stories from her parents, had old newspapers and magazines her parents had managed to keep, it wasn't a complete story, but I know the gist."

"Tell me." He still didn't look at her, but she thought she could detect shame emanating from him. She glanced at Leo whose eyes were widening.

"Do…do you not know?" she asked. He shook his head. "Because, Sean said, your grandfather had been alive, and that's where you got some…ideas, I guess. I thought you knew."

Derek let out a humorless laugh.

"My parents broke off contact with him when I was about eleven." He was staring so hard at the ground Melody thought the floor would start to smoke, "I tried to reach out to him when I was older, but he never returned my calls."

"He was probably afraid," Leo said, "Afraid of what your parents had put in your head, afraid you'd only try to corner him, afraid he'd say something accidentally. It's not easy to hide all the time." Melody let the boys stare at each other for a few moments before breaking the silence.

110

"Be that as it may," she sidestepped to block Leo from Derek's line of view, "It's a bit off topic. We were talking about getting you to stop using me as a mascot."

"And I was telling you that's not happening." Derek took a sip of his beer.

"So, you're going to ignore everything I've said, use my name, and watch more people die?" Melody snapped.

"If you're so upset that more people might die, you might as well try to help us. Come to the meeting tonight. See where we stand. We're not going to be put off because that bastard Covington is trying to scare us. We all know the risks. You're either with us, or against us." His stare bore into her, but she didn't back down.

"You can't make me an enemy when you're trying to use me against the Party. You can't make me a symbol and an omen at the same time." She glowered at him.

"I suppose not. But there's very little you can do to stop us apart from running around shouting 'Stop!' is there? And, really, you can't do that without drawing attention to yourself, and I doubt you want to do that." Derek's lip curled up into a slight smirk. It was taking a good deal of Melody's self-control not to punch him in the nose.

She looked at Leo one last time, then back at Derek.

"When's the meeting tonight?"

———

Leo stood awkwardly to the side as she coughed. He'd offered to hold back her hair, but it was too short for that to be of any real use. She pressed her palm against the brick, supporting herself as she gasped for air, trying to ignore the smell of the contents of her stomach on the ground beneath her.

"You're not actually going to go tonight, are you?" Leo asked.

111

"He's going to get everyone killed."

"And you're going to burst in and stop them?"

"I want to know what the hell he's saying to everyone." She spat on the ground, trying to clear her mouth.

"You good?" he asked. She raised her eyebrows. "No, I mean, to walk somewhere. We got to get the car, check into a hotel, lie low until tonight."

"Oh, yeah, I'm good." She tried to take a step, but swayed, and had to support herself against the wall again. "Okay, give me a minute." She bent forward, her head between her knees, and willed herself to breathe. "I don't get what he's playing at, why he won't listen to me, to us."

"And it's your name he's using."

"It's not really about me though," she muttered.

Leo tilted his head. "What are you talking about?" He took a quick look around, then lowered his voice, "*Free Melody*? What else would it be?"

"You heard him. He only gave a damn about his friend. If he thought he'd get the same effect with *Remember Sean*, he would've done that instead." She looked to the side, making sure they were indeed alone, "Look, we need to get out of here." Leo nodded, and she tried walking again.

They found the car and drove until they found a motel with free parking. Leo checked in while Melody stayed in the car. He texted her the room number so she could meet him outside the door with the bags and avoid any management seeing her face. They hadn't packed much, preferring to leave a chunk of stuff in their rooms back in New York and create some confusion as to whether they had actually left. By the time it was realized they were indeed gone—which wasn't unusual, given the harsh environment

112

of reconstruction cities, people up and left frequently—it hopefully would not be understood that they had left the day after the D.C. executions. Only Liz and Greg would know when they saw the missing car, but, hopefully, they would understand, in time. They knew they couldn't speak to Leo's parents before leaving, a fact they silently agreed not to discuss.

Leo had turned already turned on the TV when Melody knocked on the door to the dank room. She tossed him his backpack and sat on the bed watching the news, using her bag as a pillow.

They passed the next few hours mostly in silence. Leo ran out to get dinner for them, sandwiches from a nearby store, and grabbed Melody a newspaper which she thanked him for. But other than that, she watched the news through blurry eyes, dozing off now and then, checking the clock every few minutes.

Finally, around 7:30, Leo said, "We'd better start heading over, yeah?" To which Melody gratefully agreed. She quickly touched up her make-up while Leo did up his boots and handed her a baseball hat. She gave him a questioning look.

"Saw it at the gas station when I bought dinner and thought it was a good idea." She nodded, and shoved it on, tightening the strap in the back as they walked out the door. Leo double and triple checked he had his ID and the keys, and Melody shoved her hands in her coat pockets, head down.

She'd forgotten how much warmer it was down in this city, compared to New York, as she watched a few late-night bike riders come flying past her and the evening breeze gently blew her hair. It was still cold, but not the frigid degrees she'd had to become used to. Given that the housing was free for reconstruction workers, the heat was kept on to a survivable level, and no higher. It was

113

certainly never comfortable.

They walked the familiar streets to the bus stop, having already agreed that once they settled somewhere, they'd use the car as little as possible until they could get rid of it. As they boarded, Melody did a quick scan for anyone she might recognize, or who might recognize her.

She'd never felt so intensely vulnerable. It was different when they were running in the beginning. There was only raw fear and panic. They'd driven off course, circled around to Ohio, before heading back up to New York. They'd switched license plates multiple times, doing whatever they thought they could to throw anyone who might be following them off the trail. The first night, they'd snuck Melody into the dingy hotel room, and had chopped off most of her hair. She remembered watching it fall to the floor around her, feeling nothing, thinking that it had been smart that Greg say they do it over trash bags to make sure no traces of the process remained.

But that had been months ago, with Leo's parents guiding the way. Without Liz, with no way to contact her, Melody felt lost.

She couldn't dwell on this, though. There was the much more pressing problem of a group of assholes trying to kill themselves and using her name as a rallying cry, and that was more than enough to occupy her mind as she counted down the stops to the news station.

They climbed out of the bus a couple blocks away, and walked the remaining distance, keeping their heads down. The security guard had changed, but as soon as Leo said they were there for a meeting with Des, they were given visitors badges and sent to the elevators, with a quick whispered warning about the camera positions. As they entered the lift, Melody adjusted the hat

114

to hide her face more thoroughly, and Leo turned towards her, so his back was to the camera while obscuring her at the same time.

She took a deep breath when they reached the basement, and saw the hallway still brightly lit. Some late–night workers were ducking in and out of rooms, carrying giant piles of files. They paid Leo and Melody little attention as they started back towards room B41.

There was little fanfare. Nothing to suggest what was happening in this room. It had a conference table, a projector, and around a dozen people scattered around.

Derek was already there, at the head of the table, rolling a cigarette.

"I understand, but she's still not coming," he was saying to a disgruntled looking man who looked a few years older than Derek.

"But she's safer with us than she is on her own!" The man crossed his arms in front of his chest, frowning at Derek.

"I understand that." Derek sighed, digging in his pocket for a lighter, "But she's not talking to me. As far as I can tell, she's not left her house for a couple days. She's really shaken up. They did their job well. Morgan's out, at least for now. Give her some time. Jackie will work her magic eventually and get her back here."

The man opened his mouth to protest, but caught sight of Melody and Leo, and bent down to whisper something to Derek that Melody couldn't make out.

"They were very insistent," Derek said calmly, not bothering to keep his voice down. They'd agreed that afternoon they would not be introduced by their real names, or have their true intention revealed until the end of the meeting. But, standing here now, Melody wasn't sure if that had been the smartest plan. She wasn't sure if she'd be able to contain herself.

Derek blew out a puff of smoke. "Shall we begin?" The man looked uncomfortable, but took a step back and sat in a chair a few spots away from Derek. The rest gradually made their way to seats, leaving empty spaces here and there. Melody and Leo hung back, leaning against the wall, waiting with nervous energy. A few around the table shot them curious looks but said nothing. Apparently, if Derek had cleared them, they were alright to be there.

"So," Derek said, as way of calling the meeting to order. "We've had a tough week." Every eye watched him intently. He put the cigarette down in the ashtray, clasping his hands in front of him on the table, "I'm not going to pretend to you that this was not expected. We knew this was coming since Lena, Benji, and Fred were caught. They were strong. They didn't give us up. They knew what they were fighting for. Please, join me for a moment of silence for our friends, three more who will never have a proper funeral, whose families will have no proper place to mourn, who died as nameless enemies of Our Dear Jamison."

Melody noticed the flashes of anger that lit the faces in the room, the hands gripping the edges of the table, the look of hunger in some of the eyes as they looked at Derek. She bowed her head with the rest, until a voice broke the silence.

"We can't let them get away with this!" Someone at the end of the table exploded.

Many nodded, a few grimaced as if in reluctant acceptance. Derek grinned.

"We are not giving up," He shot a half glance to Melody, "That is exactly what Covington and the rest of those fuckers want. We are playing directly into their hands if we do. There are those that will be too cowardly to act, and that's fine. But we here understand that there is—"

116

The door swung open, almost hitting Melody across the face. "I'm so sorry I'm late!" A frazzled-looking woman with coiled brown hair and smooth copper skin stumbled into the room, her hands full of files. "I got away as quickly as I could," she looked around and noticed the people close to the door. "Oh crap, I'm so sorry, did I get you? I was just—" she stopped mid-sentence and tilted her head to the side. She peered into Melody's eyes, looking intently into her face. Her mouth opened slightly, her large brown eyes widening in shock and comprehension. She did a ninety degree turn and dropped the files at her feet. "You said you didn't know them!"

"What are you talking about, Jackie?" Derek asked, carefully.

"Don't bullshit me, Derek. What the hell is Melody doing here?"

The room went silent.

"She doesn't like what we're doing," Derek said plainly. Melody glared at him. "Well, you don't, do you?"

"No. I don't," she said quietly. Jackie's eyes went even wider. The table erupted in mutters. Melody cleared her throat and took a step forward to address the room at large.

"Please, explain this to me. What exactly do you think you're fighting for? And why are you doing it in my name? Because from all I've seen you've made me a martyr to an unclear cause that's gotten your friends captured, tortured, and killed."

There was silence for another moment. Jackie looked confusedly between Derek and Melody.

"But, we're doing it for you." She stated it as though it should have been obvious.

Melody blinked. "No, you're not."

"Yes, we are!" Jackie exclaimed, looking around the room

to the others for support, "We're doing it for you, saying that this has gone too far, that you're not a traitor, you had a right to write what you did, to talk about what you wanted to talk about!"

Melody looked from Jackie to Derek, and made a couple of quick assumptions.

"You're not fighting for me. You're fighting for an idea with my name on it. If you want to fight for political prisoners, for the people who have been stuck in jail unfairly, for whatever idealistic fantasies you have, fine. Be my guest. On your own head be it. But you're not going to die *for me*. That's what I've got an issue with. I don't want anyone fucking dying for me, or an idea of what they think I am, or what I stand for. So, figure out another campaign slogan."

"Well, great. Thank you for your support." The man sitting close to Derek said sarcastically, "But you'll forgive us if we don't suddenly change our entire strategy, considering that we've now spread out to Maryland and have heard word from Pennsylvania some are joining us in our next event as well. It's a bit too late to go changing the message now."

"You've spread out to Pennsylvania?" Leo asked quietly.

"Yes. We've started getting teams out to North Carolina, and we've got people in Ohio right now too," Jackie said defiantly.

"Why are all of you here?" Melody asked, a little desperately, "Why do all of you think this, above anything else, is worth fighting for?"

The others in the room all looked at each other.

And they each said a name, or names, one by one. Ending with Derek, who once again invoked Sean's name.

"Sean Anker, Benjamin Jones, Lena Williams, and Frank Martinez." He stared at Melody for a moment, before letting out a humorless laugh. "You're just the best mascot, to use your term."

"Why?" She asked weakly. "You could've used anyone."

"You're young, white, blonde, blue-eyed, and you were writing a letter to your mother." Jackie rattled off, "And your name was plastered all over the national news. You, quite literally, are a poster child." Melody looked helplessly at Leo, who grimaced back. Jackie glanced from Derek to Melody, before taking a step towards her.

"Look, I know you don't want this on you, and it's not. This is our choice. We know what we're doing. Think of it this way. We're not really doing it for you. We're doing it for our people, and you're just the person we can use to represent what's happening. The person people will pay attention to. It's not pretty - it's what it is. If you're here, you can help. We know you're not happy, you can't be. But you must have been doing something to stay alive, something smart to make sure that you weren't found, and were able to live under the radar for so long. You were trained by the Party; you know things we don't." Her round, deep brown eyes were filled with hope. Derek ran a hand through his spiky black hair and looked around the table again.

"Yeah, she's got a point," he said, resignedly. "We could use you."

Murmurs started around the table again, this time more hopeful, contemplative.

"Give us a second." Melody gestured at Leo, and they walked back out of the room.

Derek watched them leave out of the corner of his eye, pulling out his cell phone, preparing for a long night.

January 2093

Alexander smiled from the doorway, watching as Jordan ran the brush through her hair.

"What?" She asked.

"Nothing," he said, "You look beautiful."

"Stop," she swatted him away playfully, making her way back into the bedroom. He sat down on the bed. He wasn't sure why she was in such a good mood, and he didn't want to question it. Her smile brightened the room; made him calmer.

"You've been quiet tonight," she said, continuing to get ready for bed. "Did something else happen?"

"Jordan—"

"Don't make me go through the debate of 'Do I want to know, do I *really*,' it's just redundant at this point. So, come on, tell me."

He sighed. "We got a tip about a car today. It matched the description of the Myers' car, so we checked it out. It was sold a couple days ago for a few thousand. Much less than what they could've gotten. It was a nice car."

"Was it them?" Jordan asked eagerly.

"No, I don't think so. Registration was to a Nicolas

Thackeray up in New York. The guy said it was a John Thackeray who sold it. His son. Wanted some money to make a fresh start."

"He ran away with his father's car?" She asked, looking angry.

"No, I guess he had permission. We got a hold of Nicolas. He's working up in a reconstruction site in New York. Said he just wanted his son safe. Seemed glad to hear from us, didn't give a shit about the car. Said he gave it to John when John left New York."

"Still, though," Jordan sounded agitated, and he couldn't quite figure out why, but she continued, "So, it wasn't the Myers'. What does that mean?"

"That the only semblance of a lead we've had in months was a joke," he said bitterly. "I got pulled into the Chief of Detective's office today, me and the captain."

"Shit." She crawled across the bed over to him, putting a hand on his shoulder.

"I asked for more resources, I've been saying for months that I don't have the manpower or the capacity to handle this assignment. And that wasn't what they wanted to hear," Alexander was trying very hard to keep from shaking. His wife's hand gently running down his arm, more than anything else, was pushing him to a breaking point. He felt an edge under his feet, but he didn't know how to back away. "I was given a deadline, Jordan."

"When?" She asked.

"End of March." It hurt to breathe. There was a pain in his chest. He winced, and tried to hide it, but she wasn't fooled. She went to the medicine cabinet in the bathroom and came back with the bottle of antacids.

"They won't help," he snapped.

"I don't care," she glared at him. He grimaced, but swallowed the two tablets she was waving in front of his face.

"Did they say specifically what happens at the end of March?" She asked, breaking the silence.

"Did they have to?" He couldn't look at her, and she didn't answer. No, they didn't. If the deadline passed (with a very strong implication that even if he did manage to meet it) every single mistake would have to be accounted for. Even the mistakes that were not his.

But he didn't want to tell her that. She already knew. And what was the point of saying those truths out loud?

"Can I ask you something?" He asked, and took her silence as a yes. "Why did it annoy you so much that the Thackeray kid sold the car?" It probably wasn't what they should have been talking about, but he needed to change the subject. Needed solid ground.

She remained silent for a second, pondering the question.

"Do you remember when we got married, what you told me?"

"I told you a lot of things," he said, frowning.

"You told me you'd make detective by 30, sergeant by 35; we'd have a government salary and benefits and two kids. We could have a nanny, or I could work from home, or both. And we'd get a little puppy because there was no way you were living with a cat."

"I stand by that; I hate cats."

"Do you ever think about that, Alex?" She asked. His face fell. She was at once hopeful and heartbroken. Because she already knew the answer.

"If you want a child, I want a child," he told her. "But, in an ideal world, I'd be there to see my child born. And I can't promise you that. Not right now."

"But that's always been it, hasn't it?" she asked. She wasn't crying. She rarely cried. But she had gone to a level of sadness

123

where he could not reach her, could not help her. "It's always been a case, or an assignment, or something else where you've been afraid you might not come home. This time, it just has a name that everyone knows."

"Jordan—" He tried, but she shook her head.

"I understand," she said, "I don't want to do it without you, either. But that's why I was irritated. Because that kid had a father, and from what it sounded like, left him behind without a care. And here we are."

"It's not fair," he whispered. He wanted to touch her, wanted to hold her, but she was already crawling under the blankets, and turning away from him. He couldn't bear the thought of being banished tonight, nor could he bear the thought of his presence making her break. He went to stand up, but heard her voice.

"Don't go." He turned, not quite believing his ears. She had turned so her back was facing him. He didn't move, not sure he hadn't imagined it. "Stay, Alex. Hold me, please?"

He turned off the light and crawled under the blankets next to his wife. He wrapped his arm protectively around her, and felt her fingers intertwine in his.

"We're going to be okay," He heard her whisper, and he honestly was not sure if she wanted him to hear. He buried his face into the crook of her neck and said nothing more.

———

"You'll be in place by dawn?"

"Yeah."

"And, remember, the Southeast and North entrances are the ones to go for. Avoid—"

"Avoid the West." Derek sighed. They'd gone over this three times already.

Logan nodded, satisfied. They walked in silence for a few moments before Logan asked, "How's it all going then? Them staying with you?"

Derek shrugged. In truth, he wasn't sure how to feel about it. They weren't really in his way. They slipped out as soon as curfew was lifted and came back only when curfew was in effect. They didn't talk about where they went in the meantime, but he knew that when they came back, they always wore hats or scarves and avoided the camera attached to the door entry so that Derek and his neighbors wouldn't be implicated if they were caught. They stayed out of his way and communicated in silent gestures or expressions. It was…. weird. But they had nowhere else to go, and he wasn't going to let someone else from the group take on the danger of having them, though a few had offered.

"Why did you tell her where to find me?"

"Why wouldn't I?" Logan raised an eyebrow at him. "So, what's her plan now then?"

"I guess she's helping. That Leo guy is too. Still haven't figured out his deal. But Jackie and Marco have got her working on some media stuff, part of a new campaign idea."

"Interesting. Who's the target?"

"Philly, Pittsburgh, Cleveland, and Trenton are the newer ones we want to make sure of, and we're still hitting the old ones in Virginia. Maryland's been wavering since the executions, but we think the desire to push back is still there. Teams are going out to states West and North. We want to get a feel to see how much we can spread right now. How many cities we can get on board for this." They were walking back towards the police station, Derek helping Logan carry coffee. It had been the only way to pin him down.

"That seems ambitious. How many do you want to get?"

125

Derek shrugged. "As many as we can."

"You've got to have a lot of people, if you have that many available to go on trips."

"I'm not telling you how much we've spread, Logan."

"I'm not asking you to. I'm trying to help when I can, aren't I? And I sent her to you because you either needed someone to stop this or kick it up to something actually meaningful. It seems like that'd be a good thing after everything that's happened." Logan's voice wasn't kind, but it wasn't harsh either. Derek scowled.

"Fuck you. We were getting along just fine," he muttered resentfully.

"Just fine?" Logan stopped in front of Derek, and fully towered over him. Derek could feel his eyes boring into his head. "You were directly responsible for their deaths, Derek, and don't you dare forget it." His voice had lowered to less than a whisper, "I don't know what happened that night, but you're the one in charge. If you were getting along 'just fine', that shit at the Navy Yard wouldn't have happened. Those executions wouldn't have happened, and she never would have come back."

"Don't you dare blame me, I didn't tip off the guards, it had to have been—" Derek tried but Logan silenced him with a look.

"I am going to blame you, because you need to remember this shit if you're going to go ahead with this. You keep saying you hate her because of what she's done?" He let the idea hang as he turned around and kept walking towards the station.

Derek stared after him for a few seconds, before scoffing at no one and turning in the opposite direction.

"Where are you going?" Logan called after him, "I thought you were—"

"I'll do it later." Derek cut him off curtly, striding away.

How dare he? Derek thought bitterly. It wasn't his fault. He hadn't told anyone about the Navy Yard. It had to have been someone else. He'd heard some kids on the periphery of their group had been caught, it might've been them... but it wasn't *his* fault. He'd tried to get everyone out. He had gotten Morgan out. He should be praised for that, not blamed for everyone else.

But his stomach still churned with guilt whenever he thought about it. He knew, deep down, that wasn't true.

If Derek was being honest, the reason he wasn't telling Logan more about the movement wasn't because he didn't trust Logan. He knew Logan would help more if he could. It was really because he had no idea how much it had spiraled. He had his core group that helped with some organization, the outreach team, and the sales team that made sure they had enough money to keep spreading. But he also knew that people who he had never met were taking matters into their own hands. That there were those who had started their own factions, who had never and would never know who 'Des' was, and he planned to keep it that way.

He knew there were kids who had broken into the Library of Congress and tried to steal documents. He knew that there were people over in West Virginia who'd tried to ransack a school. He knew that there were numerous groups springing up all around because of the rumors that filtered in during the meetings, and that these teams that were going out to see the cities weren't necessarily recruiting new members, but to see if they already existed.

He would never admit it aloud, but he had no idea how to control what he'd created.

It had started out simple enough, talking to Morgan after they'd all been fired, showing her the letter. She'd been obsessed. And with Morgan came Jackie, who'd still been working at the station for a different show, who knew exactly how to tell the right people. Who had gotten them jobs at her station, so they maintained access to the building.

Logan had been right. Everyone had lost someone.

From there it was just knowing who to bring together and sorting out who wanted to do what. He was definitely happier working at night, spray painting houses and giving a massive middle finger to all the laws that had regulated his life, that had separated him from his grandfather, that had made him lose his friends. He operated angry. He needed Jackie and Morgan to help run the outreach and sales sides, to help keep track of everyone. But Morgan was out, or so she claimed, and Jackie couldn't do everything, couldn't take on all Morgan had been doing. It didn't help that her continuing without Morgan had caused a lot of tension between the two of them.

He liked being thought of as the leader. Reality just didn't play out like it had in his head. He'd imagined the beginning, the initial time gathering support, and he'd pictured an end of some sort, a vague promise of reform. But, late at night, in that space between waking and dreaming, when he could be honest with himself, he could admit that he liked the idea of doing something much more than the process of actually doing it. This middle, this work, fumbling in the dark, he felt like an incompetent child. He wanted someone else to tell him what to do, and now with Melody and Leo coming in, thrusting all of his doubts into the spotlight...

He remembered Melody's first couple days, being briefed by Jackie, attempting to build a firmer understanding of their operation.

"Where do you go?" she'd asked Jackie as Jackie and Marco counted the little bags of white powder, marking them against a ledger of clients.

"The parks near the Senate building, mostly." Jackie said absentmindedly. "We started hanging near the Prevention Unit too. The guys going in for shifts sometimes want a hit."

"Do you mind?" Melody asked, looking at the ledger. Jackie shook her head, and Melody pulled the book towards herself. She frowned, running a finger down the list of names.

"There were a few bars near where I used to live," she said, "The ones that were known as afterhours places for Party people. I had to know which ones to avoid, so they wouldn't find my fake. You'd get a lot of clients. I could come with, tell you who to go for."

"If you could give us names, that'd be great." Jackie nodded eagerly, "But, I don't think you should come with."

"Oh, I don't think they'd recognize me." Melody shrugged, continuing to flip through the ledger.

"No, it's just..." Jackie cast around, looking for the right word, "Our team has an aesthetic."

Melody looked up at her, an eyebrow raised.

"Party members don't look like me," Marco said, shoving on his coat. "They look like you."

"So, they think it's safe to buy from you." Melody closed the ledger, pushing it back across the table. Jackie gave her a shrug of a goodbye, and Derek saw no emotions in Melody's face as her eyes followed them out the door.

Two days later, Jackie found a list of names in the ledger, with vague descriptions and where they worked. And he could do nothing but try to swallow down the resentment that she had been useful. That she now probably knew as much about the workings of the movement as he did.

He reached the basement of the station to find Jackie and Melody sitting at a laptop, poring over a picture. Jackie smiled

129

brightly at him, and Melody gave him a cursory nod.

"Come look!" Jackie said excitedly.

"What is it?" He asked, coming around to peer over Melody's shoulder.

"The new flyers. We've got to move on from spray paint, and we're not getting enough traction with just the letter anymore," Jackie explained.

It was a picture of a girl; it could have been Melody, it was hard to tell, sitting under a bridge, looking cold, scared, and alone. Her skin and hair, blonde again, looked dirty. A few strands flew in an invisible breeze, and her blue eyes pierced through the camera. Derek could see the real Melody, sitting right in front of him, and if she ever made such a pitiful expression in front of him, he would laugh in her face, knowing it was fake. But, in the photo, it pulled at something within him, making him want to reach out to her. The next photo was a different bridge, the one after that, her on a park bench. Every image was a different landmark for the corresponding city they would be distributed to.

"How'd you do them?" Derek asked Melody.

"Marco did it with one of the green screens upstairs. Gave me a wig and I took off my contacts," Melody said absentmindedly, skimming through the pictures quickly against a list of cities written beside her. Jackie ran over to the printer.

"This is what we're thinking for the back, what do you think?" She held it up for him.

In clear, bold text, it said,

Over the land of the free and the home of the brave?
Freedom of thought, freedom of speech, freedom from fear
FREE MELODY, FREE ALL

"We can't print enough for each city, but we'll give the

proof, and the teams can print them when they get there. It'll look better that way."

Derek nodded. He flipped the flyer over, and it was a picture of Melody in front of Lincoln Park, beside one of the new statues of Jamison. There was moonlight shining off her hair, glinting in her eyes. He made a mental note to congratulate Marco on the realism.

He smiled his approval at the girls and tucked the flyer into his pocket.

"Where's the fake bro?" he asked Melody. She spared a glance for him before going back to checking off the list of cities.

"He's running some errands with Charlie. I didn't ask."

He sighed and pulled a chair towards himself, sitting beside Melody, looking over her shoulder at the list of cities.

There were at least twenty-five names on it.

Shit.

He looked over at Jackie.

"We've got the teams for all those covered?"

"Yeah," she said, looking at him slightly confused. "We covered that at the last meeting, don't you remember? We have established people at half of them, and growing numbers at most others. We're only sending feeler teams to a couple."

He could feel Melody's eyes boring into his skull and he cleared his throat.

"Just double-checking." He covered himself.

"It's difficult to keep track of it all." Melody said quietly. A foolish man would take her tone for seriousness.

He knew better, but said nothing.

"I think that's everything, yeah?" she said to Jackie, shutting the lid of the laptop. Jackie nodded.

"I'll see you later then." She grabbed her jacket and hat, gave Jackie a quick hug, another nod in Derek's general direction, and walked out.

"Wow. So warm," Jackie laughed.

"Does it have to be?"

"You know, when this first started, I thought you were kidding that you didn't know who she was."

Derek sighed.

"It wasn't entirely true."

"So, you did know her?"

"I'd met her. Once."

"And?" Jackie pressed.

"She dated Sean. Well, you knew that, you read the letter."

"Yes, so?"

"Well, she lied about who she was," Derek said bitterly. "We thought she was an accountant named Sam. We - me, Sean, Logan - all had drinks with her one night. He wanted us to meet her so badly, we knew he was crazy about this girl. She seemed a little cold, but she was alright. And then, well." He met her gaze then quickly looked away.

Jackie's look could have set something on fire.

"You know, Derek, sometimes I think I get you, I really do. Sometimes, I see the person who decided to do this, to put this together, to fight for something. None of us really knew what this was going to be, what we were getting into. That's fine. But you blamed her, from the beginning, you blamed her, and used her anyway. How does that make you any better than Covington, or the other assholes?"

"Jackie—" He tried to reason with her, but she just shook her head.

"She didn't ask for any of it. Neither did Benji, or Fred, and Lena. Neither did Sean. Neither did Charlie's mom, or my cousin, or Morgan's brother. None of them. You saying she had any blame is like saying you don't believe in any of what we're doing. And if you don't, then I don't know what the hell we're doing here."

Derek stared open mouthed at her, not sure of what to say or do. He hadn't expected the 180-degree turnaround and wasn't sure how to make it better. He hadn't told anyone exactly what he thought of Melody before—it hadn't seemed to matter. Before he could string a sentence together, Jackie had packed up the laptop and was striding from the room, but she turned back around to look at him.

"I never blamed you for putting Morgan in danger, Derek. Should I?"

Not waiting for a response, she disappeared from the room.

———————

"Erin?" He cautiously called out to the living room at large. "Le–Jack–Joh–Whatever?" No response. He stumbled over to the sofa and collapsed onto it, his brain a beautiful whiskey covered cloud. He turned the TV on and pulled the flask out of his coat pocket.

He wasn't sure how much time had passed before the door opened quietly, and he saw the blurred shapes in the darkness.

"Ahh there they are!" He exclaimed.

"What's up with you?" Leo asked.

"Nothing," Derek said defensively.

"He's drunk." He heard Melody whisper.

"Yeah, so what?" He snapped.

"Nothing," she said calmly, "Do you need help getting to bed?"

133

"Yeah, you'd like that, wouldn't you?" He sneered. "Please, add me to your list." He pointed to Leo. "How many times has she fucked you? Sean said she had the tightest pussy, but I bet that's not true. How is it really?"

Leo took two massive strides forward, but Melody beat him to it. She stuck an arm in front of Leo, and slowly bent down in front of Derek, her hair tickling his chest.

"It's fine, Leo," her whisper was almost a purr, "I got it." She traced a finger along Derek's chin, down his neck, his chest, bending her head so her lips were only an inch from his. "He's just upset," she murmured.

Derek didn't know what was happening. Everything had stopped working. When was the last time he'd been fucked? Did she remember Leo was in the room? Did this just happen with the two of them? He hadn't meant it, hadn't really thought of touching her. He was upset, but it felt good, even if it was just because of the booze.

"You didn't mean it, did you?" She leaned into his ear.

He couldn't answer, he just swallowed.

Her fingers were dangerously low, and he didn't know what he wanted to happen anymore.

She pulled back and looked him dead in the eyes.

"Did you?" She demanded an answer, undoing the zipper of his jeans.

"No," his voice was hoarse.

And her lips were on his, kissing him, and he couldn't think, couldn't focus on anything except her lips, and the feel of her, and the desire fighting through his drunken brain—until a pain ripped through him, setting him on fire. He ripped his face away from her, trying to double over in pain, but she would not let him go, her fingernails digging into his balls, a look of dark satisfaction on her face as he looked up at her, trying to breathe through the pain.

"Say sorry."

"Please," he begged.

"Say it."

"PLEASE."

"I didn't kill Sean. I didn't kill anyone. Stop blaming me. Now fucking apologize."

"I'm sorry." He thought he might pass out from the pain. She gave him one last look of derision and let go. He crumpled, sliding down off the sofa.

She said nothing more, picking up her bag again and walking towards the bathroom.

Leo sat on the couch next to where Derek had been a moment before, giving him an almost sympathetic look.

"In answer to your other question," he said, reaching for the remote, "I haven't slept with her. I've heard stories about the ball crushing before, though I've never seen it in person. Surprised. I thought you'd start crying."

February 2093

Alexander was focusing on his breathing, and his breathing only. He'd been led down to the Chief of Detectives' office and been left to sit.

To rot.

To stew in his own incompetence.

He concentrated all his energy on inhaling and exhaling at a steady pace, keeping his heart rate under control. For the first time, he wished that Logan was with him. If the kid was here, he'd be able to pass the blame off on someone.

But that wasn't fair, and he knew he wouldn't do it. This was his fault. He'd been unable to bring Karsh in. He'd been unable to bring her accomplices in. He'd been unable to quash the movement around her. Their public stunt had stopped anything large from happening for a few weeks, but now there were flyers scattered around basically every major city in the Northeast and spreading. All with her picture—which meant that she had to be orchestrating the movement—right?

This went way beyond a kid writing letters now, and his palms were beginning to sweat again at the mere thought.

Breathe in, breathe out.

He heard the door handle turn and quickly wiped his hands on his trousers, standing up. He was in his full dress today, his hat tucked under his arm. He saluted the Chief, and behind him...

He paled.

"Detective Covington, the Secretary of Homeland Security." The introduction was not necessary.

Covington swallowed. The Secretary sat behind the Chief's desk without invitation.

"Alexander, do I need to say it?" He looked up at the detective. "This is not what we had hoped for."

Alexander gave a curt nod, not trusting himself to speak.

"There has an uptick in vandalism over the past two weeks." The Secretary gave him a disappointed look, "And you, Richard, from what I understand, have given him a minimal task force. He's had the help of some in the Prevention Unit, and nothing more."

The Chief looked stunned. Clearly, he had thought this meeting was for Alexander's chastisement alone.

"Sir," Richard protested, but the Secretary held up a hand.

"Quiet. I expected more from you. From both of you. President Jamison is counting on Covington and his team to bring down these terrorists. He is not used to these delays."

Alexander and Richard nodded.

"I trust you have heard of the upcoming nonsense they have attempted to plan?"

"Yes, sir," Alexander managed to say.

"Given the ongoing vandalism, increased spread of propaganda, and the violence that has been threatened against the police specifically, we have decided to place your wife under protective custody until this matter is resolved."

Jordan.

Jordan, who had told him to speak out initially.

Jordan, who knew much, much more than she should. Enough to get herself killed.

"Sir..."

"I trust there is nothing else?" The Secretary said, standing, with such a finality that the words died in Alexander's throat.

"No, sir," he said weakly.

The Secretary gave them both a once-over, before striding out of the office.

———————

"I don't understand why you had to leak it," Melody sighed.

They were sitting in the park again. She was wearing the same baseball cap, flicking through a magazine. Logan was on the other side of her, with a book.

"It's not really a secret Derek and I are friendly." He sighed. "If Derek is arrested, it'll look very suspicious if I've said nothing."

"You don't trust him." It was a statement, not a question. Logan took a moment before responding.

"I don't know what Derek will be like under pressure."

"His begging face is cute."

"Don't joke about that."

She didn't look at him, turning a page over.

"I have enough to feel guilty about without him looking like a lost puppy. They weren't going to listen to me about pulling the plug on it and he's the leader of it all. He needed to pull his shit together."

"Has he?"

"Sort of." She shrugged. Logan sighed.

"Do you regret it?" She asked, "Showing him the letter?"

"Sometimes," he admitted. "Sometimes I wonder if it would've been better, but it's started something, hasn't it? I don't know what that counts for. But I wonder...Derek was going to do something regardless, but given how reckless they've been I'm amazed they haven't all been killed."

"I don't know if that speaks to their brilliance or your boss's incompetence."

"Hey," Logan looked defensive. "He's not the best, but he's not a terrible person, or detective. He's trying. They've given him shit to work with and—"

"Logan, do you want Derek to be taken out?" Melody said quietly.

"No," he said, regaining his composure.

"So forget it."

"Okay."

They sat in silence for a minute.

"How are you?" he asked. His voice had changed. It was almost worrying. Caring.

"I'm fine."

"Erin."

"I'm keeping my shit together. John's keeping it together. He misses his parents, I know that, but they haven't tried to contact him. They know it's better not to."

"Do you know what you want to do? After Thursday?"

"Yeah," she looked up from the magazine for a moment, towards the little pond. There wasn't anyone out today, it was too cold, the ground covered in a layer of frost. "I want to find Derek's grandfather."

"What? Why!?"

"I want Derek to know what he's started, what they fought

for before, what he's fighting for again. Hell, I want to know as well. I don't know the full story. I know bits and pieces, but I don't know the whole thing. If we can find someone who still remembers what it was like before the War, how it started...." She trailed off, picking up the magazine again. "I just think it'd be useful, to give him a frame of reference. Give him something beyond his current anger."

"You almost sound like a concerned parent."

"Don't you want to know?" She had to fight not to look at him. She wanted to look into his eyes, push him for a true answer.

"No, I don't. It's either an answer that will haunt me, that will make me want to fight more for Derek's side, which I can't do, or it's an answer that will make me regret everything I've done for you and him up until this point, which would be even worse."

"Why wouldn't you be able to fight more?" She pressed him.

He shook his head; she could see it out of the corner of her eye.

"You may think Derek's not afraid to die, but he is. I've known him for a long time. The guy's scared. And you know what? I am too. You're the one walking through this with nothing to lose anymore. The rest of us? We're fucking terrified. I don't want to die alone in a cramped little cell with the shit kicked out of me, so numb I can't feel what finally kills me. I want to live, even if it means living with Covington screaming at me every day for the next 30 years. I don't care. It's better than the alternative."

"So, this brings me back to my original point. Why did you leak it?"

"Why did you come back?" He challenged her. "What are you actually doing here? What are you gaining from helping in this?"

Melody looked out into the gray sky.

"Well, they feed me, don't they?"

141

"If that's all you care about, why do you even leave the house?"

"If you're so terrified of dying, why do you?"

"For no other reason than sheer necessity."

She had no response to this, and he stood up and left a few minutes later, leaving her alone in the freezing, sunlit afternoon.

Leo caught up with her, handing her a cup of coffee, which she accepted gratefully. They'd agreed it was too dangerous for her to do the patrols with the rest of them, but Leo occasionally went with Charlie in his sweeps of the five or so blocks around the police station.

"Anything new?"

"Yeah, actually," he muttered, wrapping an arm around her shoulder on the pretense of bringing her closer, whispering in her ear. "There were a ton more guards out there today, and I saw Covington."

"You did?" They had not seen this man who was trying to kill them since the televised executions in December.

"Yeah. He looked awful, something's up." He took out his phone and showed her a picture.

He looked like he'd aged a decade in the months since Melody had first seen him, the day that seemed so long ago, back in Arshem's office. His hair was streaked with gray, and his uniform was hanging off his frame. His skin looked sickly pale, like he rarely saw the sun anymore.

"Why did you take this?" She muttered. "We have Marco for this type of intel. He's been collecting photos and videos of the place for a month."

Leo studied the picture hard for a minute before deleting it.

142

"In that broadcast, back in December, he looked so determined, so strong. It was so strange to see him like this, looking so.... mortal. It was just nice to know that he could be struggling too."

"Yeah, I get that." Melody sighed, leaning against him. They walked in silence for a minute, and she drank more of the coffee.

"I have to go over to Morgan's tonight with Jackie," he said, after a while, sounding apologetic.

"Okay, why?"

"Morgan's nervous about tomorrow. She doesn't want Jackie to go. I understand that, but Jackie's not going to be sitting on her ass while this goes down. She wants backup, to try to get Morgan to understand why she's got to go."

Melody grimaced at him.

"And she asked you to explain your side of it."

"Pretty much. But that leaves you with your very best friend tonight."

"It'll be fine. I'll keep him calm before tomorrow."

"That'd be a first."

"I'll make sure he gets there in one piece."

"More believable." Leo chuckled. They walked together back towards Derek's apartment, running through the plan for the next day in hushed tones. When they were within a block of the building, they looked at each other, and gave each other a tight hug. "I'll see you after," she said.

"Yeah." He sounded confident, "Of course." He gave her another hug, and she watched him walk around the corner before going into the building.

The place hadn't changed too much in the two months since they'd arrived. The kitchen was now consistently in use, and clean. Blankets lined the couch in the living room. Their bags sat beside the TV.

She walked over to the kitchen and pulled out some ingredients for dinner that night. She wasn't sure when Derek would be back, but thought it best to make sure there was enough for him. He'd been off the past couple of days, nervous about what was to come, she was sure, but he needed to pull it together. The others needed a leader, and he needed to be calm to perform the role.

She made chicken and stir-fried vegetables. She knew he liked garlic, so she added in a few extra cloves. He had enough boxes of macaroni and cheese and cans of beans that they'd be okay if they needed to hide out for a while—so she felt okay using up the fresh ingredients he had on hand.

He came in when she was scooping a helping onto a plate.

"Hey," he said, looking surprised.

"Hey," she called over to him. "You hungry?"

"Um, kind of? That smells really good."

"Thanks." She brought down another plate from the cabinet and scooped some food onto it. He got his own cutlery and thanked her as she handed him the plate. They went to the living room, and he grabbed the six pack he'd brought home with him. He handed her one, and they sat in silence for a while.

"You okay?" She asked, finally. He shrugged.

"Sure."

"You can talk, you know. I'm not going to rip your head off." She put her food down and took a swig of the beer. He ripped off an enormous bite of chicken and chewed, not looking at her.

"This feels too weird," he finally said.

"Explain."

"Sitting here. Having dinner with you. Drinking with you.

Pretending that we can have a normal evening. I don't...I don't know how to deal with this."

Melody grinned.

"You know, when we were away, Leo and his parents, they loved these moments." She took another sip and looked around the apartment. "There weren't a lot of times when we could be alone, and when we were, they insisted we make the most of it, pretend it was how it used to be: pretend to be a family. Have dinner together. Greg would get off his ass, drinking bottles dry, start reminiscing about Leo's first steps, and the house back here. I didn't want to hear about it. It made me sick to think that they weren't back here because of me." She took another long sip of the beer, "Look, I get that this is weird, but sometimes you have to take a step out of all of it. The planning, the rebellion, and all this being the figurehead business. You are still a person, and you can relax sometimes. Otherwise, you're going to collapse under all of it. So tonight, maybe we're just two people who need to eat dinner."

He considered her words for a minute, "You never talk about them, Greg and Liz. Leo's mentioned them a couple times, but you never do."

"I don't like thinking about them. They had to leave everything behind because of that stupid letter, and then we left without saying goodbye. I took their son away from them. I was never that close with Greg, but Liz was like my mom. I'll never be able to ask for their forgiveness. I just have to live with that."

"How long have you known Leo, then?"

"As long as I can remember. My mom was best friends with Liz. I guess Mom made her promise to take care of me."

"Why did you start writing the letters?" She could tell by his tone he'd been dying to ask this for a while. She finished off the bottle and gestured for him to hand her another.

"You ask a lot of questions."

"You can ask me some too," he offered. She hesitated, twisting off the top of the bottle before deciding to answer.

"Mom left when I was two. I was old enough to talk, to know something was wrong. Dad was due for a promotion at work. He hadn't told anyone. He couldn't risk having a toddler blab—you know kids, they don't have a filter. So, he said she was traveling. He helped me start writing letters; he got me asking her the questions I would've bothered him with. When I was six, the Party finally figured out she was gone. Their investigation into a ship that ICE sunk had finally uncovered the names of the people aboard being smuggled from New York to the UK, including my mother. Dad went through hell for it. They took him in for questioning and found out he'd already filed for divorce by the time she left, and demanded keeping custody of me so I'd go through the Party system. They couldn't prove he lied about knowing where she was going, either. While they had him in custody I went to live with Liz. That was when Leo and I got really close. Of course, by that point, I'd been buying the whole 'she's traveling' thing for so long. When Dad got out, he couldn't deal with having to explain it to me as well, at least, that's more or less what he eventually told me. He said she was in the UK, and wasn't coming back, which was why he'd been arrested. I was stupid enough to believe him. For years I wrote letters, and he said he'd take care of getting them to her.

"Then, when I was sixteen, he wanted to talk about my future with the Party. I told him I didn't want to go down the traditional Party track, that I wanted to go into Executive, to work with the Pentagon. He was surprised, but proud. See, it's not that big of a deal if you leave your parent's track if you're going to work in

146

the military. Serving your country, and all that. But then, he realized why. If you make it far enough in the Pentagon, you can travel. We were just starting to re–establish our former economic and diplomatic relations with the UK. It wasn't too much of a stretch to believe we'd be trying to regain that intelligence relationship as well. I actually ended up working against that, with Arshem." She cut off, eyes looking at something Derek didn't see, and she took another sip of her drink before continuing.

"So, he told me. Told me he wasn't having me chase a fairy tale anymore. Told me he'd never sent any of the letters, that he'd destroyed them all as soon as I'd given them to him. That they were childish and dangerous and that I needed to stop—that I needed to focus on reality. That she was a dangerous woman who never wanted me, who believed in extremism and put us all in danger. That she'd been killed, and how it happened.

"We didn't have the best relationship, but, after that, we never talked. I finished school, went to the fast-track program for Legislative, essentially as a fuck you to him and the whole thing. But I never stopped writing the letters. Even though I never got a response, obviously, they'd become so habitual for me, a catharsis in a way. Like I could put anything into it, and no one would judge me. I could say what I wanted to say and be done with it. I never intended for anyone to read them. They were just for me to vent." She took another drink. They didn't speak for a while, until she finally said, "Okay. Enough about me. Your turn."

"Fair. What do you want to know?"

"I want to know about your grandpa."

"What do you want to know about him?" His tone had changed; it was suddenly defensive.

"I want to know what he told you, what he didn't tell you,"

she said carefully. "What's the deal with him?"

Derek shifted uncomfortably.

"He's, well..." He fiddled with the label on his bottle, "I'm not sure where he is now." She said nothing, just waited for him to continue. After a few moments, he finally said, "Look, when I was really young, like, eight or nine, I was over at a neighbor's. She and I were friends, and she lived with her parents and her grandma. Her grandma was watching us, making us lunch or something, and was telling us these stories. About before the War, or whatever you want to call it. I guess before you could get so much more from other countries, imports weren't so fucking expensive. She was telling us about all these traditions they used to have, and how Asian families used to celebrate the Chinese New Year. She told us all about the reunion dinner, giving each other red envelopes. My parents aren't exactly, well, they aren't poor. You know, my trust fund is what got the movement going in the beginning, not that they know what it's being used for, but... anyway, when I got home, I asked them if we could buy rice dumplings or sesame seed balls. They're not popular anymore, but you could find them if you tried.

"They freaked out. Wanted to know how I heard about those things, wanted to know why I wanted them, and what the hell was wrong with American desserts. They made sure I knew that New Year's was on January 1st, and blah blah blah. Obviously, I didn't know what the hell was wrong, so I told them.

"The next time I saw my grandpa, I told him what had happened. I told him about the grandma, and what she'd been telling us, and how Mom and Dad had been upset. I told him how I'd seen the grandma being arrested. I asked him what a grandma could have done to be arrested. He didn't really answer me. Thinking back on it, I don't think he would've known how.

He would've been about...twenty or so at the time of the War, definitely would've known what was happening. He would've seen it all, how it all changed. Would've had to figure out how to survive. He told me not to think about it, that I should be happy with what I had, to focus on the history my teachers taught me, and not some old woman's fantasies. It was only then I noticed my dad was listening at the door. You know, in school, they tell us to talk to our teachers if we hear anything weird, anything that doesn't sound right, that goes against what they've taught us. It was the first time I realized people actually did that. That my dad did that.

"I tried to ask him questions a couple times after that, when my parents weren't in the room, but I know he was scared. Hell, I was scared. I knew something was wrong. I don't know if they knew or suspected but eventually my parents stopped letting me see him, and he stopped contacting me. I haven't spoken to him since I was about eleven. I don't think he's dead, but he might be. I hope not." He didn't look at Melody, just kept picking away at the label of the beer bottle. "My brother and sister, it's not even like we really talk, they're still in Boston with my parents, but they never really met him. Never really knew him." She said nothing, continuing to drink in silence. There was nothing else to say.

They finished eating and drank the rest of the beer before moving on to Derek's whiskey supply with the news whispering in the background.

"Leo said there were more patrols around today," Melody said, finally.

"Yeah, should be okay, though. With the time we're going," Derek said, as though if he said it with enough determination, it would be true.

"Derek," she said, placing her empty glass on the table,

"Just because I didn't agree with what you were doing, doesn't mean I don't realize it took a shit ton of bravery to do."

He cracked a smile.

"Melody Karsh gave *me* a compliment?"

"Stranger things have happened." She smiled back.

"Oh, that reminds me." He stood up and crossed to the door, grabbing something out of his jacket pocket. He tossed it to her as he plopped back on the sofa beside her.

"What's this?"

"For tomorrow. If you use the hat you keep wearing, you won't be able to keep it afterwards." He shrugged. She unfolded the square he'd tossed her and found a black knit beanie.

"Thanks," she told him.

"Don't mention it."

The sirens rang, blasting through the city and echoing through the apartment. They looked at each other in the silent seconds following,

"Was Leo not supposed to come back?" He asked. She shook her head. He tilted his head to the side, studying her face.

She had a moment to decide whether to agree, as his lips met hers. And she decided she didn't care. His fingers knotted in her hair, and she let her mind clear.

"Why?" She heard his whisper and wasn't sure if it was a question for her, or to himself.

"Does it matter?" She asked. Because it could have been any number of things.

What they'd just talked about, what they'd just shared.

What was facing them tomorrow.

The alcohol flooding their systems.

Sheer opportunity.

A combination of any or all of it.

He gently tugged her hair, arching her back, her eyes still closed.

"No, it doesn't." And he brought his mouth to hers once more.

Melody was already dressed when he walked into the living room the next morning. She was standing in front of the mirror, placing a fresh pair of colored contacts into her eyes. Derek looked away, trying to find his boots. He laced them up as she placed the beanie on her head, her bangs still covering one eye. He reached under the coffee table and extracted the guns. One was Melody's—her party-issued one. The other he'd obtained from Charlie' contacts. She'd taught him what to do, how to aim. He hadn't fired it, hoped he wouldn't have to, but at least he would, theoretically, be able to. He watched as she bent down and attached the holster to the inside of her calf, then tucked the sweats back into her boots. Hopefully, she wouldn't need to use hers either.

He shoved his into his jeans, next to hip, and shrugged on his black leather jacket. He put on his own hat, tucking all his hair underneath it, and shoved the black half mask in his pocket.

She looked at him, and he nodded. They crept quietly out of the apartment, and, making frequent checks around corners and behind themselves, made their way to the Prevention Unit.

It was a brick building with absolutely no windows. It was barred from public access. This was where serious interrogations occurred: those who entered did not exit. About a block away, they paused, ducking into an alleyway after making sure there were no officers anywhere nearby. Melody wrapped her white and black scarf around her face, and Derek pulled his mask on to cover up

151

to his nose and mouth. They put on black gloves and began to slowly make their way to their designated point near the Southeast entrance. Leo, Jackie, and Charlie were going to the North entrance. Marco was already inside the news station.

Derek swallowed: the stupidity of their mission washing over him. He looked over at Melody—she was staring straight ahead at the doors, her expression completely blank. He took a deep, steadying breath, and tried to stop his hands from shaking.

His phone vibrated, and he looked down at it.

"North door set," he whispered, and a second later, "And Marco's set."

She looked at him; she was waiting for him to take the lead. He gritted his teeth.

Two guards stood by the doors. If Logan's tips were right, they only needed two words. The guards raised their guns as they walked up. Before they could speak, Derek, hands raised, said, "Independence Day." His heart was beating so loudly he thought it might burst through his chest. It took so much willpower not to take the gun at his side and start shooting. His fingers twitched, unconsciously moving closer to the gun. He was terrified, and could feel Melody beside him, tensing, but still looking determinedly ahead.

The guard on the left was at first too shocked to move, the audacity of their actions rendering him temporarily speechless. He managed to raise his gun higher, but before he could do anything, his partner raised his own gun, hitting him on the back of the head. The guard crumpled to the ground, dripping blood onto the cement under his skull.

"What's the plan? I can't be caught, man, I've got kids. I support what you're doing but—" Derek's lagging brain kicked into overdrive. He couldn't be worrying about this guy's kids right now. They had too much on the line as it was.

"We're going to lock you in an office," he interrupted. "Pretend we got the upper hand on you somehow."

"Take our guns," the guard said. "Don't keep them, put them somewhere else in the building. Make it look more real."

Melody nodded. She took both the guns as Derek entered the code to get in on the electronic keypad on the right side of the door.

"Don't want to know how you know that," the guard muttered.

"No, you don't," Derek replied. The guard, with Melody's help, lifted his partner into the building. The first office they saw, they carried the unconscious man inside. They were handed a key ring, and Derek locked the door.

They hurried along the corridor, to the main lobby. He checked his phone for the time: 5:34. They waited another minute and saw Leo, Jackie, and Charlie, similarly dressed in black with their faces covered, hurrying along towards them.

"Everything okay?" Derek asked.

"Yeah, both our guys were on our side," Jackie said happily.

"Only one of ours was, but the other handled it." Melody told them. "Do you have their guns?" Leo nodded.

"We'll find a place to dump them on the way out; for now, we keep them. Right, let's go." They hurried along the corridor, to where Logan had told them the office would be.

Sure enough, there he was, sleeping: Lieutenant Fritz Parker, head of the Prevention Unit. From what Logan had told them, he'd been here more often than he'd been home lately, and it was worth ensuring that he was incapacitated before moving forward.

Barely breathing, Derek went to work on the keyring, going

through them one by one, trying them in the lock, trying to make as little sound as possible.

When the lock finally clicked, Parker made a little snort in his sleep and Derek winced, sure he'd woken him up, but Parker's head merely lolled to the side, and they all breathed a sigh of relief. Derek and Charlie entered the room, and he took the gun out, holding it so tightly his knuckles turned white. Charlie held one of the guard's guns; it was larger, clunky, not suited to what they wanted to do. Charlie gave Derek a nod and kept the gun fixed on Parker as Derek snuck behind him. He wasn't sure exactly how to do this, but he'd seen it done before, during arrests, when looking out his window after curfew. Outside the building just a moment ago. He had an idea. He tried not to think of what would happen if he got it wrong as he twisted his grip on the gun and slammed the butt into the side of Parker's head.

His face lolled to the side, his eyes bleary. He tried to open them, and without thinking Derek hit the gun against Parker's skull again, and then again. His glove was bloody, as was the butt of the gun, and Parker's body slumped forward, falling onto his desk.

They took a few steps back.

"Did you kill him?" Charlie whispered. Derek swallowed and held his fingers in front of Parker's nose.

"He's breathing." He said, with more relief in his voice than he intended. "Right. Charlie, Leo, you're up here. Melody, Jackie, with me. Five minutes, in and out." They all nodded at him. Leo handed Jackie one of the taken guns before Jackie followed Melody and Derek down the stairs. Derek entered another Logan–given code into the panel that greeted them at the bottom of the staircase. The door clicked and he raised up the gun.

The two guards were not expecting anyone to come until

154

the shift change at 7:30. They were sitting on stools at either side of the door, waiting out the end of the night. Whereas, for the three intruders, adrenaline had kicked itself into overdrive. Melody and Jackie jammed their stolen weapons into the sides of the guards' faces, while Derek waited in the doorway.

"We will shoot you, and we outnumber you," Jackie's voice was cold. "We will leave you to bleed out in these cells just like one of your prisoners. Or you can let us do what we came here to do, and no one needs to get hurt."

The guards raised their hands in surrender.

"Please, don't kill us. You don't have to—"

"Shut up," Melody shoved her target out of the stool. She took the handcuffs off his belt, and secured his hands behind his back, then came around to help Jackie with the guard she was holding still. On their knees, hands bound, Derek came behind them with his gun. Again, he crashed the butt of it over one head, surer of himself. He went down, unconscious. When Derek turned to the second guard, his shaking hand lessened the impact. The guard screamed in pain, but before Derek could raise the gun again, he met Melody's eyes.

"Let me do it," she said, and he saw more than the exasperation her tone would suggest. He saw a glint of malice in her eyes he'd never seen, or at least, never noticed, before. It was a desire, not just to get the job done, but to cause the necessary pain.

He handed over the gun, and she struck without hesitation.

He swallowed, looking away from the fallen guards, focusing on the gray, cement hallway. "Okay, let's get it set up." Melody took his phone, Jackie pulled out hers. Both started filming and nodded to Derek.

"This is Des, with the Free Melody movement, and we're

reporting to you from the Prevention Unit in Washington, D.C. This is not a place where the public is allowed. This is not a place the police, the government, or Our Dear Jamison want you to see. This is a place where prisoners are taken, interrogated, tortured, and executed. We're here to show you what this place is, where they wish to take Melody Karsh for the crime of writing a letter to her mother, where they have taken thousands of people for similar actions, only to be called terrorists, to be told they have committed treason against the government and must die for their offenses." He paused, walking towards a cell, and peeked inside. A tiny window of bulletproof glass, covered in bars, let him see a glimpse of the room. It did not hold a prisoner, but he could see scorch marks, and dried blood caking the walls. He did not want to know what had happened in that room. He gestured for the girls to video the inside.

"We can't know the horrors that have occurred here, but we can take some educated guesses." He looked in another cell, and saw an emaciated man huddled under a thin blanket. This room bore similar signs of the torture that occurred within.

"We do not have the ability to release anyone here, as much as we would like to. It would require the type of force we do not possess, and the ability and power to protect these prisoners, which we do not have the capacity to do."

He walked to where Logan had told him to go, the room with all the instruments. He fumbled with the key ring but managed to find the right one after several moments searching. He opened the door, and heard Jackie try to suppress her reaction.

He couldn't have imagined what was inside, even after Melody's and Logan's warnings.

Medical tools, tubes, metal instruments of every shape and size.

Brass knuckles, so many knives, he couldn't keep track of them all, something that looked like pincers, a blowtorch, something that might have been a branding iron.

Ropes, chains, and zip ties.

What looked like a small pair of hedge clippers, cleavers, and several bats.

A box of rubber gloves, several shelves of cleaning equipment, and a container labeled "SHARPS. SAFE DISPOSAL."

He couldn't look at the girls. He was trying hard not to vomit.

"Do we need to say anything?" His voice was hollow. He saw the girls carefully document everything in the room on their videos, giving him a second to gather himself.

"If you think these are fine practices for a government to use on its citizens, then go ahead, and ignore this report. But we believe that we have witnessed enough, that these atrocities have gone on for long enough. If you, like us, want to demand a better government, one that does not hide in the shadows turning its prisoners into rotting, shattered corpses, then join us. Free Melody, Free All."

He nodded to Jackie and Melody, who shut off the videos. Jackie looked at her phone, and her eyes went wide.

"Leo said Charlie is freaking out about Parker."

"What happened? When did that come in?"

"A minute ago."

"Let's go."

They dashed for the door, and sprinted up the steps, stopping across from Leo and Charlie.

"Charlie, come on!" Leo was whispering frantically. He was

pressed against the wall, trying to get Charlie to back away, but Charlie was pointing his gun directly at the door, where Parker was starting to feebly stir. This wasn't the plan. If Parker woke up, they were supposed to run, regardless of where he, Melody, and Jackie were. The point was no one was supposed to get caught. *What the hell was happening?*

"No, this son of a bitch is not getting out of there." His voice had cracked. Derek wasn't sure what had happened in the minutes they were downstairs, but something had set Charlie off.

"Charlie, please," Jackie whispered, "Please, we can go, please, let's go." Charlie spared her a glance, before turning his attention back to the door. Derek wasn't having any more of this. He was going to get everyone out this time. He took three quick strides to Charlie, determined to wrench the gun away, knock him out, carry him over his shoulder if he had to, he was getting him out of here. But before he could reach Charlie, the sound of gunshots echoed off the walls, ringing in his ears.

Charlie was clutching his chest, blood pouring from him, his mouth open in surprise as he fell to the ground. As he did, Derek had a clear view into the office, and saw Parker, blood falling into glazed eyes, trying to steady a gun that was pointed directly at Derek's heart.

Time seemed to stop. Derek couldn't process anything beyond the barrel of the gun.

"Run, you idiots!" Melody shouted, grabbing Leo and dashing for the North door. Derek ducked his head, the sound of the gun firing again reverberating in his skull. A hand was pulling him forward, towards the Southeast door.

They sprinted outside, down the street. Eight movement members had their houses on standby if they needed to get into shelter quickly. Melody and Jackie needed to get the videos to Marco.

158

What would Parker do? Was he able to call for help? Could he stand? Give chase?

He pulled Jackie into a sharp right turn. Another member, Arla, lived in a building down this block. He paused long enough to give Jackie a boost up the fire escape.

"Upload...video...I'll...keep going..." He turned back around and sprinted away. He hoped she would climb onto the roof and send it off before trying to get Arla to let her inside. They couldn't let that danger go for nothing, and who knew if Parker alerted the West door guards, or if Melody and Leo were being chased down too?

He didn't dare risk going back to the apartment, he was sure Parker had called for backup by now, that someone had sounded the alarm. He knew a couple other members nearby, he just had to make it in time.

He ducked between a couple of parked cars and risked looking behind him. He couldn't see Parker, but saw a couple officers coming towards him. He cursed under his breath, and bent down, pressing his body underneath the cars. Had they noticed him already? It was only then he realized—he was still carrying the key ring. They jingled every time he moved. Shit. He might as well have been carrying a billboard saying, *"Catch me!"* And now he'd seen what they did to those they did catch.

He shook his head. No. He wouldn't go down like that. He carefully, deliberately, crawled between the cars, and rolled out onto the street side of the next one, hoping the officers still hadn't seen him. He gently took the keyring and looked over to the officers again. They were a bit behind him, about a block in between him and them, their backs to him. There was a gap, where the streets intersected, about twenty feet away, with a sewer drain. If he could

159

throw it just right, if by some miracle he could get them there, maybe he could get away.

He ground his teeth together, took a deep breath, and threw the keys towards the drain.

He didn't pause to see if the officers had gone to see what had caused the noise, or if the target had met its mark, but kept himself bent low against the cars, running as fast as he could in the cramped position away from them.

He ran to the next safe house four blocks away. It was a basement apartment, rented out by Sonja and Tyler, a couple that were fairly new to the movement but who had agreed to help for today. They had kept their window open in case someone needed to slip inside quickly, and Derek tumbled in, faster than he had anticipated, and landed on the floor with a crash.

"Derek? Derek, you okay? What happened?" Tyler came running over to him, helping him to his feet. Derek couldn't breathe: the stitch in his chest and the fall were too much for him. He clutched his chest and wheezed as Sonja stumbled in from the adjacent bedroom with sleepy eyes.

"Honey, what…? Oh, Derek! What's wrong?" She helped Derek sit down, and Tyler hurried to get him a glass of water.

"Parker shot Charlie. Don't know if Parker got word out he needed help in time. We split up. Jackie should be safe at Arla's. Not sure about Melody and Leo." He managed after a minute and a few gulps of water.

"Well, at least one video is safe, right?" Sonja looked from Tyler to Derek.

"That's what we needed, at least one safe copy." Derek agreed, sitting back, trying to regain control of his breathing.

Now, there was nothing but to wait.

From the case file of Melody Karsh: July 2092-April 2093 September 2089

Dear Mom,

I finally let Chase come over. We were supposed to go over to his place, get some pizza, watch TV, but his parents were having some book club thing to promote their store. They invited us to stay, but Chase's face—that boy basically sprinted out of the house.

So, he suggested we come here, which made sense. Dad wasn't supposed to be home until later on. And it was fine, for a while. We had fun. But Dad came back early, and just had this look on his face. We called it an early night, and he kissed me goodbye. Dad asked me who he was, what his parents did. I told him, they lived above a bookstore they owned, I went to school with him.

He told me, "That's fine," and I was surprised, but then he said, "He knows it's not serious, right?" I didn't answer him, at first. I asked him why that was something that needed to be clarified. He got real quiet for a bit and didn't want to look at me. He told me, "Melody, you need to find someone in the Party." I was fuming. Furious. I shouldn't have said it, but I snapped at him. Is that a new rule, now?

He just blinked up at me, and Mom, for a second there, I could have sworn he looked sad. "No, Melody. It's not. But do you really want to end up with someone like your mother?"

And I thought, for a moment, that there was something there, something for you, that might make me want to forgive him. A memory we could hold on to. But then he said, "Besides, once you go to training, he won't want you anymore."

You know, I wish I could talk to Greg about this. Would be nice to hear what he has to say about it. It's not that me and Chase are serious, by any means, and I don't intend to be. It'd just be nice to talk to another parent about it, ask what they would want their son to consider before dating a Party member. But Greg and me aren't like Liz and me. There's never been that level. It's not his fault, and I do love him. I just don't know how to interact with him the same way. But I've said this before, it's probably boring you by now.

Greg's having a rough time at the moment, too. More of his contracts are being cancelled, more projects frozen, apartments half-built. It's not him; it's the city. They don't have the money. He keeps joking he can always work at a store or something, but he's not really joking. There was an interview on Channel 7 the other day with someone from Jamison's cabinet and the Secretary of Homeland Security. They were talking about taking back our claims in Puerto Rico and the Virgin Islands, expanding to be Our Great Nation again. Seriously? Fucking seriously? You want to take on more when you can't keep your people alive as is? We can't handle the territory we have, can't rebuild it, can't prosper in it, and you want to take on more? It's happening everywhere, Chicago's reconstruction funding is barely hanging on; they already cut half the meals they provide to the labor out there. I don't know how many died outside this winter, they never keep count, but we know it's worse than last year.

There's probably a reason behind this expansion, some resource they want. But still. Such bullshit. They'll get it and leave the people there to sort out the mess they leave behind.

Love,
Melody

IV

"Would you mind elaborating on how the fuck you let this happen?" The video shot in the basement of the Prevention Unit was playing on repeat across every screen in the news station studio. The boy, well, they couldn't really tell his age, but he looked younger, had been muted. They could see him gesturing to the instruments across a dozen screens. See the revulsion in his black eyes, see his already pale skin grow paler.

The body of the man officers had shot without a second thought when they saw what he was doing in the mixing booth was still there, oozing blood onto the carpeted floor.

If anything positive could be said about the situation, it was that they'd been able to stop the broadcast in D.C. about halfway through the video. The same could not be said elsewhere, as calls began to flood in from the rest of the East Coast, and some cities from the Midwest.

Alexander looked over at Logan, who'd tried to warn them, who'd said he'd gotten a tip that an attack from the Free Melody movement might be directed at either the Prevention Center or the police station's intake center. But he'd thought it would occur mid-morning, during a shift transfer. Not dawn; not before curfew had been lifted.

He wanted to be furious at Logan. He really did. But the kid had tried.

He was, however, furious at Parker, who was currently unconscious. How could he have let his guard down? Let himself be hurt?

He was furious at the guards, who somehow had let little more than children obtain their guns and lock them into their offices.

He was furious at Richard, who was yelling at him as though he had any control over what happened at the Prevention Unit, when it was not even remotely under his jurisdiction.

And he was furious, most of all, with the terrorist in the black mask.

"I let nothing happen," he snapped, "I told them to put more guards out there. They did. For two days. We kept more guards at the station. It's not my responsibility what Parker does. We should be much more concerned about getting this under control. We need to find out what those guards know, who saw what. Logan," he turned around and found the kid right behind him, "You get on that. Take their statements. I'm going to check on Parker. If he wakes up, he's the only one that might've seen all of them together." Logan nodded, walking out of the station.

"You were not dismissed!" Richard was puffing out his chest, but Alexander had had enough.

"You were the one who decided to punish me by assigning minimal people to this. You're the one who let this all blow up. So, when Homeland calls, I'm giving the phone to you. And if anything happens to my wife, it's you who's going to answer for it, not the Secretary. Now, sir, I'm going to check on Parker." And without looking back, he strode out of the studio.

———————

"You told him that?" Parker managed a weak laugh.

"Yeah."

"He's going to demote you."

"Good. Get someone else to deal with this shit."

"Don't say that. Think of Jordan."

"Right," Alexander sighed. "How are you feeling?"

"Like I was run over by a truck, but other than that," Parker tried to sit up a little straighter.

"Listen, we need to go over what you saw. What you did."

"Yeah," Parker grimaced.

"So, what happened?"

"Near as I can tell, the little shits got the key ring from one of the guards. Don't know how they managed it; must've sneaked up on my guys at the Southeast entrance, knocked down the one, pulled a gun or something on the other, made him let them in. He's got a family, you know, it wouldn't have been that hard, got his keys. Doesn't excuse it, but. I must've passed out around 4, 4:30? They had guns, Alexander. Didn't know how to use them, took the kid a couple tries to knock me out; it wasn't pretty. Anyways, I guess they went downstairs, don't know how they figured out that code, unless they made a guard give it up. You know, they'll never admit it. Too scared of what'll happen to 'em. Made that fucking video, came back up. Now, while this is happening, I start to wake up. I've been through worse, I think. And I hear something, like muttering. And I try to get my brain and my body to cooperate. Finally get my eyes open a bit and see this guy staring at me. Just pointing this gun at me and *staring*.

"Now, I don't forget faces. This guy, I knew his mom. Real

167

piece of work." He grinned at Alexander, "Do you remember Debs?" Alexander let out a groan.

"Fuck, that was when you were in ICE, yeah?"

"Yeah, Debs, was, well..." Parker's eyes went glassy for a moment, "But you know, she wanted more. She wanted a daddy for her little Charlie. She wanted some stability, she wanted all of it. And I was willing, I was willing to put up with her teenage brat if it got her to calm down. But, man, she was not happy with what I did. She bought my lies about finance and working long hours for a while, then she wanted to drop by for lunch one day, and clearly, I didn't work where I said I did. She did some digging, found out the truth. I'd told her a fake last name. ICE, well, you know. It gets rough. People trying to sneak out left, right, and center. Good practice for getting into Prevention. But she didn't like it. Wanted me to leave. Found a bunch of my files and threatened me. She knew people, she said. Knew reporters, knew people out of the country. I doubt even half of it was true. But, still, you don't threaten an officer, you don't threaten anyone with that sort of shit."

"So, you had her arrested?"

"Yeah," Parker sighed, wistfully. "Shame, really. She was so...well." He grinned sideways at Alexander and laughed.

"So that guy recognized you?"

"Oh, I'm sure it took him a while; it must've been a couple minutes before he had his little temper tantrum. It's been...oh fourteen years? Something like that? But he started whispering to whoever was with him that I was done, that I needed to die. At that point, I wasn't sure who it was. I just saw these eyes staring me down. You know they were all dressed like that, scarf or mask around the face, hats covering hair, all black. Like a bad movie. Wasn't sure who it was until after I'd shot him, and I saw his face after stumbling out there to get a look. Most of his friends, they were smart, they were quiet. I couldn't figure out how many there were. Knew they were trying to get him to back down, eventually he starts shouting, they get louder, I see this other guy come up, and I think, this is it, they're going to kill me, or they're all going to get out of here. Either way, this can't happen. I have to do something.

"They weren't looking at me. I managed to pick my head up enough and get my gun out. Shot the one aiming at me, Charlie. He went down, and I was aiming for the next one when someone, a girl, I think, had the sense to yell at them to run. I couldn't get a shot. My head was killing me. I tried to call for help, tried to stand, but whoever it was did a real number on me." Parker's face was contorted, his anguish palpable.

"I failed, Alex. I let them get in, I let them escape. You tried to warn me, Logan tried to warn me, and it happened anyway. And we've got nothing." Parker sighed. "It was a mistake. I understand that. I'm going to pay for it. If this doesn't kill me, Richard, or someone else will. Or they'll blacklist me, which is essentially the same. I don't know how to explain this to Vic." He let his head fall back against the pillows. "When you were questioning Marco, did you say his name was? What did you ask? What did he say?"

"We didn't interrogate him, Richard shot him the second we got to him." Alexander was sorry he couldn't give Parker better news. "Stopped him, but we didn't get anything out of him first."

Parker shifted on his pillows, turning his head to look at Alexander. "Did it really spread all up the coast?" Alexander couldn't bring himself to speak, but the lack of response was enough for Parker. "Can you just kill me? You'd make it less painful." Parker grinned, weakly. And Alexander was sure his friend was not entirely joking.

"I'll check back in later," Alexander said, patting Parker's shoulder, "Stay strong." Parker nodded, head moving back to stare at the ceiling again.

"It's too good for him," Jackie said viciously. The newspaper was spread on the basement table, bearing the headline *Former Lieutenant Sentenced to Execution*. The article blamed him for allowing terrorists to create "false propaganda," saying nothing of Charlie or Marco's deaths.

"Well, at least it fully got out almost everywhere else," Derek said, passing the paper cups around. Tonight, they were drinking a toast to all those that had died for the movement. Melody followed the others, and drank the whiskey, savoring the familiar burn in her throat.

The silence rang for a moment, before Jackie spoke again. "So, what's the next move? We can't let this go for nothing. If people believe Parker did this, they won't believe he died for nothing, and if they don't believe he did it, they'll want to know the truth. And we need to capitalize on the success other cities did have in spreading the video."

"Exactly," Derek agreed. He looked around the room. "I think we need to have a rally."

Melody looked at him, surprised. A few murmured, in agreement or disagreement, she couldn't tell.

"A rally?" She asked, "A rally saying what? How are you going to organize this and not expect to be shot? Do you not remember the Anthem Riot?"

"But that was only about a dozen people. This will be hundreds," he said confidently.

"My point stands. There are also hundreds of pissed off police officers that know we're responsible not only for the death of a lieutenant but also for multiple brain injuries of guards."

"We've got guns too; you guys managed to get away with a couple," Tyler suggested.

"Yes. That'll work. Two shotguns and two guard rifles, with only one person who knows how to use them, against an army." Leo rolled his eyes.

"No, no. We are not resorting to violence," Jackie cut across him. "We're not using their tactics. That's the whole point."

"No, the whole point is to bring attention to the fact that they're imprisoning people for no fucking reason, and we need it to stop!" Someone else down the table spoke up.

"Why can't we use violence? We've seen the stuff they're using against us now; a couple of bullets is nothing compared to what they're doing."

"But this isn't a competition of who's more creative at being despicable," Melody tried, but another voice spoke over her.

"We should be prepared, bring the guns just in case, bring any weapons we can, and if they get violent, we get violent too!"

"*Stop!*" Derek had stood on his chair, standing over them. He looked down at everyone, his eyes flickering for a moment to Melody, who recognized the moment as one of the rarities in which he reminded the group of his authority. He waited for every last face to turn to him before he began to speak. "I understand that you're scared," he told them, "I understand that there is a desire to get our revenge after what happened to Benji, Lena, Fred, now Marco and Charlie, to some of the others in Philly, Boston, Annapolis, and Charleston—look, I get it. I want to rip Parker limb from limb myself. But we have to keep our heads clear. If we go in thinking we can take on the entire D.C. police force, we will get plowed down. That's not how this can go. Take protection, sure. Don't go down willingly. But don't act *offensively*. That's not what this has been about, and it never will be. If we start acting like the aggressors, we'll lose the support we're gaining. Hear me?" He waited, and they nodded, a few gave reluctant grumbles. A couple crossed their arms, or sat further back in their seats, looking unconvinced.

"I know you're upset," he said. "I know you want more. But we haven't gained anything yet. We're still hiding out down here, nine floors down from where one of us, one of the founders of this thing, was murdered. We can't afford to get cocky. Alright? We have to plan this carefully. If we're going to start taking to the streets, we need to make sure the other cities that are with us are doing it at the same time. That we share a common message, a common demand, and we're trying to broadcast it to as many people as possible."

He shot Melody a half-glance. A "how's that?" sort of look. She gave him a small smile. He was taking it seriously. That was good enough for her.

They were sitting in Derek's living room having dinner when she broached the subject.

"Derek, you know what you were saying about a common message?" she asked carefully.

"Yeah?" He asked, through a mouthful of bread.

"I want to talk to your grandpa."

Derek froze, looking between her and Leo. Leo, who was still focusing on cutting his chicken, said, "Why would you want to do that?"

She saw Derek visibly relax, taking it as a sign she had not told Leo any of what had happened or been said the night before they broke into the Prevention Unit.

"His grandfather was alive during the War," she explained. "I think it would be good to see what he has to say, to finally get the full story of what happened, of why it happened."

"I agree. Would be good to see if there's a common thread somewhere. Could get the older generation involved, maybe. Get more people on our side."

"And if there *is* a common thread, it makes the argument stronger. We pick up where that failed. We try to build where that left off."

"Hey, not to put a damper on this, but could you stop planning as though I'm not here?" Derek's agitated voice brought them out of their excited discussion. She turned to him to see him scowling, his plate now on the coffee table, and arms crossed over his chest. "Sorry," she said, realizing their mistake, "I think, worst comes to worst, he refuses to speak, which is nothing he hasn't been doing already. At best, you get to talk to him. *Really* talk to him. Doesn't that seem worth it?"

He considered her argument, and she met his eyes, trying not to betray her nerves. He opened the drawer of the coffee table and pulled out the bag of cocaine she knew he stashed there. She refused to let her face show any judgement as he took a hit, waiting for his answer.

"For starters, what makes you so sure he would be willing to talk? And even if he is, why do you think he'd be easy to find? I lost track of him years ago, and it's not like my parents would be willing to help."

"I think he'd be more willing than you'd think. I think he was terrified of your parents, not of you. And we have Jackie and the archives for your second point."

"I'm *not* getting her involved in this." He shot her down, shoving the bag into his pocket.

"I'm not trying to get her involved in this," she said calmly. "I just need her access. If I say I'm doing something for the movement, trying to recruit specific people, whatever, I'll think of something, she won't question me."

"Look, I would love to see that man again. I think you know that, but I—" his mouth twisted slightly, and he took a second, as if trying to find the right words. "I just don't think he's going to be the same man I told you about."

"Even if he's not, it's better to have tried, isn't it? Don't you want to know what happened?" The three of them looked at each other, but Derek shook his head.

"Yeah, yeah I do. But it's not worth it, for any of us. It's not—"

"Don't you even try to pull that 'it's not safe' bullshit on us." Leo interrupted, not bothering to hide his contempt, "We've done much more stupid shit than this. I want to know, Melody wants to know, you want to know. So why isn't that enough?"

"Do you ever drop that 'mighty protector' crap, or must you wear it like a badge of honor every waking hour?" Derek snapped back. Leo opened his mouth to retaliate, but Melody was going to stop it before it began.

"Hey!" Melody stood up. "We're not doing this. Both of you, calm down." She waited until Leo gave her a nod, and Derek shrugged. "We don't have to decide anything right now. But we're not going to bitch about it, alright?"

"Fuck this," Derek muttered. He stood up and walked into his bedroom without another glance in her direction.

She stared forlornly at the door, then shot a glare at Leo as she started collecting the plates and moving to the kitchen.

"I wasn't finished, you know," he told her, keeping his voice low.

"Yes, you were."

"How was I supposed to know he'd snap like that?" He followed her into the kitchen, where she began putting the leftovers into plastic containers. "You didn't tell me you were bringing this up," he reminded her. She felt a prick of guilt at that, but pushed it away.

"He would've felt like we were teaming up on him even more if I'd told you first. I knew you'd agree with me."

"I could've pretended you hadn't."

She grinned at him. "Leo, I love you, but you're not that good of an actor." He snorted.

"Fine. But, saying it's dangerous? After that trip to the Prevention Unit?"

"I realize he was just making excuses, but that wasn't the way to call him out on it. You know how he gets, even when he doesn't take that shit."

"What would you have said, then?" He was irritated, she could tell, but he was listening.

"That we understood it would have been their first time seeing each other since Derek was eleven years old, that it would have been a difficult reunion in the best of times, let alone because Derek was asking for something. That we understood the fear of him being distrustful of Derek, of being rejected. His grandfather would probably think Derek was sent to spy, to see if he had any connection to the movement or something. His own children were suspicious of him, didn't believe him, kept Derek away, probably threatened to turn him in. He'll be paranoid. He has reasons to be. We'll go together, convince him that we're all on the same side. And, if it goes poorly, we'll be there to support Derek, no matter what."

Leo looked at the ground, running a hand along his neck. "I'm sorry."

"It's okay." She gave him a quick hug. He moved to her left to start washing the dishes as she put the containers in the refrigerator, and they were straightening the living room before he caught her eye again. He turned his head to the bedroom door in a silent gesture that she understood perfectly.

We're okay, but what are you going to do about him?

She shrugged.

Partially because she didn't know, and partially because she was sick of having to worry about it.

———

It took her three days before she approached him again. Derek was sitting in the conference room, going over a city map, marking all houses that they knew contained supporters, when she strode in, clutching something under her arm.

He gave her a quick glance before continuing to stare at the map.

"What?" He asked, more harsh than necessary.

She pushed a file towards him. "I found him."

Her words didn't reach him, he was concentrating, knowing he was forgetting something. He could feel her impatience but ignored her. She circled around him and bent down to look at the map too. She pointed to a spot his pen hadn't yet scribbled in.

"You forgot Carla. She's around here, isn't she? And you haven't marked yourself yet."

He looked up at her, her hair, grown out slightly, covering the right side of her face. He was aware of her, even if the words coming from her were still taking a while to process. She gave the map another scan, then looked at him. "Why are you doing this?"

"Trying to find the best place to start our rally, march, protest, whatever."

"It's a many-headed monster." He could hear the smile in her voice. He nodded, giving the map up for another time. It was the kind of thing Charlie would have done, not him. Maybe Jackie could take a look at it, help him decide.

"What were you saying?" he asked, trying to clear his head. She pointed to the file.

"Where'd you go? I lost you there." She peered into his face. He made a noncommittal grunt and swiveled his chair away from her, pulling the file towards himself, on top of the map.

He looked much younger than Derek remembered. His hair had not yet turned gray, his eyes looked much more alive, but there he was.

Aiden Lin.

Derek's fingers traced the paper, following along with the information written about the man he had not seen in over fifteen years.

Status: Fully naturalized American citizen. Child of first-generation Americans.

Husband, Oscar Lin, deceased, also American citizen. One child, three grandchildren.

Known dissident at time of Transitions. No known foreign government ties or pre–transition government ties.

Placed under watch 2076–2079 under suspicion of son, Daniel Lin. No charges brought during this time.

He was still at the same address; hadn't moved in all these years.

Derek's brain seemed to speed up into overdrive. He didn't know what to do with the anger and sadness building inside of him. He looked at her, wanting to forget what the file contained. What Aiden had never told him, what his father had done. He realized just how close she was to him. He wasn't sure what he wanted to do, other than release some of the tension building inside of him.

"I told you I wasn't doing this." He cast a look around. Searching for anything in the room, apart from her.

"And I chose to ignore you." She stood her ground, her voice level, not a hint of emotion, just statement of fact. "This is too important. You were angry."

"No, I was frustrated. Now I'm angry." He shoved the chair away. "You completely ignored me. You didn't care about how I felt about any of this, you just did what you wanted to do, not caring about—"

"You weren't thinking about the movement, about anyone other than yourself." Her tone didn't change. Her expression stayed the same, just cold objectivity. "You were only focused on how you would feel. You still haven't fully understood—this is bigger than you. This affects so many people other than you. You have yet to grasp this concept." Her voice was so calm. He wanted anything from her, condescension, anger to match his, repulsion, any emotion, other than this stone she gave him.

"Don't you fucking dare." He towered over her. "I'm the one who built this. I'm the one who made this. I've done what no one else has managed to do. You were the coward who ran. You were shitting yourself, scared out of your mind, when I had the courage to—"

178

"To what?" She was right in front of him, in his face. Her voice was a dangerous whisper, "To what, exactly?"

His fingers twitched.

"You need me," he said. "Without me, you have nowhere to go. Nowhere to stay. No one would take you in but me. What would you say to Leo if you couldn't come back to me?"

She gave him a look he could not decipher, but he knew instantly that his words had not had the effect he'd wanted.

"I thought we were past this, Derek." He wanted so badly to break her calm. To hear her scream. To hear her angry, to hear her *anything*. To feel a distraction out of his mind trapped between the map, the file, and those that were gone. The night they'd had too much to drink. "We would find someplace else to go. I don't know what the other members would say if you suddenly threw us out, though."

He felt his stomach clench. He wanted a hit.

"What do you actually want to say?" She asked.

She was too close. Much, much too close. He could feel her chest against his, as her breathing made it rise and fall.

There was a moment of silence, when he felt like she might have been trying to burn a hole through his skull, before he grabbed her and forced his mouth on hers.

"Derek, what are you doing?" She pulled her face away, as his right hand was moving to circle her waist, and his left moved to where her neck met her cheek. Instead of speaking, he kissed her, which she returned. He kissed her more furiously, wrapping his hand into her hair. He felt her hands on his back, slowly felt her melt.

"Melody," he whispered. It was almost a whine, a plea.

She was pushing him, twisting away from him, and he

released, not wanting to look at her, not wanting to be within a thousand miles of her. He tried to storm away, but her voice called to him.

"Derek, if you want to fuck me so you don't have to think about anything for a minute, that's fine, but can you be honest about it?" He stopped, feeling a part of himself shrivel. She took a hold of his wrist, and came around to face him, trying to keep his face in her view even when he looked away.

"I understand it. I understand needing to hold someone without it meaning anything. I understand wanting to drown it all out. You have people that depend on you. You have something built up around you, whether you like it or not, whether you intended this or not. And because of that, people have suffered, and died. You've lost people, they've lost people. You need to find a way to deal with that. Is this what you need? Because if it is, that's okay. But don't act like it's because you actually give a damn about me."

It took an age before it clicked in his brain.

"You're here." He finally said, "And I want to hold you."

"Hold me, or fuck me?"

"Both."

"We have time, if you make it quick. Leo will be waiting for us. I told him to meet us at Aiden's."

He cast her a shadow of a smile.

"You were so sure I'd agree to go?"

She didn't answer.

"Make sure the door is locked." He told her, his voice low. She complied, moving back around the table to the entrance to the room. He rolled up the map and pushed it and the file into her bag underneath the table. When he looked up, she was standing a step away from the door, pulling her shirt up over her head. He took her in—the slight curve of her breasts, the muscles in her shoulders, the beginnings of biceps, the protruding collarbone, the line of her legs.

He crossed the room to her in long, quick strides, and he placed his hands on either side of her face, pinning her to the wall. Knowing what he wanted, he said, "I'm not going to be gentle."

"Okay." It was acknowledgement. It was agreement. It was consent. His lips met hers: needy, angry, punishing, wanting. His hand tangled in her hair and pulled her head to the side so he could kiss down her neck as her hands began clawing their way under his shirt. He bit down, and felt himself twitch as she gasped—whether in surprise or pleasure he couldn't tell. His hand trailed down from her hair, down her waist, and to her thigh. He hooked her leg around his hip and pushed her more forcefully against the wall. She wrapped her other leg around him, pulling herself more tightly to him.

With an arm wrapped around her chest and another supporting her ass, he carried her back to the table. He set her down to sit at the edge of it, releasing his grip slightly, lips grazing along her collarbone, her chest, her stomach. Her fingers were anxiously digging underneath his shirt, trying to find a grip on him, her moans soft in his ear. He paused, finding the edges of the fabric and ripping it off over his head. But he hadn't wanted to stop. He hadn't wanted to remove himself from her, break the contact from her, especially for something so trivial. He found a spot on her breast and bit, harder than before, forcing her head into his shoulder to stifle the cry.

His mouth found hers again, as his hands found the waistband of her jeans. She helped him slide them down her legs as he lay her back on the table, his lips and teeth tracing patterns

181

down her chest.

He unzipped his jeans, letting them fall around his knees, positioning himself in front of her, and looked down into her face.

Her hands were braced against his shoulders, one leg dangling over the edge of the table, one wound around him again. Her eyes were shut, with an expression on her face that told him that she was a thousand miles away. He could have been anyone, anyone at all, and the expression would have been the same. And he hated it, but was grateful for it, because then he could pretend she wasn't who she was, and disappear into a different moment.

He pushed into her, and he covered her mouth with his again to stifle the noises escaping from her. He felt her fingers move around his arms as he found a remorseless rhythm. He knotted his fingers into her hair again and pulled her head back, feeling her arch into him, her nails clawing into his back.

Through the clouds of tension and heat, he felt himself release, and for a few, glorious moments, there was nothing more than the feel of her, the smoothness of her skin, and the way her arms entwined around his body.

———

She didn't understand how a house could look so foreboding, yet it did. They were lurking on the sidewalk, waiting to go to the door. She ran her fingers through her hair for the tenth time, looking between Derek and Leo.

"We can't just stand here all afternoon," she said, rolling her eyes at the two boys.

Leo nodded. Derek straightened his shoulders and took three strides to the front porch. He raised his hand, and she saw his finger tremble slightly before he hit the doorbell. They waited in silence, hearing nothing, before Derek jammed the button again.

"Maybe he's not home?" Leo suggested, giving Melody a look.

"He's an eighty-two-year-old retiree whose family doesn't talk to him. He's home," Derek said shortly. The silence dragged on, but, finally, they heard the sound of footsteps beyond the door.

It opened a crack, enough that Melody was sure whoever was behind the door could see Derek, but no one else.

"Hello?" It was a woman's voice.

"Hi, is Aiden in?" He asked.

"Um, yeah, he is. Who are you?" She peered out looking to the side. Melody caught a glimpse of black hair and pale skin.

"I'm Derek Lin. His grandson."

"He didn't say you were coming. Who are the others with you?"

"Erin and John Thackeray. They're friends of mine. They know I haven't seen him in a while so…" He let the sentence hang. She was too skeptical for Melody's liking. She wondered if Aiden had told her to be suspicious of anyone coming to call, or if her awareness was why she was here.

"Can you please just tell him I'm here? Let him decide if he wants to see me. This wasn't planned," Derek continued. He shot her a smile but judging by the way his shoulders sagged when the door closed again, it had not been returned. Melody leaned against the side of the house, keeping an eye on Derek as he shoved his hands into his pockets, looking the epitome of awkward. Leo crossed over to stand beside her, looking up at the porch roof.

More shuffling, and the door opened fully.

"Derek?" Though his face betrayed his age, his voice did not. His hair had gone gray, his face a mass of wrinkles. He pushed his glasses up his nose, looking into the face of the much younger man. His oversized button up sweater blew slightly in the breeze, as the silence seemed to stretch for an age. Melody reached behind her, not quite conscious of her hand moving, but Leo caught her fingers and squeezed as they both waited for Derek to reply.

"Hi," Derek finally said, taking a step towards Aiden. Aiden hesitated.

"Callie said you had friends?" Derek nodded and gestured over to where Melody and Leo were standing. Melody pulled her hand away and took a step closer.

It was like the moment when Jackie had walked into the conference room when they'd gone to that first meeting. Aiden looked at her, taking her in from top to bottom. His eyes passed over Leo too, and he seemed to peer through them, silently understanding.

His face split into a wide smile, and he pulled his grandson into a tight hug.

"I knew you'd be okay," he said quietly.

Derek, though he initially looked stunned, returned the hug, and they stayed quiet for a few moments before Aiden let go and gestured them all into the house.

"You'll have to forgive Callie for not letting you in right away," He said, shutting the door behind Leo, "There were too many years of visitors who I had not asked to see."

"We saw your file," Melody told him. "We understand."

He looked at her again, and shook his head, turning back to Derek, "I have to ask, how?"

"It's a long story." Derek sighed.

"I wondered if you were involved, if you were doing anything," Aiden began to move through the house, to a small living room in the back of the first floor. "You always were the most curious child. I knew you wouldn't be sitting still while this was happening. But now I have to wonder."

"It's his movement," Melody told him. Derek gave her a funny look, but she ignored him.

"I don't think so. Seems it's as much yours as anyone else's."

"Nope. All Derek's. We came back to try to stop him, and well, that obviously didn't work out," Leo supplied.

"You're the boy that left with her? I'm sorry, I don't remember your name."

"I'm Leo. Leon only when someone is very angry." Aiden smiled at the pair of them.

"Come, sit. I'll have Callie make tea." He left them in the room as he went off to the kitchen, and they sat awkwardly on the couch and loveseat. Aiden came back a couple minutes later and eased himself onto the armchair, saying,

"Callie's got the kettle going, won't be too long."

"Who is Callie?"

"Callie Zhao. She was assigned to me a few years ago, part of the initiative to assist the elderly population." The corners of his mouth twitched, "Keep an eye on the ones they were afraid of, more like."

"So, she's...."

"Heard more stories than you, by this point." He cast a look at Melody, "Well, actually, I'm not sure about that."

"Why were they afraid of you?" Melody asked.

"Well, it had a lot to do with how they started educating, in the beginning." He sighed, "Daniel, my son, Derek's father, was a part of a test group brought into Party schools. I didn't have a choice; they knew my name from the Transitions, and my ties to China. So, it was either send your kid to the school, or your kid is taken away from you and sent to the school regardless, and you'll be arrested." He sighed, "I was very wary, after that. I asked Daniel every day what they were teaching him. My husband, when he was alive, was nervous as well. After Oscar died, I tried to hold on to him, I tried to tell him.... He said I was a foolish old man clinging to fantasies, of a past that never existed. He said I was dangerous and that he would have me arrested. I think Oscar dying had something to do with it. He was a teenager; he didn't handle it well.

"But, that's neither here nor there. I don't know who he told, if it was a teacher, or the police, but they raided the house. They found nothing. They kept tabs on me, I knew I was being followed, for a time. When Derek here was born, I didn't dare try again. Daniel wouldn't leave me alone with him for longer than five minutes once he could talk. But there was a neighbor, a grandmother that was arrested, who told Derek and his friend about Chinese New Year, old traditions, you know. Things they've tried to quash, tried to bury. We were all living here at the time. After the Transitions, this was a different neighborhood. So many were the children of Chinese, Japanese, Thai, Filipino immigrants. Daniel said point blank he was moving, taking Derek to a different, less dangerous, environment.

"And what could I do? I'd already seen what my son would do. It took so long to build up that tenuous relationship, but there was nothing resembling trust. I knew he thought I'd tell Derek the same things I told him. After you all moved away, the house was raided again, and I knew they didn't really go away this time. They kept tabs on the neighborhood for years. Some got scared and moved away. Some were arrested. Some stayed, but not many. Those of us left just don't know where else to go.

"But, I'm sure you didn't come to hear me reminisce about

186

that. What can I do for you? Why have you all come here?" He jogged himself out of his memories, looking around at them all.

"Actually," Derek cast Melody a sideways look, "We did."

"If Derek is to have any hope of succeeding," Melody continued for him, "We need to know what happened during the War. What it was like. How we really got to where we are now."

Some of the color disappeared in Aiden's cheeks.

"I... I don't know." He looked between them all again. "That's a big story to tell. And, I just said——"

"I don't give a damn about my dad." Derek's tone left little room for doubt.

"Mel and I, we're dead regardless," Leo said. "We won't be taking anyone else down with us."

Aiden let out a grunt of laughter.

"You say that now," he smiled, not unkindly, at Leo. "And, after they've had you for a few days? Weeks? When you're nothing but a pile of broken bones and blood?"

Melody caught Leo wince.

"I saw it, I saw it all. And you think you can just say you'll be strong and that'll be the end of it?"

Melody could feel the tension in the room, but she had eyes only for Aiden.

"Tell us. Please," she said quietly, "Tell us what happened back then."

He took a moment. Callie came in with a tray and handed him a steaming mug of tea. He gave her a wordless thanks as she left, and he scanned the room again.

"So, you want to hear a story?" His tone was indecipherable, and he turned his eyes back to the mug in his hands, "And you want it to be nice and clean, with a beginning and an end. With a good

187

and bad side, sides that are easily discernible. You can tell who's who, who's right and wrong, and you can raise the flag again and pick up the cause where they left off and ride into a victorious sunset."

"It wasn't like that?" Derek asked.

"It's never like that. Innocents die, children, the weak, the sick, the starving, and who can say why?"

"Because—" Derek started, but Aiden quickly interrupted.

"No. No 'because.' Whether because of a soldier, a fighter, a neighbor, doesn't really matter. It still is."

He sighed and took a sip of tea.

"I was twenty-one when it all began. It had been building for a while, you understand. It wasn't one incident and it just all exploded. It was like building a fire. You need to build it up. Fuel wood, tinder, kindling, only then can you light a match and expect it to burn and stay burning.

"There was so much wrong. I wouldn't know where to begin. There isn't a context to explain it to you, or the time. You'd need the right history, but there were centuries of oppression, of hatred, mistrust, and greed. It just built and kept building. We'd take a step forward then five steps back. At least, that was how it seemed to me. I was," he broke off, and looked at Melody and Leo carefully.

"You're twenty?"

"Twenty-one, later this month." Melody said.

"Twenty-two, why?" Leo asked.

"I want to excuse it by being young, but I look at you and I can't." He hung his head. "I thought I'd have time, after college, maybe, when I was an adult, with a job, when money and taxes and things mattered. My parents, they worked so hard. I didn't want for anything. Paid for me to go to Georgetown, and I spent my first three years coasting by. The kids there studying politics, foreign affairs, you could see some of them walking around looking like they hadn't slept in weeks, haunted by what they were studying and seeing every day. Some thought everything was fine. Others drank too much. It wasn't anything I really thought about because I didn't have to. Some would try to get us involved, make us sign petitions for this or that, try to get us to march in the city. My friends and I, well, we were well off, had jobs waiting for us on the other side. What did we care?

"My junior year, 2031, that was when it started to get bad. See, there had been this thing called 'tort reform,'—it was changes to the civil justice system that basically controlled how much a normal citizen could sue a company or entity for. There was an accident, a group of elementary school children going on a field trip. The bus, whatever company made the brakes, they should have been recalled. They weren't. Nineteen children, five dead. But see, they were crossing a state border, and some kids got airlifted to Indiana, some to Illinois, some stayed in Kentucky.

"One of the little girls that was treated in Kentucky... it wasn't just the brakes. It was the hospital too. They didn't perform the right tests, or they didn't treat the right things, I don't remember exactly. It was so long ago. She was paralyzed. A little boy who was treated in Illinois, he was injured, but not as severely. He won his lawsuit and was paid something like $1 million. The girl was only paid something like $250,000. That barely covered the medical expenses, and she needed physical therapy, occupational therapy, and a nurse so her parents could work. And people wanted to know why a little black girl was treated one way when a white boy was treated another, when it was the same case, the same circumstances. It was children, riding a bus, on a school trip.

"It sparked riots in Kentucky, in Illinois, and states where

189

there had been protests before—Maryland, Missouri, New York. People were angry. People were confused. Like I said, it wasn't just one thing. It wasn't just about the kids, or race, or money. It was about all of it. So, you reached a point where you weren't sure who was on your side. It wasn't one side against the other, it was supremacists fighting against minorities, it was religions fighting against each other, science over religion against religion over science. Men against women, old against young, poor against rich. You didn't know who to trust, where to turn.

"That summer, one of my friends, Roy, was supposed to be doing an internship in New York. The city was still trying to plow along; the financial institutions were trying to convince the rest of the world that this was a temporary situation, that it would smooth over soon, that business as usual would commence soon, we were still a smart investment. He was nervous to go, but he went anyway. We were going to go visit him in July, and my parents were all for it. The fighting had come from Maryland to D.C., where there was more than enough unrest. We were set to take the train into Penn on the day it happened.

"Roy lived in a loft in Brooklyn, he'd take the subway everyday into Midtown. He said he liked Brooklyn; he was excited for us to see his place. We were in Pennsylvania when we heard the news. Our train stopped. The lights flickered on and off. And the conductor announced there had been a massive attack in New York and we were being rerouted to Philadelphia to await further instruction.

"Now, bear in mind that all sorts of groups were taking advantage of the situation as the chaos began, trying to get vulnerable, scared people to listen to their message. Fringe groups on both sides of the political spectrum grew. Fascist groups rose and sparked violent demonstrations. Hate crimes, rioting,

190

bombings, shootings, hackings that could cripple a city, you saw everything, and every group took credit.

"That day, the day I was supposed to meet Roy, there was a large shipment of oil inbound to Manhattan. The trucks were crossing the Williamsburg Bridge and met a group of eco-terrorists protesting the use of fossil fuels. There had been a bill put to the New York City legislature, whether or not the city would move entirely to renewable energy. The city felt it wasn't feasible, that the sources then available weren't reliable, and the city that was such an international financial and economic center could not rely on intermittent power. But that did not go over very well. Gas prices were rising after a fair few years of record lows, and many were not all that happy about the decision. So, this group decided to take out a few trucks, and send a message. Hurt people in more than just their wallets.

"They miscalculated, though. Meant to hit the trucks in the center of the bridge, but mistimed the bombings. Took out a chunk of Williamsburg, at the worst possible spot. They hit near the entrance to the bridge, the Brooklyn Queens expressway, and near the Marcy Avenue train station. At least a thousand died. Roy died. Hundreds of millions in damages. And, not too long after, a hate group saw an opening, figuring that they should have their say in punishing the city for its sins. They bombed parts of Greenwich Village, a well-known area for the LGBTQ community.

"Well, after that, New York got angry. The city could always be counted on to bounce back, but there's a breaking point. Across the country there were riots everywhere. Panic and confusion. The mayor tried to quarantine Manhattan, declared a state of emergency, and brought in the National Guard. There had been other attempted terrorist attacks in the previous years, but these were two incredibly destructive, successful ones, within days of each other, and they came from home. They couldn't spin it a different way, though many certainly tried. People demanded action. They were terrified.

"With Manhattan under attack and in quarantine, financial centers didn't know what to do. The city couldn't function. New Yorkers were known for being resilient, but this was different. They couldn't move within the city, couldn't get outside the city. There was paranoia that there would be another attack. Other financial centers, Chicago, Boston, Charlotte, San Francisco, tried to take up the slack, but international investment all but stopped. Chicago had its own attacks to deal with not long after. Stocks plummeted. The President started to blame the international community, immigrants, refugees, and foreigners for the violence, which of course made the violence worse and other countries even more reluctant to help. Some countries started to impose embargoes on US goods. Others started to charge more for their exports. With a lack of foreign money, exports stalled, and necessary imports to create goods rising in cost, the economy stopped functioning. Some industries collapsed within days. The violence got worse. A march stormed the capital, raided Capitol Hill. Congressmen and senators were slaughtered; the President was hidden underground.

"It wasn't too long before some states began begging the federal government for help. They asked for security forces, for money, for anything, to help quell the violence, to make it stop. And, well, that had happened before. When given a choice between stability and freedom …people don't tend to think of anything beyond their immediate needs. What did a curfew really matter if it meant that we were safe at night? What did increased security at state borders really mean? Surely everyone had a driver's license anyway, what was the harm? And if protecting the national border to prevent people from getting in meant preventing people from leaving, well, surely, for a little while, that could be okay too."

Aiden paused and took a long sip of tea. Melody was waiting on the edge of her seat, not sure she could handle where the story was going, but unable to stop listening.

"There are some people who can fight because it's the right thing to do. Because they know people are suffering near or far, because they know they have to. Then there are those like me, who need to see it up close before they have a reason to put themselves on the line. Other people never understand why, even when it's right outside their door. I'm not proud it took me as long as it did. And honestly, even after all this time, I don't know what hit me more, Roy, or Greenwich. I'm not proud of that either. But, either way, after the attacks I wouldn't stand still. I went to marches, stood outside and against police barricades. We screamed against injustices of all sorts. Not that it did any good.

"When the states handed over control, the government said it would just be for a little while, until the fighting died down. It didn't take too long, not with the authority the National Guard and the Army, eventually, were given to stop protests and rioting. They bombed parts of Chicago and Detroit deemed 'battlegrounds.' Boston, Houston, Los Angeles, Denver, they didn't fare much better. But, after it was somewhat suppressed, the states demanded a Constitutional Convention. Not all agreed, but most, something like forty did. Many in power at the time wanted to see the changes stay. Just before the convention started, the President and Vice President were killed. The Cabinet assumed power. We didn't know what was coming but knew it couldn't be good. We knew we had to keep fighting.

"Not all the states could physically send delegates; some were attacked on their way to the convention. But it happened, and three months later, they came out with what you now know as the Constitution. I'm still a bit hazy on the details myself, but I know it was led in large part by the Cabinet at the time. The Secretary of Defense was made the President; you know him as General Foster. It united the military in a new, more symbolic way, made it a bit easier to control when states weren't so happy to ratify. It didn't take too long before everyone agreed, and then, well. The House of Representatives, one of the bodies of Congress, was destroyed. We saw the establishment of the Party. Over the years, they've amended it so it looks like it does now, with the kids and the branches and the emphasis on lineage.

"I was arrested soon after they announced the new 'President.' When they established the new Senate. It had been seven years at that point. Seven years of uncertainty, violence, chaos. I was okay, because of my family's position. But those that depended on government assistance? They were never able to, or never bothered to, count how many died. No telling how many people were killed in the fighting or trying to cross the border. The homeless population rose, I know that. So many suffered. No one bothered reporting crimes after a while, not when the police were trying to lock up those who needed help. I don't blame those who just wanted it all to end. Who were so tired. They just wanted a home and peace. They wanted a job and stability. I was able to keep fighting, not everyone was. The ability to be political is a privilege, to be able to pay attention because your focus is not on feeding yourself, not solely on making it from one day to the next.

"But I was arrested, and they threatened my husband. He was at home with Daniel, and I couldn't risk them both. We were afraid they might take Daniel away. So, I went home to live a quiet life. Those who didn't... well. Who's to say how much they suffered? But the streets were cleared quickly enough. We tried to make do. We tried to keep the past alive. They'd raid our house for old books and things from time to time. Daniel would help them look."

He looked into his mug again, and Melody could see tears in the corners of his eyes.

"Is that enough of a story for you?" He asked, quietly, draining the last of his tea, and setting the cup definitively on the coffee table. Melody didn't look at him. She stared at the mug, the ring of moisture staining the wood. The pictures he'd painted burning into her mind.

She nodded.

"Yes, Mr. Lin. That's the story we wanted."

From the case file of Melody Karsh: July 2092-April 2093
December 2091

Dear Mom,

Arshem's at it again. Though, this time, I could see his point. Never thought I'd say those words. There's this new phone that China released not too long ago, and tech companies have been basically begging for it to be allowed in. A week ago, the first shipment came through. And the thing is—they're so cheap for what they are. Supposed to be top of the line—I think they will flood the American market, which is easy enough when you have no real competition. Arshem's fine with them being imported, but he wants a blanket ban on Party members owning one, and wants a deal with China to share any intelligence that could be gathered from citizens owning and using the phone. The ban went through immediately, the intelligence deal has been an ongoing debate.

I told Liz this was happening, and she just grinned at me, and said it sounded like an interesting fight to be a part of. Then she pulled a brown paper bag out from the top of the refrigerator and dumped it out onto the kitchen table. And, sure enough, she had four of them already. It's a piece of glass—clear, transparent, shatterproof. And in each corner a little piece of black or gold metal, just enough for you to actually see the thing if it's laying

197

out. It operates off of voice recognition, and it's such a beautiful little thing. She got it under an alias, as a part of a family plan, so it can't be traced back to me. And she said that my reaction was worth the cost.

So now I'm sitting in my apartment, playing with the settings, as I'm supposed to be drafting Arshem's next plan for negotiation. It's the little things, right?

Honestly, why I'm this excited about a phone, I don't know. Maybe because it's one thing in no way attached to me. I can't be tracked as a Party member through it. I won't live in constant fear that Arshem or someone in Judicial will pull up the records of my conversations and see who I was talking to, and what I was saying.

Because the phone doesn't exist, just like Sam doesn't exist. And I'm so fucked if either of those things change.

    Love,

    Melody

V

The cold air bit at her face as she stood by the open window. So many things she'd taken for granted were thrust into sharper relief. Like the cigarette in her hand—she'd always taken it as a given that rolling was more popular because of the stark price difference between that and packs. She considered it for a moment as she held it against her lips. Had there been a change? When had the imports gotten too expensive?

Liz had told her there had been a War. A war between the government and the people, and that everyone had lost. She had told Melody that the people had wanted stability after the fighting and had caved in to fear. Every clipping she had in the library had confirmed this telling of the story.

How much had Liz really known? Had Liz's parents given in? Been subjugated to the same treatment as Aiden? Surely not, or else Liz would have gone to the same sort of school as Daniel. Liz's parents must've stayed on the sidelines, out of sight. Or maybe, there had only been so much the new government could do? Maybe Liz had gotten off easy.

So many times she'd wanted the story, but Liz had been

so unwilling to provide what details she did know. Of all the information of the past she would happily divulge, between the library and knowledge she'd personally obtained, she was so tight-lipped about the War. Greg had been no use; he knew even less than Liz.

Melody wanted to understand. Years of panic and confusion, in many cases starvation, homelessness, basic needs unmet. A promise of stability would be met with open arms. *But then it would go from bad to worse to this fucking mess.* She flicked ashes from the cigarette out the window.

Derek had been talking quietly to Aiden, Leo in the kitchen doing dishes with Callie. So, she was here, looking at a gray sky, lost in thought.

It wasn't a fruitless mission, but it wasn't what she'd hoped for. She'd wanted to believe that there was some common goal before, a message, a rallying call, something. But it sounded so similar to what was happening now under Derek's leadership. He didn't know who these people were, operating under his banner. So many kids would say they were a part of it without having ever met Derek or having attended a meeting. He couldn't control their actions. And what about those in other cities? In other states? How was he supposed to manage that? Political prisoners would only unite so many people for so long. There was so much more wrong. So much more suffering. So much more that hadn't been fixed, that had been left unanswered in the battles before.

"Melody?" She felt a tap on her shoulder and jumped. She turned to see Aiden standing near her. Derek had left the room; she hadn't heard their conversation end.

"Hi, sorry," she ran a hand through her hair, trying to clear her head.

"I don't mean to be, well I don't want…." he was twisting his hands.

"What's wrong?"

"I want to ask you something. I sent Derek out for a moment, so I could talk to you."

"What did you want to ask that you couldn't in front of him?" She was wary of this conversation. She didn't like to think he either trusted her more than his grandson, or didn't trust her at all.

"How's he doing? Derek, with all this," he looked at her, and she could see a mix of hope and fear in his lined face. She opened her mouth, but she couldn't think of any words.

"I'll rephrase." He thought for a moment, "Can he lead this? Is he going to keep it together?"

A part of her wanted to lie. She wanted to give him his hope. Instead, she took a drag from the cigarette, and blew smoke out the window in a long, slow exhale.

"He's…getting there." She said carefully.

"When they catch him, will they break him?" She almost dropped the cigarette. His words were stated so plainly.

"You—"

"I've seen this before. I've lived through this. Lived it over and over again." His eyes met hers. "I don't want to die. I don't want Derek to die. But he will be caught. He's told me what you're planning. He will be arrested, either because someone gives him up, or because the police will finally figure out who he is, or he puts himself in a position where it's obvious. Regardless of what happens, he will be killed. I want to know, for the sake of his legacy, will he crack under the pressure. Will he survive their torture? Will he give you up?"

They looked at each other and understanding passed between them. In this moment, he wasn't a grandfather. He was a survivor: an old dissident talking to a new one.

"No. He won't. I don't know who he'll give up, who will pay for him, but I know he will break. He'll want an easy out, in the end." Saying it out loud was surprisingly easy, for how often she'd tried to bury the thought.

He was silent for a moment but took her hand in his.

"Melody, please. Help him. Support him. I can't see this die again. I don't know if there's anything I could have done before to help him, to stop Daniel from...well. I don't know. But, please. He's started something impossible. Don't let it end with him."

"I'm marked for dead too." She felt the edges of her mouth twitch against her will.

"I know," he nodded. "But I know that while you're here, you can help him."

"You're putting a lot of faith in a stranger."

"A stranger who gave him the courage to come here and ask for help. A stranger who helped him plan the intrusion into the Prevention Unit. A stranger who is helping him plan what comes next. A stranger who, with others, I am sure, is propping up someone who should not be the leader. I knew him as a child. I trust that he has grown into a man, but he was headstrong and foolish then. He was not one to sit back and plan out a strategy, and he isn't one to do so now. Please, for as long as you can, help him become the leader he needs to be."

She took a final drag of the cigarette and stubbed it out on the windowsill.

"We will do everything we can to help him," she said, finally. "We already are."

Aiden nodded and clasped her shoulder. But, before he walked away he leaned in closer, and whispered in her ear.

"It's always good to have a plan, just in case." He shuffled away from her to his armchair. She stayed by the window, feeling the air on her skin, staring blankly into the back of his head.

———

She told Derek she and Leo would go pick up food when they left a little while later. She was sure he was grateful for the time alone, and she wanted the chance to talk to Leo undetected.

Ideally, she would have had Logan around for this conversation, but since the attack on the Prevention Unit, he had been unreachable. She wasn't surprised. She assumed he was lying as low as possible until the heat wore off, but she knew she owed him a warning of what was coming next, of what she and Aiden had finally said aloud.

Leo drew her out of her thoughts.

"Erin?"

"Huh?" She jerked at his touch on her arm. They'd been quiet the entire bus ride back towards Derek's, but now on the walk to the store they would have a chance to talk.

"What do you think?"

"Of what?"

"What Aiden said?"

"I'm trying to absorb it all."

"It's quite a story." Something in his tone set her on edge, and she narrowed her eyes at him.

"What do you mean?"

"Well," his mouth curved, almost into a smirk, "think about it. If that really happened."

"Really happened?" She tried to interrupt but he kept going.

203

"Mom would've told me. She said it was one side versus the other. That guy—going on about everyone fighting each other? I don't know what he's thinking. Maybe it's just so he feels better about himself. Maybe it's so that he doesn't feel guilty about caving in. So that he could have a story to tell where he wasn't the bad guy, because everyone was the bad guy? I don't know, Mel, but it's a load of crap."

Melody had stopped walking with him as his rant concluded, but realized the danger of it, that it could call attention to their conversation, and caught up with him again.

She didn't speak. She wanted to weigh each word carefully.

"John," she started, "she might not have known."

"Whatever she did or didn't say—it was all to protect us." His face was set, shoulders square, as if bracing for more than just this fight with her.

How far did she need to push this? How important was it for him to accept the truth, rather than letting the memory of his mother, unfailing in giving knowledge and wisdom, remain intact?

"That's true." Melody nodded, and whispered, "And the idea of one side versus the other is not incorrect. The way Aiden told it," this time she plowed on past his attempts to interrupt, "once the military took over, it was one against the rest, yeah? The difference is just in how it started, which Liz never really told us."

He didn't respond, just kept walking. He said nothing as they shopped, apart from whatever was necessary to get in and out. She tried to process it in her mind. What would cause him to shut out the truth? He'd been so level-headed throughout everything.

But maybe that was it, the thought crossed her mind as they began the walk back to Derek's apartment, *maybe he can't be so calm anymore.* If he'd been holding on so tightly to that image of Liz, and it was broken? The picture of her as an all-knowing, perfect entity…

She sighed, and Leo turned to look at her. "What?" he asked, a bit more aggressively than necessary.

"Nothing," she said quickly. "Just tired."

"Here." He reached to take one of the bags from her. She let him without complaint.

"Hey," she started cautiously. "Aiden and I talked, while you were talking to Callie," she could feel him instantly raise his guard. "It was about Derek, and what he would do, if he got into trouble."

"Oh," she sensed him relax slightly. "What did he think?"

"The same thing I do."

"What do you want to do?"

"We need to help him."

"Why?" he snapped. "He's shit at this. He can't do anything."

"He's the one who started it," she argued. "People respond to his name, his voice, more than anything else."

"They respond to his message, not him."

"It's his delivery of that message. He was the one who—"

"Jackie could do his job. Jackie, and Morgan, they should be the ones in charge. Hell, you should be in charge more than him."

"Me?"

"You're the one propping him up. You, and them, he's nothing without you. Can't tie his own damn shoes. Can't do anything without you."

"I can see Jackie, she could maybe take it on after him, maybe with Morgan, but in the meantime—"

"How do you even want to help him?" He was growing angrier and angrier. "Do you want to fuck him into power? Your magical pussy of leadership ability?"

"Le–John, what the fuck?"

205

"What the hell else are you getting out of this?"

"Don't you dare."

"Yes, I fucking dare. Do you just want to sleep with the one in charge? You could spread your legs for Covington, maybe he'd let you just be his whore, instead of—" He stopped, and saw her expression, the fire in her eyes, the lips set into a thin line.

"I didn't—" He immediately started to backtrack, but she pushed past him, grabbing the bags from his hands.

"Sleep somewhere else tonight. Any other member's. I don't care. Stay away from me."

She was sure he was calling after her, but she could hear nothing past the roaring in her ears.

The moonlight coming through the window made her skin shine. Her hair fell into her face as she methodically rolled the cigarette, licking the edge of the paper to make it stay.

"Do you mind, or do you want me to go to the window?" she asked, holding it up.

"No, it's fine," Derek reached behind him to the bedside table, finding an empty coffee cup. He passed it to her. "Here."

"Thanks," she held the cigarette between her pointer and middle finger, searching for the lighter. He looked for a moment with her, finding it at the edge of the bed. He held it up and lit the cigarette for her. He could see her visibly relax as she inhaled, and exhaled smoke.

"When did you start?" he asked. It was the first time she'd ever done this in here. She'd always gone out into the living room, or hallway.

"Seventeen," she shrugged, "it was rare, though. I liked drinking more. But we didn't get to as much—when we left. Just with the work we were doing. Smoking was easier." He gently ran a finger down her thigh, absently tracing swirls.

"You ever going to tell me about where you guys went?"

"You ever going to actually forgive me for Sean?" They smiled at each other. He knew she was serious, that she knew how he felt, but he also knew she wasn't angry at him. She blew out a puff of smoke and offered him the cigarette. He took it and watched her as she gazed out the window.

The first night, he thought she might kill something. She had dumped grocery bags in the kitchen, and he could hear her shoving items into drawers, opening and slamming closed the refrigerator door. When he went to tell her to be quiet, to be mindful of the neighbors, she'd given him a look that could've turned the entire apartment into ice. He'd backed away as she marched towards the bathroom.

"Where's Leo?" he'd managed to get out.

"I don't know." It was more than cold. He couldn't figure it out. He didn't try to.

"Is he coming back tonight?"

"No." She spoke from behind the closed door. He heard the shower turn on, and he had the distinct impression it would be better for him to be in his room when she came out.

The second day, they'd been cordial to each other during the planning meeting. They didn't mention meeting Aiden to anyone, Leo and Melody sat next to each other, but Derek noticed that every time he got too close, her shoulders would stiffen. Or she might turn her chair slightly, or back away. Nothing too obvious to anyone else. But Derek, who had lived with them for several months now, could tell.

He'd suggested to Melody that they stop by the liquor store

on the way home. Since then, she'd slept in his bed.

They were on day five now. And he knew he should ask why, what made those two who were willing to charge into death together break so suddenly, but was also sure that this wasn't the time. Or maybe, he needed that to be the truth. Tomorrow, Melody had finally managed to pin down Logan for a meet up so they could warn him of what was coming. And then, the day after...

He knew, from a very confused Jackie, that Leo was staying with her and Morgan. Jackie had no more answers than he did. But that was enough, surely? That they knew he was safe.

He handed her back the cigarette, and kissed down her chest, to playfully bite at the skin on her inner thigh. He heard her appreciative sigh and looked up at her. The cigarette lay just so between her fingers, her lips still slightly pink from their last round. Her eyes met his; expectant, exasperated.

"Do you ever get tired?" She asked.

"Sometimes."

"You're restless tonight."

"Don't I have reason to be?"

"Several." He wanted to taste her, to feel her break under him again. He couldn't tell if she was thinking too hard, or if her mind was as blank as her expression.

"You can say no," he watched her carefully. Seeing if anything changed. She wanted to say something, he knew it. She took a final drag on the cigarette and dropped it into the cup.

"Tell me if you need this," she said quietly. "Tell me what you want."

She let the cup fall on the bed as he began to work, his tongue drawing her out in slow, deliberate motions.

"Did you need words, or was that enough of an answer?"

He asked, moving up to nip at her neck. She just smiled and pulled him up to kiss her.

He woke when he heard the door open. He looked over and saw Melody still beside him, curled up on the other side of the bed facing away towards the window. He got up, and stepped quietly towards the bedroom door, listening hard. Whoever was out there was creeping around, or so it seemed to him. He wasn't sure, but he didn't want to take a chance. He reached carefully under the mattress where he'd hidden one of the guns after the day at the Prevention Unit. Melody grunted in her sleep and rolled over, her hair falling in her face.

He opened the door as little as possible, holding the gun slightly in front of him, peeking around the frame. Seeing it clear, he took a few steps, and heard movement in the kitchen. He stopped again, peering around the corner, but couldn't get a clear view from his angle. He took a deep breath, and stepped into the room, holding the gun out right in front of him.

He heard the glass shatter before he registered who it was.

"Fuck, Derek, what the hell, get that thing away from me!" Leo stood in front of him with bags under his eyes, hair on end, and clutching a bottle of vodka. Derek let out a breath, and let his brain catch up as he watched Leo stoop to pick up the broken pieces of a tumbler.

"What the hell are you doing, sneaking in here?" he asked, lowering the gun. Leo scowled.

"I'm not sneaking, I was staying here. I had clothes here, my bag."

"You came here this early… for your shit?" Derek gestured to the vodka.

"No, I—" Leo seemed to cave into himself. His shoulders slumped. His head fell. "Jackie kicked me out," he finally said.

"Jackie wouldn't do that."

"Kick out might be too harsh. She finally got me to tell her what happened, and said I had to get my shit together and fix it." He stood up, taking the pieces of glass to the garbage can, "I'm assuming you've heard by now?"

Derek shook his head. "She didn't want to tell. I didn't want to ask."

Leo grabbed another tumbler from the cabinet and poured a healthy dose of vodka into it. "Well, that's something, I guess."

"Look," Derek rubbed a hand over his eyes, "Whatever this shit is between you and Melody, can you two just deal with it? We've got enough crap without you two doing, whatever the fuck you're doing."

"Could say the same to you."

"How do you figure?"

"You're the one fucking her. Do you really have time for *that* while you're leading a revolution? Is that why you're doing this? For the perks?"

The way he said 'perks' made Derek take an involuntary step towards him.

"I thought she was like your sister. Is that how you talk about your sister?" He said quietly.

"I'm not talking about her. I'm talking about you."

"Are you? Or are you just pissed that she'll touch any dick but yours?"

Leo took a long sip of his drink.

"I don't know where to start on that." He said, finally, "I've never looked at her like that. I've only wanted her safe."

"Bullshit."

"I've known her since I was born. She's my sister, first and always." He took another sip. "But I don't know why she picked you. I don't know why she thinks you're worth this lapse in judgement. We need to stay focused on this fight. She knows that. We came back to stop it. We can't, we won't, and that's probably for the best. But we've got to see it through as long as we can. And she's letting that focus go to fucking you, why? We've got one more day. She's still got to talk to Logan, there are areas we still haven't gotten the word out to yet. But she's holed up here with you. For what?"

It was too much, much too much, and much too early, for Derek's mind. He couldn't talk to Leo about this. More than that, he had no reason to.

But the guy was right about one thing, at least.

"Say all that's true. Tomorrow, we could all be caught or killed. Are you really going to fight with her because she wanted to get laid a couple times before then? That's really how you want it to go down?"

Derek didn't wait for him to reply. He started back out of the room, leaving Leo to his drink. He opened the door and saw Melody changing into jeans and a long-sleeved black shirt.

"He's back," she said, tying up the laces of her boots. He nodded.

"You going to meet Logan?" he asked.

"Yeah,"

"You're okay with this?"

"It was going to have to be sorted eventually. We'll deal with it out of here. After I finish up with Logan."

"Thanks," he was grateful. He would be having a long enough day.

"I'll see you tonight," she said, zipping up her jacket and grabbing her hat.

"Bye," he said, but she'd already walked out the door.

She was bent over the pond, crumbling bits of her muffin to feed to the ducks when he found her.

"You weren't at our bench," Logan said.

"I've been here for a while." She handed him some of the muffin and gestured to the ground beside her.

"It's cold." He grumbled, but he knelt next to her, tossing bits of food into the water.

"You get used to it. I have coffee. Probably cold by now though."

"We don't usually do this," he said warily.

"It's probably the last time I'm going to get to see you. I recognize that. I didn't want it to be so impersonal."

"Why?" He looked at her.

"We're marching tomorrow." She expected more of a reaction, but he just grimaced, and returned his gaze to the pond.

"About damn time." She opened her mouth, but before she could say anything, he continued, "He's had people riled up for weeks, months, really, and it's time he did something with it."

"He's—" But he cut her off again.

"I think the thing with the Prevention Unit was a good idea. But he should have done that after a protest, with a couple of arrests. Let people see what was happening to those who'd just tried to speak. It would've made a greater impact, I think. Or..." he sighed. "Maybe, it's better this way. Let people know what they're facing. Let them get upset over what their friends and families have had to face. Are facing. Who knows? We heard that there was already a protest over in Boston. A group of women, I think. I don't know too many details, Covington just heard word from the police there that you weren't among those caught. Point is, if Derek's really going to do this, he should fucking do it."

Melody nodded, throwing the last bits of the muffin into the water. She took one of the coffee cups beside her and passed it to Logan, taking the other for herself. She sat back on the grass, stretching her legs out in front of her.

"Are you worried?" she asked him.

"About what?"

"What happens if we're caught?"

"Derek? I told you before. I don't trust him. I think he's been in over his head for some time. I've had to make my peace with that." He sighed. "You? I think you should be proud."

"Me? Why?"

"No matter what happens, you started *something*," their eyes met, and she could see the sincerity in his gaze.

"I started nothing. I ran away. And when I came back, it wasn't to fight with them."

"I know. But by running, you gave him time to get it off the ground. You avoided capture longer than anyone that we know of. It's given this time to thrive. And coming back, telling them to stop, you made them refocus. Gave them a reality check and help when they needed it. Gave Derek grounding and gave inspiration for the others."

"I haven't—"

"You don't want to see it, but you have. You're not in that station, looking at the damage you've caused to our credibility. Looking out at the streets, seeing people look at you more warily. Listening at the bar, hearing that toast less often, hearing more whispers, hearing just... more." The corners of his lips twitched. "Did you ever find his grandfather?"

"We did," she returned her gaze to the water.

"How was it?" he asked, cautiously. She remembered his trepidation of knowing the history.

"We got the truth. I don't know how you would react, whether you'd want to fight more or not, it wasn't anything that would really help the cause, but I know it was the truth."

"How do you know?" he asked. She shrugged.

"Why did you warn me when they were raiding my apartment?" she asked him. He stared at her, momentarily stunned. She hadn't ever asked this. "Sometimes, you just trust people. Even if you don't want to trust anyone. You know what they're saying is the truth."

"I knew you didn't deserve to go to prison for that," he said, quietly.

"You chose your side when you first met me, whether you want to admit it or not."

"I suppose so."

They didn't speak for a long while. They drank their coffee, and watched the sun try to shine through the clouds. Eventually, she said,

"Well, I just wanted to warn you, and I guess, to say goodbye. I know it'll be too dangerous to try to get to you after this, if...well. Yeah." She let the sentence drop with a shrug.

He stood and brushed the dirt off his jeans. "Yeah. Thank you. I'm... I'm glad you did." His eyes looked down into hers, green into false brown. They let the moment linger, before she turned around, and finally walked out of the park.

"Erin." He caught up with her after the meeting as they began walking out of the building.

"John," she said politely. The meeting had been tense enough, as they discussed the starting positions, safe places to hide when the protest was broken up, and reiteration of the messages they wanted to communicate. It had been drilled out many times already, but everyone was nervous.

"Please, can we talk?"

"Yeah," she eased up on her tone.

"This…is this really what we need to be doing before tomorrow?" he asked, running a hand along the back of his neck.

"No, I didn't think so."

"Don't be like that,"

"Really?" She glared at him. "You told me to whore myself out for a pardon."

"Yeah, I did,"

"And you want me to forget about that?"

"No, I just," he sighed, "I just—" He tried to say the words, and she realized she didn't need to hear it.

"I know." She spoke. His eyes were over bright. She opened her arms and he pulled her into a hug, burying his face into her shoulder.

"I didn't mean to."

"I know."

"It was just…"

"I know."

"There was so much."

"I know." She ran her hand along his back.

"I miss her. I miss her so much. And Dad. I just, I couldn't, and I thought, well, I don't know what I thought. I'm so, so sorry."

"I know you are." She ran her fingers through his hair, gently shushing him as he cried into her shirt. She guided him to a side street where they weren't in the way of passersby.

"Have you, have you been okay? Are you doing okay? That sounds so lame, but," he wiped at his eyes, trying to bring her back into focus.

"Are you kidding?" She couldn't even grin at him. "We're about to do this thing and you—"

"How many times can I say I'm sorry?" he asked.

"Mm, a few more, I think," she laughed as he squeezed her into another hug, holding her so tightly it felt like her ribs might crack.

"It's your life, you live it how you want."

"Thank you for finally saying that," she said. "I'm here for you too, whatever you want to do. To deal with whatever you need to deal with, however you need to do it."

"I know you are." He slung an arm around her shoulder, and they continued walking towards Derek's apartment.

————

He was surprised to see them in such high spirits as they entered together.

"Do I want to know?" Derek asked.

"Probably not," Melody said, shaking her head, traces of laughter still on her face.

"Look, Derek, I'm sorry about this morning," Leo said, his head slightly bowed. "I know tomorrow's, well, we don't know what's happening tomorrow. So, for everything. I just want to say thank you." He offered his hand. Derek looked at it for a second, then took it.

"Don't worry about it. We've all got our shit to deal with," he said. Leo nodded, giving him a smile.

"You guys are going to make me tear up," Melody said from the back, waving a hand melodramatically in front of her face.

"Call me when that happens, will you? I want to be here to see the apocalypse." Leo laughed.

They shared laughter that night, and well into the next morning. Drank Leo's vodka, the rest of Derek's whiskey, and tried not to think of what was coming. Derek had almost forgotten what it was like to have them both in the house. But now, it felt like a new normal. A normal he knew wouldn't last, but a normal all the same. And, as he and Melody finally said goodnight to Leo, both going into his bedroom, as he buried himself into the warmth of her, letting all fear of the morning be forgotten for a few, beautiful moments, he found himself hoping that he would not be the sole survivor when this was finally over.

March 1, 2093

His fingers were twitching beside him, waiting for Jackie, who had the spare bullhorn. He'd forgotten his. Jackie had prepared for him to forget it. He'd promised he wouldn't, but of course he had. He didn't know where the others were. They were along Constitution Avenue now, a mass covered in hats and face masks or scarves, screaming into the sky. Signs painted with FREE MELODY, or, WE WILL NOT BE SILENCED, or variations thereof.

He felt someone press against him, and something metal touched his hand.

"We're with you," Jackie's voice was thick with anticipation, with emotion, and he saw her dart back in the crowd towards Morgan, Morgan's red hair visible under the navy beanie she'd tried to tuck it under.

He fought his way through the crowd, up the steps. There were police surrounding the crowd, but no one seemed to know what to do. When was the last time there had been a rally at all, let alone with this many people? There wasn't a count, but he was sure it was in the thousands. More than he'd prepared for.

He stepped up the stairs, he wasn't sure if people knew

who he was, but they let him through without much struggle. He found the spot where three in the group were waiting for him with a wooden box. He nodded, and they placed it down for him.

He took a deep breath, wiped the sweat off his palms, and took the step up.

Alexander got the call from the police commissioner as he was on his way into the office. It was a mass, a giant mass of people, beginning 15 minutes before the end of curfew, when the officers were heading in at the end of the shift. Before they'd gotten their shit together, gotten a hold of enough backup to tackle the group of a hundred or so, it had expanded, exponentially. It had started, they were guessing, as far out as Deanwood and Fort Totten, and had moved through the city to end here, in front of the Senate buildings on Constitution Avenue. He couldn't see where the crowd ended. The police had them well surrounded now, but they had never dealt with something of this scale.

He didn't understand it—how he was now in charge of controlling this riot—but he was. He assumed it was because it was the same people he'd been put in charge of rounding up. Because it would be one more fuck up the higher ups could pin on him, another nail in his coffin, not theirs. He was on the phone with Homeland now, who were trying their hardest not to sound as confused, afraid, and pissed off as he was.

"...We're on the other end with Boston and Philadelphia PD that they've got massive turnouts as well. It sounds like there was an attempt in Chicago, but that's been suppressed, we think. Not sure about New York, can't get a damn answer out there. Might be something in Annapolis too. Maybe Detroit." The officer, Taylor, Covington thought his name was, was doing nothing to reassure him that the situation was under control.

"How do you not know?" Covington couldn't stop himself from asking.

"Because President Jamison issued the order that there was to be no media coverage of this, and precincts are scrambling to figure out what to do as is. They're not sure which phone calls to take. Sometimes we get through, sometimes we don't. If they're trying to recruit forces from nearby precincts, that's their priority. If they're trying to go rogue and take out every protestor, well, I can't say I blame them."

"But you're fucking Homeland. If you call, they answer. Besides, surely you have some sort of, I don't know, satellite imagery of what's happening," Covington wanted to scream into the phone.

"We're working on it," Taylor snapped back at him. "Right now, your focus isn't on those other cities, it's on D.C. It's on those people in front of you, threatening the safety of those you swore to protect."

Covington swallowed the dozen or so curses he wanted to hurl at Taylor before saying, "What does Homeland think the strategy should be?"

"Since the movement originated in D.C., we think there will be some sort of indication as to who the leader of the movement is. Wait until that sign, then take him out. Send the rest scurrying for cover. Bring it down, bring them in dead or alive, we don't give a shit. Just get it contained."

Covington saw movement towards the front of the crowd, a young man with a mop of black hair heading up the steps of the most prominent building, the one renamed after General Foster.

"Right. I see him."

"What?"

"Taylor, I need to call you back."

"Detective Covington! Don't you—" But Covington ended the call and opened up the camera on his phone. If this wasn't being reported, he wanted a recording of it. He kept it trained on the Senate building steps, where the man, God, he had to be Logan's age, was stepping up onto a wooden box. Covington passed the phone to the nearest officer he could find. Seeing the bullhorn in his hand, he felt his stomach soar in self-satisfaction.

"He's going to speak," he said to the officer. "I want every word he says, do you understand? Everything that happens. I want it on there. Got me?" The officer nodded, taking the phone.

"I stand before you," the man began, "and I am honored, beyond honored, to be here, able to speak today. Because I know many of you are afraid. I know many of you have lost those you loved because they dared to speak. Or they knew someone who dared to speak. I knew one such person. Who dared to know Melody Karsh. Who dared to care for Melody Karsh. Who died because he sent her flowers."

"What the fuck?" Covington couldn't help but say out loud. Who the hell would know that? Parker knew that. Logan knew that. The people who had picked up that Sean kid had known that. How the fuck had this guy known that? He stepped around the perimeter of the crowd, coming closer to the steps.

"I am not alone in my pain. I am not the only one who has suffered at the hands of a tyrant. At the hands of a police state. I am one of many. We are all hurting. We all demand more. We all demand answers. We all demand the right to speak, to be free!" At his words, an overwhelming roar sounded from the crowd, so loud several officers covered their ears. There was something familiar

222

about this voice though, that Alexander couldn't put his finger on.

"We demand the freedom of those who are tortured, who are imprisoned. We demand our freedom. We demand freedom for Melody, a girl who has done nothing other than feel what we all feel. Who said what we all wanted to say. I ask you all, to say to these men with me, FREE MELODY, FREE ALL!"

"FREE MELODY, FREE ALL!" The chant rang through the crowd so loud it was deafening, and Covington had had enough. He knew who to target, and it was time to act. The crowd was beginning to rush at the officers, who were still unwilling to move against such a large number of people, but he was not so cowardly.

He pointed his gun and shot the man who had tried to start a revolution.

From the case file of Melody Karsh: July 2092-April 2093
June 2091

Dear Mom,

Leo and Liz—they want to know what it was like. I came back and went straight to their place. Lined up appointments to view apartments near the Hill. Liz looked at me, and just said, you're home now, it's okay. And I nodded. And smiled.

But now it's been long enough that they're worried. Leo is always trying to hug me, remind me he's there. Liz keeps telling me I need to come over for dinner. I want to talk to them, but what do I say?

They tell you, "This is what you were born to do." Or, "You are becoming who you were born to be." And this is repeated every day, multiple times a day. Until you say it back every time. This is who I was born to be.

They tell you that you are so fortunate, that you should thank your lucky stars that your family, that past generations, made the choice to join the Party. That there is no higher honor than supporting the reign of Our Dear Jamison. That we are born into our duty, and we are now working to fulfill it. And our reward for it is to live lives better than the rest.

225

They give you a gun and teach you how to shoot it. The dark cardboard cutouts used as targets look like people you knew in high school. They're your enemies now. You were made for this, they were not.

You aren't a soldier. There is no saluting, no jumping to attention. Instead, you sit in a classroom for eight hours a day, learning how to properly perform the role you were born to fill. Until you answer back all the questions correctly without blinking.

There is no emotion for you. Not anymore. It is a luxury for those beneath you, one of the few they have that you do not. You are carved from stone. You do not react when they show you interrogation techniques. When they teach you what happens to those foolish enough to go against the Party. Against Our Dear Jamison. You do not cry when you watch a prisoner die.

Every moment is watched, every movement, every feeling, every twitch of your fingers.

There is no graduation ceremony at Quantico. There is only your teacher pulling you aside to tell you you've received your assignment.

And on the way home, you're finally alone. Away from the cameras, away from prying eyes. And still, you do not scream. You do not change your face. You do not act any differently when you are given this moment, this privacy. Because if you do, if you break the second you think no one is watching, if you shed a single tear, they will take you back. And you will watch blood pouring, skin on fire, bones broken, and shots fired, until you no longer react. This is your final test.

This is what they made you.

This is who you were meant to be.

And that's not a story anyone wants to hear.

Melody

VI

It was panic. But Covington was calm as he radioed the officers on the other side of the perimeter. He rushed through the crowd, the officers around him, emboldened by him, shooting at anyone within reach, who began to scatter instantaneously. He was fighting to get to the steps. He had to get there before the man's cult–like followers got there first.

He pushed and punched and shoved his way violently through the crowd, finally arriving at his destination, where officers were trying to stop the group attempting to help the wounded leader escape into the crowd. In the mass of people, it was harder to pinpoint the right targets, but Covington was situated in a better spot, and managed to shoot one in the stomach. He went down, blood pouring from the wound.

Something plowed into his side, so hard and so fast he could not react in time. It knocked the wind out of him, and he fell to the ground.

"MORGAN, NO!"

"HE CAN'T GET—"

"NO!"

Something trampled on top of him, but he managed to

cover his face with his hands, blocking his head from damage. He struggled to stand, but his gun had been knocked out of his grasp. No matter, his target would be wounded enough. He wouldn't have been able to find Karsh in this mess anyway. If she was here, she could wait another day. He managed to get back to his feet, and saw, to his great surprise and joy, that the leader and one remaining helper were heading directly towards him. They tried to charge course, but too late. He hit the helper with a right hook, sending him to the ground, and the leader came crashing down.

It was a look of terror. He had seen it before, but never in a form so pure. Every particle of the man, (well, boy really, how old could he be?) seemed to quake in fear. He tried to inch away from Covington, but the detective moved around him and stepped onto his hand, ensuring the captive would not escape.

"Get him wrapped up, I want him to survive," he said to the officers who had finally arrived. He grabbed the radio at his waist. "We have the leader," he said to the rest of the forces, "Take down as many as you can. We don't need any other survivors, apart from Karsh. Karsh is to be brought in alive."

He released his foot from the man's hand, watching disdainfully as his men half carried, half dragged the man away. He started to follow, but out of the corner of his eye he saw something that made him pause. He turned around and saw someone staring at him with large brown eyes completely devoid of any expression. The bottom half of the face was covered in a black and white scarf, and the hair was covered with a black knit cap. By the slight curve of the body, he guessed it was a girl hiding under the layers of baggy clothing. Then his eyes traveled down, and he saw the gun in their hand.

Pointed directly at his heart.

His brain stopped.

But then there was a yell from behind the person, and she whipped around, going to the aid of one of her fellow terrorists. She was pointing the gun at someone else.

Alexander felt himself stumble back, as though her looking away had released him from a spell. He should have had more bravery. He should've been able to move, to react, do something. But that look, beyond cold, had shaken him in a way he couldn't quite describe.

He shook his head. He needed to get out of here, and away from whoever that was. And, he added a mental note, he needed to ask whoever they'd just taken in, just how many Party members they'd corrupted, or how many people Karsh had taught to use a gun.

———

Melody could feel fury pulsing through her veins. She'd had him. She'd *had* him, but when she'd heard Jackie scream, she'd had to turn away. Leo had fought to pull Morgan away from Covington, but she'd had him, a perfect shot on him, and missed it.

It was a panic. Some marchers were fighting against officers, trying to battle with whatever mediocre weapons they'd brought. Some officers were backing away, but most were charging forward, keeping the marchers scattering in different directions. There were dogs beginning to run towards them as well, catching on to the arms or legs of some marchers.

She needed to get the fuck out of here.

She had, the previous evening, before they'd gone back to Derek's, discussed their own plan. She'd told Leo she had more than a feeling everything would go haywire.

"He won't make it down into the crowd in time," Melody

had said. "He thinks he'll be protected by the members at the front, and they'll try, but there will be one or more half-cocked cops who won't wait for an instruction, or the instruction will be to take him out before he's through. Derek thinks he'll be able to get through it because of what happened at the Anthem Riot, where there was too much happening, and the cops there didn't know what to do. And they didn't, until one, or more, finally pulled a trigger. Once one does, they all will."

They'd staggered their exits in the morning, and they'd taken the few minutes after Derek had left to quickly pack Melody's things from his room, to wipe down the bathroom and Derek's room, to remove themselves from the apartment as much as they possibly could. Leo had cleaned the rest of the apartment after Melody and Derek had gone to bed the night before. In the best-case scenario, they had merely been cautious. They had no reason to think Derek would be observant enough to suspect, or be annoyed, that they had tried to protect each other. Protect themselves in having a backup plan and protect him by not leaving evidence he'd been harboring fugitives. Things he had not thought about or considered seriously. She'd tried to tell Derek, in the nights they had alone, that he needed a story if he was caught. To blame Parker, Charlie, Marco, have a name in his head of someone who was dead and could not dispute the story. He'd walked away from her every time.

If she and Leo were separated, they were to meet at Lincoln Park, which they assumed would not be being watched too closely, given the necessity for officers elsewhere. They'd find a motel for the night, just while the noise died down, and then they'd move to a member's house, or somewhere else.

She fought through the crowd, keeping one hand to the

scarf on her face, shoving the gun back into the waistband of her jeans. She saw an opening a bit up and to the side, and sprinted towards it, running down the street. She saw others similarly fleeing, the crowd thinning as she kept going. There was a massive stitch in her side, but she ignored it and kept moving.

She hoped with everything in her that Leo was okay, that he had gotten out safely as well. But, until she could get to a spot where she could check her phone safely, there wasn't anything she could do. Melody paused, taking in the street signs, trying to figure out where she was.

She was three blocks away from her old apartment. For a second, she had the overwhelming urge to turn that way, to stop and go and see the place. To have her bed back, the clothes, to see the kitchen, to sit on the couch that had taken her and Leo so long to get up the stairs when she'd moved in. She took a look around.

Why did it feel so foreign here? Why did it feel so wrong? She must have walked down this way over a thousand times but.... this wasn't hers anymore.

She had a brief picture in her head, of a different future. If her apartment had never been searched. If the letters hadn't been there.

Melody pictured growing older. She pictured Leo graduating college, and watching him as he went on to do whatever he would do. Going out in a suit every day. Getting an apartment near hers. She pictured her days in the park with Logan, going to get coffee, as he ranted about the friend, Derek, that she didn't really know. As he poked her about Sean, their breakup. And maybe the teasing led to something more, and maybe it didn't. She imagined them all going to Black Thorn for drinks after work. She imagined Liz and Gregory, and the discussions in their basement about the contents

231

of the library. She imagined time etching itself across her face, of crawling her way through Legislative, working on writing bills in a back office with other nameless faces. And she pictured herself wrinkled, and graying, coming home to that same apartment, just a few streets away.

She blinked. The picture was gone. She checked the street signs again and took off towards the park.

The park was fairly quiet. Melody had found a place near one of the new statues, flicking ash off her cigarette. The park had been one of the few places that had retained its pre-War name. Lincoln, a uniter of the country, a controller of agitators, of course had his place in history remembered. But most of the statues had been replaced by the presidents that had come in the last few decades. Jamison's latest had been unveiled in 2091, to celebrate his tenth year in power. It was where she was sitting now, stubbing out the end of the cigarette and beginning to roll a third, when he appeared.

The black jacket, scarf, and gray hat he'd been wearing were gone, an old blue pullover replacing them, and his backpack on his shoulder.

Melody didn't run over. She raised a hand in greeting, feeling her heartbeat begin to slow to a normal pace for the first time in hours. He walked over to her and pulled her into a hug that was not suited to the emotion either of them was feeling.

"Hey," Leo greeted her.

"Hi," she smiled.

They began to walk, calmly as possible, around the park.

"I could kill you right now," he said in barely more than a whisper.

"What are you talking about?" she asked, linking her arm through his and coming closer, the better to hear.

"What the hell were you thinking, waving that thing around?" he hissed.

"Did you see what Covington did to... Des?" They hadn't discussed speaking of Derek in code, but it wasn't hard to switch.

"No, I didn't. But I'm assuming he's the one who started it off." He cast a wary look around at the others in the park, still blissfully unaware of the event that had occurred so close by. They began to make their way to the exit. The sooner they found a place for the night, the better. Melody had a sneaking suspicion that Covington would put out a curfew notice as soon as he had Derek safely locked up. It would be the easiest way to catch stragglers from the rally.

"I think so too. He got rid of those around him, let him fall, and stepped on him, John. Stepped on him like he was nothing more than an annoying bug. If I could take him out, then, it would have been over. Des would have been safe. He couldn't hunt or hurt anyone else. We could—" she wasn't sure what she wanted the end of that sentence to be.

"Erin." He let out a sigh, "That's not how it works, and you know that. If you took him out, they would have been on you before you could have moved. And—" he stopped her interruption, "even if that wasn't the case, if he's gone, someone will take his place. Someone who might have more contacts, more resources. We've been in a good position with a friend by his side. We will never be that lucky again. The replacement may be smarter, more ruthless, more cunning. Taking one down is like trying to take down a hydra. You will never win by slicing off heads."

"So, what the fuck are we doing, then?" They started down

the street.

"I guess," he let his shoulders sag, "I guess we're trying to weaken it in other ways. But we're not killing anyone. You're not a murderer. You are not letting that be another nail in your coffin."

"That, back there? That was my coffin. It's been built and having nails shoved in it for months. Anything else is just extra roses thrown on top."

"You really would do it." It was a statement, not a question.

"Yeah, I think I would." She replied.

"I think that, more than anything, is what scares me," he said quietly. "That you could become what they say you are."

"That's not fair."

"That is fair." He glared at her, "It's completely fair. You, talking, you, trying to give others a voice, you, standing up in the face of bullets, that's on them saying you're a terrorist. The second you start firing bullets back? That's on you. Then you are no longer innocent. Don't be what they say you are. Don't become what they want you to be."

"Damn it," she ran a hand through her hair, almost determined to pull it out by the roots. "I'm keeping it, though." It didn't matter. He'd won, and he knew it.

They found a motel about ten minutes from the park. They came inside, posing as tourists from New York. The receptionist took their money, keeping his eyes on a tiny television screen.

"Have you seen this shit?" he asked, handing Leo the change.

"No," Leo said, keeping his voice calm. "What happened?"

"It's a good thing you came in when you did. Jamison is imposing a nation-wide curfew from 12:30, in the interest of national security. People in California won't have even fucking woken up yet. Or they'll be arrested for getting stuck in traffic on the highway." He paused, giving them a once over, "I'm just saying, it's unusual, I'm sure there's a damn good reason, Our Dear Jamison's got our best interests at heart."

Melody took in his shifty look, the way his eyes moved back and forth between the two of them and was uncomfortably reminded of a night so long ago, when she sat across from Derek in a bar.

"Of course," Leo took the key, and hesitated. "Stay safe," he said before they walked out the door, out towards their room on the second floor.

As soon as they'd closed and bolted the door, Melody felt Leo's arms around her, and she sagged into his embrace.

They didn't have to say anything. The fear and paranoia of the last few hours came crashing down on them.

Melody turned on the TV, and they lay together, holding each other, waiting for their suspicions about Derek to be confirmed, and hoping against hope that they wouldn't be.

He woke with a searing pain in his head. He let out an involuntary groan, and tried to straighten himself, but found he couldn't. Jerking his leg caused another moan, and he struggled to open his eyes. He blinked in the bright light and let his head fall to his chest. His arms and legs were bound to a silver metal chair. His leg had been haphazardly wrapped with gauze to stop the bleeding, but he doubted they'd done anything more for the gunshot wound than that.

He tried to make sense of what was happening.

He'd been at the rally, finished his speech. He'd been shot—he'd been *shot*, carried, and then—

Someone was clearing their throat. He looked around,

desperate to see who it was, but the light shining in his face was blinding him. There was the sound of metal scraping, and a sigh as someone sat down.

The light was adjusted downward, and Derek tried to blink, clear his vision of the spots that appeared afterwards.

Detective Alexander Covington was sitting in front of him, looking tired, but calm.

"Derek Lin." It was a statement, not a question. His eyes, a dark, murky brown, bore into Derek's with an intensity Derek had only ever seen in Melody's. But this was not Melody. This was not someone trying to help him, making him face his fears and doubts for his own good. This was someone with the power to destroy him.

Derek nodded, hesitantly.

"That was some stunt you pulled today, Derek." Covington pulled out a hand from the darkness and set a file on the table. He thumbed through it, never breaking eye contact. "Son to Daniel and Cassandra Lin, who have lived in Boston since 2078. We've contacted them. You were using their hard-earned money for your little…. activities, weren't you, Derek? We've gone through your cell phone records, and theirs. It doesn't look like you've talked to them in about a year. A call at Christmas, your birthday. That's it. Nothing from burner cells."

Derek shook his head slowly. But Covington had finally broken eye contact to take out a collection of photos.

"We had a bit of a problem about a month ago, didn't we, Derek?"

"Wha—" Derek tried to speak, but Covington held up a finger to his lips, and spread out the photographs on the table. He pushed a couple towards Derek. They were stills of the video they'd taken in the Prevention Unit. Derek swallowed but tried not to show any emotion.

He would not say anything about what had happened. Who had been there, who hadn't.

"That's you." Again, statement, not question. His eyes seemed to peer right through Derek. Sensing the impending lie. "You went by the codename Des, but that's you."

"That's not me," Derek stated boldly.

Covington raised one eyebrow, and leaned himself slightly onto the table, his face out of the light. He reached into his pocket and pulled out a packet of cigarettes. The manufactured kind. He placed it between his lips and held up a zippo lighter. The flame cast a light across his face, illuminating the harsh line of his jaw, the shadows under his cheekbones, the gray growing through his hair.

"It's not?" The tone was laced with restraint. His eyes came back into focus, came back into the light. They stared down at Derek, daring him to deny it again.

"No, I wasn't there."

Covington's eyes never left Derek's, as he made a wordless gesture to the blackness surrounding them.

A phone was placed in Covington's hand. Derek took a shaky breath, unsure of what was coming. A voice rang across the room, reverberating off the walls, so that Derek's own voice threatened to deafen him. Covington took a long, slow, drag of the cigarette.

"This is Des, with the Free Melody movement, and we're reporting to you from the Prevention Unit in Washington, D.C. This is not a place where the public is allowed. This is not a place the police, the government, or Our Dear Jamison want you to see. This is a place where prisoners are taken, interrogated, tortured, and executed. We're here to show you—"

"That's not you?" Covington leaned across the table, his

fingers curling against the metal, "Are you absolutely sure?" He was a time bomb of enmity, impatience, and contempt.

"—*What this place is, where they wish to take Melody Karsh for the crime of writing a letter to her mother, where they have taken thousands of people for similar actions, only to be called terrorists, to be told they have committed treason against the government and must die for their offenses.*"

The recording seemed to be getting louder, though Derek was sure Covington had not adjusted the volume. His focus had not left Derek for a moment.

"It's not me," Derek stuck out his chin defiantly. He would not go down without a fight.

Covington sighed, taking another drag of the cigarette.

"What a fucking waste."

He was across the table and an inch from Derek in a second, his hand a vise around Derek's wrist. He twisted the arm against the bindings and shoved the cigarette into the bare skin.

Derek let out a howl, trying to breathe against the pain but the smell of his skin and ash made his eyes water.

"That really wasn't you?" Covington threw the butt of the cigarette into the shadows, and with another gesture, so small, Derek thought he might have imagined it, his chair was pulled back from the table.

A fist collided with his stomach with such a force he thought he might vomit. A hand pulled his hair and forced his head up, and he was again met with Covington's face.

Covington's fingers wrapped around his chin, forcing Derek's eyes to meet his.

"So, you piece of shit, you really want to say that wasn't you?"

Derek tried to speak but couldn't against Covington's grip. Another fist landed against his rib, and then another hit the side

238

of his head.

"Derek?"

"It was me," he managed. They knew that anyway. He could confirm what they already knew, he justified in his mind.

The chair was dragged back to the table, and he was presented with the pictures once more. His head swimming, he tried to bring them into focus. They were taken from different angles, showed different views of the room of tools, opposite sides of his covered face.

"Marco received two files." Derek could feel Covington behind him, and he tried to turn his head to face his interrogator. Covington gripped the back of his skull and made Derek stare at the stills.

"Two people filmed your break in. We know at least one of those people was a girl. Who was with you, Derek?"

How did they know that? Derek's thoughts were frantic.

His head was slammed forward into the table, his cheek shoved into the cold metal.

"Come on, Derek, it's not that hard."

Derek couldn't speak. Faces flashed in front of his eyes. He couldn't say their names. He wouldn't say their names. They'd been shot for him, might've died for him.

His head was lifted up and slammed back into the table.

"Derek, I am not a patient man." Covington's voice had softened, but it sent shivers up Derek's spine. "You were the leader of this organization, yes? You know who was there."

Derek shook his head frantically.

Guards appeared on either side of him. A hand on his hair, holding up his head, and a punch to the jaw that sent him reeling.

The room swam. He tried to get his bearings, but they'd

dragged the chair back, and a sudden force smashed into his side. He wasn't sure whether he heard or felt the cracking of several ribs. He couldn't breathe. Couldn't inhale. The corners of his vision went black, before his body figured out how to function again.

"Who was there?" Covington's voice was a growl.

"I don't know!" Derek gasped, "I wasn't in charge of planning it."

"So, who was?" Covington's eyes were all he could see, "Who? Was it Melody Karsh? Was she the girl with your team?"

Derek stuttered.

"N–no. I haven't ever met her."

Covington's head tilted slightly.

Another punch hit Derek's jaw and snapped his head to the side. He spat out a mouthful of blood.

"Try again."

"I haven't met her," Derek said thickly, "I don't know where she is."

"Your movement is based on her, and you don't know where the fuck she is?"

"No." He knew it was unbelievable. He knew it.

A different picture was shoved into his face. The picture they'd created to hand out in the different cities, the one with a full shot of Melody's face, with her blonde wig, her blue eyes clear and pleading.

"How did you make this, then?" Covington asked, "If you never met her, didn't know where she was, how the hell did you make those?"

This he could easily fabricate.

"That wasn't made here. Those were distributed to a dozen different cities, a different background in each one. I don't know who made them."

This made Covington's jaw twitch. Another punch to the ribs. A door opened and shut.

"Which cities?"

"I... I don't..."

Covington grabbed a handful of Derek's hair, and shouted in his ear, "Which cities, Derek?"

The door opened, and in the strip of light that came from it, Derek could see a guard wheeling in a metal tray.

He didn't want to know what was on that tray.

"Philadelphia," he said. "Chicago, New York, Boston,"

"And?"

"Annapolis, Hartford, Frankfort, Colombia, Providence, Harrisburg, Charleston, Raleigh, Indianapolis, Nashville, Columbus, Trenton..." Derek babbled, the tray coming into view. There were knives on that tray, Knives that still shone brightly in the dim light of the cell.

Covington held up a hand.

"How fucking far did you get to?"

"I— I'm not sure. Pretty far West. I don't know."

"You were leading this thing you piece of shit. *How far did you spread?*"

"I don't know!" Derek yelled. He didn't know. It was honest. Truly honest. He had no idea.

"You don't know," Covington finally looked away, and drew his attention to the tray. He examined each tool in turn.

Brass knuckles.

3 knives of varying sizes.

A hammer.

"I'll tell you what I know, Derek," Covington said carefully,

241

considering the knives, "I know that you are either incompetent, held up by nothing more than luck and the sheer will of those around you, or you honestly believe that you can lie to me. That you can outlast whatever I choose to make you endure. And personally, I'm hoping it's the latter, because you are nothing more than a worthless piece of shit that can't even call his fucking parents."

The words hit Derek like ice water. They elevated his fear, just as much as the vision of Covington's intense examination of the knife blade in his hand. His heart was pounding so violently against his chest he was sure Covington could hear. He couldn't help the images forming in his head of what would happen if Covington fully let loose the barely restrained malice in his voice.

He held up the middle-sized knife and passed the brass knuckles to one of the guards.

"Broken zygomatic bone, or do I get to have fun with this?"

Zygo—

"Or we choose for you."

"That's not a choice!" Derek screamed.

The fist connected with his left cheek and eye, and all he could see was a white light. It was fire in his head.

He heard a mumble, like flies buzzing, before he felt something hit his right side, and heard something crack. He couldn't breathe to scream.

"How far did you spread?"

"I don't know." He gasped for air. "I swear, I swear, I don't know, I didn't pay attention, I wasn't ever in charge of that, I helped get people in the beginning, I never had any part in getting people from other cities, I swear, I swear—"

A hand covered his mouth and he jerked at the touch but fell silent. He managed to open his one good eye.

242

"So, if you weren't in charge of recruitment, what were you in charge of?" Covington had come back into his vision. He was a blurred outline, but he was there.

"I... I helped with the...the raid of the Prevention Unit. And I helped plan the riot today."

"Obviously," Covington snorted, "so, let's try again. Who was at the Prevention Unit? Who else planned those events?"

"I don't know," Derek tried again, "I was just told where to go and what to do."

Covington didn't bother to threaten him or clarify this time.

Hands appeared on Derek's shoulders, holding him in place. The knife directly in his field of vision.

Covington's eyes locked onto Derek's. "I told you, I have no time to spare."

Derek opened his mouth to speak, but instead shrieked in pain as the knife crossed his chest; once, twice, three times.

Blood trickled onto his lap, onto the gauze covering the shot leg, onto the floor.

"Who?"

Derek shook his head, tears falling from his eyes.

"Different question, then," Covington sighed, setting the knife back on the tray. "Who the hell told you how Sean Anker was caught? Who told you about the flowers?"

A scene flashed in Derek's mind. A moment from months ago, when he'd been someplace warm, and safe, having an argument with a friend. A friend who swore they wouldn't go down for whatever Derek wanted to do.

Covington pulled out the hammer, wheeling the tray closer to Derek. The hands moved from his shoulder to his right arm.

"We will be here as long as it takes, Derek," and Derek

knew he was not bluffing. "Who told you about Sean? Because whoever it was, must have been the one who gave you Melody's letter in the first place, right?"

Derek nodded, very slowly.

"Who was it?"

"Please," Derek didn't know what to do, didn't want to speak, but needed it to stop.

His screams and pleas nearly deafened them all as the hammer came down on his fingers. Each one, broken.

Covington didn't ask again, before he moved to Derek's palm.

Derek could taste blood in his throat.

"One more chance, Derek. It'll only get worse from here." Out of his one working eye, he could see Covington, with the bloody knife, one guard with the hammer, the other with the brass knuckles.

He muttered the name.

Covington grabbed his chin, nearly pulling him from the chair. Ignoring Derek's feeble cries, he whispered, "What did you say?"

"Logan," Derek managed, "It was all Logan."

"Logan Madden," Covington was a million miles away, though Derek couldn't tell. He was talking, and now he couldn't stop.

"It was all his idea. He was upset Sean was dead. He came to me, wanted someone to pay attention to Sean, but no one would. Melody was a better image. He gave us the letter to distribute, gave us the codes for the Prevention Unit. It was all his idea; everything was his idea. Please, you have to believe me, he was the one—"

"Shut him up," Covington said, already halfway towards the door.

The coroner's office had called him before he'd made it back to the police station. He'd been frantically calling Logan, desperate to find him before someone else did.

Though of course, the only people who had heard the name were still in the cell with Derek. And Derek, blubbering, crying, shitbag that he was, could easily have been lying. He usually didn't go that far, in initial interrogations, but his restraint, perception of timing, hadn't been their best.

It was only now, in retrospect, he could remember seeing the face. Logan had been friends, or at least friendly, with that asshole. Though Covington tried to reassure himself, Logan had always seemed annoyed in his presence.

That's all it was, right? He would get his hands on Logan, make him confirm it. Make him get his hands dirty in his first interrogation, prove his loyalty, and that would be the end of it. No one would possibly consider that Covington had had the true leader under his nose for nearly six months and been none the wiser.

But then, he'd gotten the call, and rushed to the morgue to identify a body.

Logan looked peaceful in death. The gash in his head has been cleaned. He could have been sleeping. His skin was tinged a slight blue. Covington was told this was from the water, but he wasn't really listening.

He'd jumped into the Potomac. Must have hit his head against something. Rocks, probably, or other debris. A few had seen him jump and immediately called for help. He had no ID. He had abandoned his badge, or it had been lost in the jump.

"Who else knows about this?" Covington asked the coroner.

245

"Just me, my assistant, and the two paramedics that brought him here."

"He's a John Doe." Covington said simply.

"But—"

"John. Doe. Until you are otherwise informed."

She nodded, and he was content she understood.

From the case file of Melody Karsh: July 2092-April 2093
March 2092

Dear Mom,

I met someone at Black Thorn yesterday. His name's Sean. He was sitting at the other end of the bar, and he looked over at me, and just had the cutest little smile. His skin was so smooth, and he had a tattoo, and in the darkness of the bar he let me lean in really close, and run my fingers along the letters, the black ink so closely matched his skin.

He told me it was for his mother and sister, that they'd 'died before their time'. The safe way to say what he wanted to. I could tell he wanted to tell me it all, but we're supposed to disown those that are arrested. Say they deserved their punishment. Alienate anyone who acts against the government or is thought to. So, it's not their names, it's just letters that could stand for anything.

And for a moment, I thought of what it would be like to really be Sam. To really be the person I was telling him I was. Then I thought of what it would be like if I just told him the truth.

It's that snap back to reality. That for those moments, you are someone else. Someone who won't trigger their memories. Someone who they won't resent based on your mere existence, even if you weren't the one responsible. But it is still your fault. Your existence allows for the continuation of what is happening. It doesn't matter that you were ordered to do whatever you did. You still did it. Their feelings towards you, towards anyone with that badge, is justified.

He thinks I'm an accountant. He works at a bank. He made a joke that any children we had would never have a problem doing their taxes.

He took me home, and he held me. He didn't want me to go in the morning.

Is it bad I want to see him again? To embrace this reality just for a little while. I can be Sam, to him. For now. Someone uncomplicated, just trying to get by.

Or is it better to stop this now? Better to stop it before it gets started.

But I liked being held, even if I don't care that it's him doing it.

There was a guy, at Quantico, we would sneak into each other's rooms at night. It was a common thing. There were maybe two hundred when I entered? Maybe seventy-five for Legislative? You more or less knew everyone. This guy—we never really talked. He looked at me across our classroom one day, and that was it. As it came closer to us getting our assignments, he told me he couldn't wait to introduce me to his parents. And I laughed. I didn't mean to—and he looked so hurt. But I told him, I'm not meeting your parents. And he just scoffed and walked away. I wanted to be sorry. But at the same time, we were not together. We were holding onto each other because it was the only thing we could do. And pretending otherwise was idiotic.

Maybe I'll just let myself give into this a bit. Just a little bit. See Sean one more time. And maybe I won't tell Leo.

Love,
Melody

248

March 2093: VII

They were nearly out of money.

Two weeks after Derek's arrest, they were desperately low on funds.

The motel manager was willing to let them stay for an additional week, understanding that with the quarantine still in effect, he was unlikely to get much business, and they were unable to go home. But they could not trust his kindness to hold out, nor did that solve the problem of finding food.

"We need to find Jackie," Melody said finally.

"I told you, we're not putting her and Morgan in danger," Leo's eyes flashed. It was the one point on which he had not budged—that they would not take shelter with another member.

"I'm not saying stay with them, I'm suggesting we meet up with them. They might be able to get us some food, update us on what's happening." Melody ran a hand through her hair. Her roots were beginning to show, another problem to add to their list.

"Fine. But I think it's too dangerous for us to venture out together. We'll call, and you can meet up with Jackie somewhere, and I'll meet Morgan somewhere else. Or you stay here." He told her.

She raised an eyebrow at him, and he held up his hands

in surrender.

"Nice try." She pulled out her phone, and began dialing the number, trying to ignore the creeping nerves that made her fingers twitch over the buttons.

———————

Melody stood beneath the bridge, a fire crackling in an empty trash can, figures huddled around its warmth. She blew on her fingers to warm them up, trying not to look too out of place, but knowing she was failing miserably. The sunset cast shadows, hiding the faces of everyone in sight. In the distance, she could see a figure bending down, talking to a couple huddled together on the ground. The figure handed over two cellophane-wrapped packages and stood back up.

Melody began to walk towards Jackie, trying to keep a distance so as not to disturb what Jackie was doing. She leaned against the cement of the underpass, waiting. They'd started doing this about a month ago, in the lead up to the rally. The money from selling to Party members now being used to pass out peanut butter sandwiches to those who lived here, or places like it. They claimed to ask for nothing in return. Only to remember who made sure they were fed.

"Hi," Melody said quietly, as Jackie approached her. The women looked over each other for a moment, checking for signs of residual injury, outward harm. Jackie looked more or less the same—more tired, her hair a bit frizzier, but with an air of excitement about her. She pulled Melody into a hug.

"I'm so glad you're okay," she said.

"Me too," Melody whispered back. They broke apart, and walked a little further along, away from any eavesdroppers.

"You've been holding up okay?" Melody asked.

"Oh, yes. Better than that, though," Jackie beamed at her. "We've been planning another rally."

"What?" Melody wasn't sure if she'd expected the next move to happen sooner, or have taken longer. She supposed she was used to Derek's combination of rashness and ineffectiveness.

"Of course, what did you think was going to happen, that we'd do the one, say okay, Derek's gone so we're done, buh-bye?" Jackie looked at her skeptically.

"No, I didn't." Melody shook her head, a shadow of a smile crossing her face.

"It's in three days. I want you there," Jackie wouldn't plead, but Melody knew what the request meant to her.

"We'll be there," she said. "Or, at least, I will be. I'm sure John will come, but I can't make promises for him."

"I'm sure Morgan will take care of that. She's got a plan in mind," Jackie smiled. She reached into her bag, and pulled out a small roll of bills, and a box of brown hair dye. Melody could feel something, some emotion in her chest, that she hadn't in quite some time.

"I thought you might need it. Morgan got the dirtiest look when she went to pay for it, the guy at the counter was making all these comments about her ruining her gorgeous hair," Jackie snorted. "Anyway, sorry it's not more, but hopefully that'll get you some food to last a little while."

Melody swallowed.

"Thank you," she clutched the box close to her chest.

"Don't mention it," Jackie pulled her in for another hug. "We'll see you soon."

"Yes, yes you will," Melody assured her, shoving the box and money in her backpack. She gave Jackie a final smile before walking back out the way she came.

They appeared as a mass of black against the gray sky.

Quietly, but quickly, they crept away in the early morning light.

Some, mostly those traveling alone or in pairs, were picked away by officers patrolling for curfew breakers before reaching the White House gates.

Melody, Leo, the motel manager, and several other guests left together. He seemed mildly surprised to see them as they were leaving their room, but said nothing as they proceeded as a group towards the rally. As they walked, others began to join them, coming out of houses, from around street corners. Other groups merging into one.

And now, they were here, standing as a silent mass in front of the gates.

The wind blew Melody's hair, back to completely brown and mostly hidden under her hat, her face behind her scarf. Leo stood beside her, his disguise also in place.

By 8AM, the police had started to arrive. It was a much quicker response time than the first rally, Melody had to nervously admit. They seemed much better prepared. She wondered if they'd managed to arrest anyone else who might have known the date Jackie had in mind for this. She thought, for perhaps the millionth time, of all the things Derek might have said after his arrest.

At 9:07, a police officer stood on a platform of some sort, Melody couldn't see. He held a megaphone to his mouth, and began to call into it:

"This is an unauthorized gathering and demonstration. Return to your homes, and you will not be harmed."

252

The crowd said nothing. This was part of Jackie and Morgan's plan. It was obvious what they were there for, but there would be no shouting, no screaming, no chanting, not even posters this time. They would intimidate with silence alone.

The police officer tried again.

"Return to your homes, and you will not be harmed."

The tension felt like electricity crackling between Melody's fingers. She turned to Leo, who took her hand, and squeezed it.

The officer turned to someone nearby, muttered something, and then held up the megaphone again.

"This is your final warning."

Melody didn't bother to look if some of the crowd had left. She was sure some would, but so long as the sea of black surrounded them, that was what mattered.

Something was thrown into the crowd, and a cloud of gas instantly made those in the immediate vicinity scatter.

Another canister, and the crowd broke apart even more, only to be met by a barricade of police.

Leo pulled Melody's hand and dived for a hole in the mass of people.

"Run!" He screamed to her over the panic of the crowd, and they clamped onto each other as they ducked and dived between bodies as the police began to close ranks, intent on letting no one out.

A large group was pushing at a section of officers, tackling them to the ground, refusing to be caged in. Three officers went down, creating a hole large enough for the protesters to push through, and they ran, en masse, out and away from the gate, away from the scene, the gas, and the gunshots.

Leo stumbled, and Melody heaved him up and down the

street, in a direction she wasn't sure of.

"Freeze!" A voice called behind that Melody was certainly not about to obey. She ducked around the next corner, sprinted down the street, then took a right. The voice seemed to be growing distant, and they took a left into a side street.

"Fuck." Leo let go of her hand and clutched his thighs, panting, looking at the brick wall of the dead end in front of them.

"Come on," Melody staggered a bit as she reached for him again, but froze, hearing the unmistakable sound of footsteps crunching on the broken pavement behind them.

"Hands up!" The voice was clearly just as out of breath as they were, but it rang with power, and anger.

Melody didn't react. Her brain seemed stuck three seconds previously, it was having trouble catching up.

"I said hands up!" The man screamed, and she made her body cooperate, turning around to face him, hands up by her head.

Alexander Covington stood in front of her, half his hair gray, eyes bloodshot, the air of a crazed man hanging over him. His eyes met hers, and recognition seemed to flash through him.

"You," his mouth twitched in what might've been a smile. "You were the one that tried to kill me last time, aren't you? Or, at least, you wanted to."

Melody said nothing. She didn't even blink. She could process nothing beyond the gun pointed at her chest.

Something crashed into her ribs as a sound exploded through her eardrums, and she was knocked backward into the ground, a body on top of her, something wet and sticky and thick soaking her, the scent of iron heavy upon the air.

She looked down, and her mouth opened in a silent scream as she saw Leo on top of her. She tried to crawl out from under him, but he was dead weight. With an almighty groan, she rolled him off of her, and saw the blood falling, bright and terrifying, from a hole in his side. She looked up, to see Covington had let his gun fall, an expression of surprise and horror on his face.

Without thinking, she pulled the gun from her jeans and pointed it at Covington. She pulled her scarf from her face and shoved it against Leo's side, trying to staunch the blood flow. He gasped and opened his eyes. He let out another moan but allowed her to pull his arm around her shoulder and heave him to his feet. She placed his free hand on the scarf, ensuring he was keeping pressure on the wound. With all his weight on her shoulders, she kept the gun pointed at Covington.

Their eyes met again, her finger on the trigger.

Leo moaned again, sinking further down her body. She cast a glance between Leo, and the detective, before beginning to half carry, half drag Leo back down the alley past Covington, the gun trained on Covington's forehead all the while, before they exited the alley, and he disappeared from view.

Three buildings up was an abandoned construction site, a boarded-up spot used by the homeless as a makeshift shelter. She kept the gun out, should Covington appear, as she shoved her way inside. She searched for a place for Leo to rest, away from windows and doors.

"I'm going to set you down, okay? It's going to be okay," she assured Leo, reaching a pillar amongst the debris of wood, sawdust, and nails, and propping him against it. He slid down it with her help, unable to stay upright. His skin was deathly pale and shone with a layer of sweat.

She tore off her jacket and took the now scarlet mess of a

scarf out from his grip, trading it out with the jacket.

She moved his head to her lap, trying to keep it slightly elevated.

"I'm sorry," she whispered, "I'm so, so sorry."

His breathing was shallow, and ragged.

"I'd do it again," he managed.

"Do what?"

"Fight with you, come back with you, take a bullet for you, protect my little sister. You'd have done the same for me. You would've shot him for me, even though I told you not to," he tried to laugh, but began to cough.

"Shh," she kissed the top of his head. "I can call Jackie, I can try to get you help, I can—"

"No, Mel, no," he shook his head, "they can't do anything, and Covington'll find us soon. You need to get out of here."

"I'm not leaving you, you asshole," she pressed harder onto the jacket, as if somehow, she could make the blood go back inside. "You're going to be okay."

"Sure, Mel."

"You are."

He didn't say anything, but shakily reached one hand up and brushed his fingertips over her cheek.

Her tears overflowed, falling down her face, as she held him close to her, feeling his life slip away from him underneath her hands.

"Please don't leave me, Leo, please," she could barely speak, her voice quiet and breaking as she cried.

They were silent for a few moments, before he shakily asked her,

"Hey, when you were a kid, and you wrote those letters to

your mom, when you wanted to run away to live with her, what did you want to do when you saw her?"

"Wh—what?"

"Tell me, please?" His voice was so weak.

"Uh, um," Melody gulped, brushing tears away. "I always thought she'd be hiding in some small town somewhere. Far away from everything. And when I got there, she'd take me in to a city— London, or Glasgow, or Newcastle—or we'd just get on a train and go. It wouldn't matter. We'd ride around and wherever we'd end up, that's where we'd end up. We'd explore, and then do it all over again. It would be freedom; irresponsible, beautiful, freedom."

"I'm going to tell her that, Mel," Leo smiled. "Her and me, and Derek—if she's your mom, she'll probably have some things to say to him—and everyone else, we'll all be on that train together."

"*No*, Leo, please," she sobbed, "please, please don't—"

"It's okay," he gasped, blood trickling from the corner of his mouth. "You'll stay strong for me, until you see me again."

She nodded. "You know I will," she kissed his forehead again, and his eyes closed. She hugged him close, shaking uncontrollably, tears blinding her.

He was gone, and she was alone.

Her head fell back, and her mouth opened in a scream. A howl of uncontained agony. A cry that pierced through the building, through to the street outside.

It was a scream that continued until Covington, along with five other officers, found the building, and the girl, and the body inside. Until he managed to pry the shaking girl from the dead boy, until he had managed to drag her away from the sight.

———————

The bag covered her head, the chains bound her to the

257

chair, but she had not tried to move or speak.

There was no way to measure time here. But she knew this was a tactic. To disorient her. She had no idea what day it was. If it was morning or night. Hell, when she'd last eaten, or drank, or slept. When she'd last washed her hair. She'd been hosed down with cold water when they'd brought her in. When was that? Not that it mattered, really.

The bag was removed, but the room was still pitch black.

A door opened, to reveal a thin strip of light. The shadow of a man entered and closed it behind him.

There really wasn't a need for the theatrics. She knew what was coming. After all, she'd been here before. Seen it for herself what felt like a lifetime ago.

She heard the man sit down across from her, and a light flicked on, illuminating a table in front of her. She sat up as straight as the chains would allow and looked into the eyes of Alexander Covington.

He looked as though he'd gotten a good night's sleep since their last encounter.

"Melody Karsh," he said. "I must, begrudgingly, admit that I'm impressed. It took us a few hours to figure out who exactly we'd caught."

She said nothing, just stared back at him.

"That was a compliment, you could at least say thank you." He raised an eyebrow.

She raised an eyebrow right back, and inclined her head as if to say, *Sure, why not.*

"Fine then. So, you and I are going to have a little chat, Melody." Covington clasped his hands together in front of him on the table.

Both her eyebrows creeped further up her forehead. If he wanted to call it a chat, sure. They could call it a chat.

"Let's start with where you've been. You've been, elusive, to say the least. The hunt for you and your friends started in July of last year. That's nine months, longer than any manhunt we have on record in the past decade, if not longer. So, where did you go?"

Melody said nothing.

"How about I answer for you?" Covington smiled at her, a smile that did not meet his eyes. "You and your friend Leo got some new IDs, didn't you? They were on you both. John and Erin Thackeray. Now, we got a call about a car that matched the description of the Myers' car a couple months ago. At the time, we confirmed it belonged to a Nicolas Thackeray up in New York. So, as you can imagine, we're already combing through New York for all traces of any Thackerays."

Melody blinked.

"You don't actually expect them to still be using that name, do you?" she asked. "Much less still be in New York. They would have moved the second you called."

Covington's jaw twitched.

"You hadn't told them you were coming back here, did you?"

"No, we didn't."

"Why?"

She measured the question.

"It doesn't matter anymore," she said.

"Oh, but it does," Covington's voice was smooth, but she could see his fingers pressing more deeply into his hands.

"How do you figure? I came back, you eventually caught me. You have no way of knowing if you would have found me, had I stayed away," she said simply.

Covington twitched again, but he smirked.

"Smart one, aren't you? No, Karsh, we don't have that guarantee. But we also have reason to believe that you are a key reason why the Free Melody movement began to instigate more violent tactics."

"How do you figure that?"

"We got the tip about the car in January, not long after the public executions of Benjamin Jones, Lena Williams, and Frank Martinez. Then, we saw the photo distribution of your face from the Movement, followed by the break in at the Prevention Unit in February, and the protests in March. It would stand to reason that following the public executions you came back here to help the movement, that you had possibly been out recruiting in other cities but were forced back when such an event occurred. A picture of you was distributed across the country. Were you working with others, other terrorist groups within those cities?"

Melody had to restrain herself from laughing.

"I was not out recruiting."

"But you were a part of the movement?"

"You saw me at both protests. That much should be obvious."

"You were a leader in the movement!"

"Nope."

"They based it around you!"

"Sure, but I had no say in that. You were the one that went on TV and told everyone my name. What others did with that information is entirely up to them. I certainly did not ask anyone to die for me."

"Not even Leon? When he jumped in front of my bullet for you?"

She bit the inside of her cheek to keep from reacting.

"Not even him," she said quietly.

"So why you? Why did they pick you?" Covington asked, leaning back on his chair, "If you weren't the instigator, what was so special about you?"

"Absolutely fucking nothing," Melody shrugged. "Except one thing."

"And what was that?" Covington asked, curious against his will.

"It's like I said before. You gave them my name. Everyone, *everyone* out there today, has lost someone, or seen what it's like to lose someone. You gave them an unintentional rallying cry."

Covington was not as effective at hiding his emotion.

"You're blaming *me* for the work of terrorists that have effectively threatened national security and put this city at a standstill?" he spat.

"No, I'm not. I'm making you examine the wider picture."

Covington grunted and stood up. He picked up the file on the desk and stepped into shadow.

"So, tell me, Melody, during the break in of the Prevention Unit, who all was there? We know Derek was, and we know at least one girl was there. Was that you?"

She said nothing.

"Come on, you were being so chatty before," he stepped around the desk, coming closer to her. She still said nothing.

A silent gesture from Covington, and a guard came forward. The guard began to slide her chair back away from the table.

"How many were there?" Covington asked. Melody still said nothing. Didn't change her neutral facial expression and didn't look away from the vague outline of where Covington would be.

"Who planned it, then?" Covington tried not to let his

irritation show. "These are simple questions, Melody. Was it Logan?"

She looked at him confused.

"Logan?"

"Was he not in charge of all of it? The whole organization?"

She could not help the burst of laughter this time. "Logan? He's a Party Kid, what the fuck?"

Covington and the guard shared a look. The guard pulled her shoulder back. Covington lowered himself so he was at eye level with her, and asked, very quietly,

"What, *exactly,* was Logan's involvement?"

"I don't know what Derek told you. I don't need to know. Derek was the guy in charge. It was Derek's idea. I am not at all surprised the coward tried to pin it all on Logan, I know they were friendly, but it was all Derek."

"So why would Logan kill himself?"

Melody peered into his eyes, trying to find the lie, and finding none. He stared back at her, trying to gauge her reaction.

"Honestly, I expected him to run, but I'm not surprised. Logan was someone who wanted to choose his own out. He couldn't handle the idea of prison. He would've known you'd tie him to Derek. He told me he would not die in a cell. He stayed true to that."

"But you did know Logan? You had contact with my partner?" Covington's jaw was set, but Melody was silent once more. "You're going to say everything he told you. Anything he said about this department, anything he told you about me or the people working with me."

"There isn't anything to tell," she said softly. She'd retreated back to calm, to a neutral, blank mask.

"Bullshit," Covington snapped, standing up, and pushing

her chair back into the guard, whose fingers inched down along her collar bone, tracing the bare skin with the tips of his fingers.

"I am going to find out every single damn thing that was said in your meetings, between you and Logan, who the new leader is and what they're planning, and where Elizabeth and Gregory are. You are going to be begging me to hear you confess by the time we're through with you."

She didn't even flinch.

So, he left her to the darkness, and the guards inside.

———————

"I want to see my wife." It came out as more of a growl than he'd intended, but after a week of no sleep, he no longer cared.

She was here. She was in custody. The rest was not up to him. He wasn't in charge of the Prevention Unit. He had been in charge of getting her here. He'd done that. Before the deadline, even. He'd brought in Derek; he'd brought in Melody. He'd done his fucking job.

"Relax, Alexander," Richard looked over his pile of paperwork at him. "I've already submitted the paperwork for her release, but it's going to take a bit with the quarantine. With Karsh in custody and Lin and Myers dead, we're working on getting the quarantine lifted. Hopefully won't be more than another day or two."

Covington let out a sigh and ran a hand over his face.

"Thank you," he said, and walked back out of the office.

———————

He couldn't sleep anymore. The screams filled his nightmares, waking and dreaming. The ones from Derek hadn't been so bad. It had been so short, the guards had taken Covington's instruction to 'shut him up,' a bit too seriously, and, after that, there wasn't anything else to do but the execution. He was all but dead by the time Covington got back from the coroner.

But Karsh. Karsh was a different story. They needed her information, and there wasn't nearly as much of a ticking clock on it. They could draw out sessions, making them horrifically slow and drawn out, or change the tempo and try to break her as quickly as possible. Sometimes, Covington would be present for the duration, other times, he would come in at the end and ask if she had anything to say.

But she no longer spoke. She only screamed.

Jordan was to be taken to the police station so that Richard could finalize the paperwork on her release. Covington refused to go down to the Prevention Unit, needing his focus to be solely on his wife. He didn't need to know what they were doing, so long as they finally achieved some results.

Jordan was led into the station by two Homeland Security agents, eyes darting around, looking at all entrances, exits, windows, and doors. He hurried to her, but the agents pushed him back.

"In a moment, sir," one told him, and proceeded to march to Richard's office. He followed behind, trying to make eye contact with Jordan, but she seemed not to see him.

Richard made him wait outside the office, and while the papers didn't take long, it felt like an eternity to him. When Richard finally opened the door and allowed Jordan to step out, he flung his arms around her without a thought.

She immediately tensed under him, and he stepped back, looking at her.

Her skin had almost a grayish tinge to it. Her long, luxurious hair now lay lank, lifeless, and frayed. Her clothes hung loosely on her frame, her collarbones and elbows jutting out against her skin. He didn't see any visible scars, but she was actively avoiding his touch. She couldn't make eye contact with him, and a wave of revulsion overwhelmed him. He felt disgusted with himself.

"Do you want to go home?" he asked, very quietly, so no one else in the office would hear. She nodded, and he led her through the maze of desks and back out the door.

He couldn't help but keep looking over at her as he drove them home, watching her like a mouse in a cage, looking frantically for a way out. He felt his stomach in his throat, and fought to suppress the nausea.

He parked the car and let her into the house. She looked around it like a stranger, pulling at the ends of her sweater.

"I..." he started, sighed, then started again, "I'm guessing you'd like to sleep? Or shower, or...just be alone, for a while?"

Jordan looked at him, curiously.

"Yeah, I would." It wasn't her voice anymore, and he swallowed back the lump in his throat.

He nodded, walked into the kitchen, and sat at the table, hearing her footsteps on the stairs. He set his face in his hands, as if trying to keep his head together.

This was not his wife. This was a broken shell that had been his wife. And he knew exactly why she was. And since Jordan was released, she would know Karsh was captured, and would know exactly what he was doing every day when he left for work.

He knew that he would never be able to touch her again, that he would be too revolted with himself to try. Even if he could, he knew that she could never forgive him, never love him, again.

April 2093

There had been two more protests, each worse than the last. Richard had assumed, wrongly, that if they announced Karsh's capture, that it would stop. But of course, it only made it worse. Covington remembered her words, and felt they, like her letters, like everything about her, would forever be etched into his brain.

You gave them my name. Everyone, everyone out there today, has lost someone, or seen what it's like to lose someone. You gave them an unintentional rallying cry.

It wasn't just D.C., of course. Information was still hushed, precincts unwilling to talk to each other, but from what he'd heard it was all up and down the East Coast. There had been a couple in the Midwest. He knew of at least a few across the West. One successful attempt in Northern California.

When he asked for the execution orders, there had been little hesitation.

"President Jamison has a request, though," Richard said, when he handed over the papers.

"What's that?"

"He wants the body moved to the morgue and kept on ice."

"Why?"

"You expect me to question the President's orders?" Richard raised an eyebrow.

"No, no sir." Covington quickly shook his head.

He had told the guards not to interrogate yesterday, or today. They had to know what that meant. She had to know what that meant.

He wanted it over. He wanted it behind him. He had no hope of moving on with his life with Jordan, but he wanted to be free of the thing in the cell.

He took a deep breath, knowing it would be the last time he entered, and opened the door. Alexander walked over to the table and took his place behind it. He stared across at her, eyes still adjusting to the darkness. He hadn't seen the girl in a few days. Her skin was a mix of black and blue, the imprints of fingers dug into her forearms. Cuts ran down her exposed skin, and he could see burns crawling up to her neck. Her bones jutted out against her skin; her frame so much smaller than it had been. She was sagging to the left, her breathing labored.

Melody didn't look at him. The chains that bound her to the chair forced her body forward, but she was gazing blankly at the opposite wall. She hadn't reacted when he'd entered, didn't seem to recognize his presence. The guard behind her was standing ready, gun in hand, waiting for Alexander's signal.

"You know why I'm here," he said, looking down at the order of execution in his hand. "You have one more chance to—"

"No, I don't," she said. It made him jump. It was the first time she had spoken since their first conversation. Her voice was quiet, and hoarse from lack of use, but echoed in the cell. "I've been dead since you first started to look for me. I could give you names and locations for dozens of people and you would still kill me."

He looked up from the papers and Melody's eyes met his. It wasn't a challenge, but her gaze sent a chill up his spine. It was the same look Jordan had. The shadow of a person that was all but gone.

"One more chance to avoid more pain," he said, "how about that?"

"You need me dead." It was not a question. "The longer you keep me alive, the longer they keep fighting. Even then, it might not stop. You know that's not my fault, but you have to deal with it the only way you can. So, if you're going to kill me, just do it already."

"Do you really not care?" Alexander asked, leaning on the table so he towered over her. "Do you really want to die?"

"No." Her voice was flat. "But I don't have a choice in that, do I?" He glared at her one final time, listening to her breathing against broken and cracked ribs, before turning on his heel and walking out of the room.

"Do it," he called, slamming the door shut behind him.

He wanted to be out of the building, or at least up the stairs before it happened, but he'd barely shut the door before the sound of the gunshot echoed off the walls.

From the case file of Melody Karsh: July 2092-April 2093
August 2087

Dear Mom,

    I don't know why I'm doing this.

    I don't know what I hope for anymore. But thinking of not writing this to you…it didn't seem like a reality.

    Dad finally told me. Well, he screamed it at me, and then Liz actually told me. Sat me down. Showed me everything.

    And you—you will never read this. You will never, have never, read any of these.

    I guess you could say that I've known for a while. But it's so much easier, when the kids in school whisper behind their hands, or straight up call you a bastard traitor to your face, that it was for something. That you were safe, and happy, and free. But you're not.

    And I guess I can be happy, though that seems like a gross misuse of the word, that you are, at least, dead. You aren't rotting in a cell. You were never tortured, you never suffered. It ended quickly enough, I suppose.

    Did you think of me, when you knew it was over? Did you know? Did you have a warning? Did you die in the explosion, or were you one of the

271

injured that drowned? Why do I even want to know? It doesn't matter. You're dead. They're all dead. And you're not coming back for me, you're not coming to help me, to tell me it was all for something.

Why didn't you bring me with you? Liz says you never really answered that. That you just asked her to take care of me if something happened. She was staying behind, and if everything went okay, you were supposed to find a way to contact her. To tell her to follow. And what, you were just going to leave me behind? Leave me behind without her, without Leo? Just with Dad?

Fuck you. Fuck you for leaving and fuck you for dying and fuck you for never reading these words.

So why do I still wish I was with you? I wish I was with you. I wish I was anywhere else. This place is a suffocating hellish pit filled with disgusting, pathetic excuses for people.

You were my escape, my dream, and you've crushed it. You've taken it away from me. It never really existed in the first place.

What do I do now? Do I still write to you? Do I still pretend that this is real? Do I still ask you questions I don't have answers to and hope one will appear? Hope that you will pop back into the universe, just because I wished for it?

And now I'm fucking crying onto a piece of paper for someone who died thirteen years ago. Because you weren't brave enough to take me with you.

So, I guess, goodbye.

Melody

May 2093: VIII

"This was supposed to have stopped," Richard peered out of the window at the people lined up outside the station. "But clearly, traitors will hold onto their own ideological whims, even when there is no hope."

Covington wasn't sure why he had been called into this office again. A week after Karsh's execution, he'd put in his papers. He was leaving the force, going to try work at the DA's office doing case research. It had been heavily hinted that he should not leave, that the man who did (albeit, after too long a time) bring down Karsh and the head of the Free Melody movement, should stay on until the entire movement collapsed, until all the Myers were caught, but he'd had enough. He'd done his part. He was getting out while he was still lucky enough to be alive. It had been a week now, and he was just waiting to hear when he would be moving.

So, he wasn't sure why he was a part of a meeting with, not just Richard, but two Secret Service agents and three agents from Homeland Security.

"President Jamison wants to speak to them," one of the Secret Service agents said through gritted teeth. "Wants a press conference, of sorts. Wants to address them, publicly."

"We have all advised against it," one of the Homeland agents said, "but it's not up to us. He wants you there, Detective Covington."

"He... he what?"

"The President has requested you, and your wife, to be at the conference, by his side. He wants to congratulate you, in person, for being the one to apprehend the terrorists Melody Karsh, Leon Myers, and Derek Lin."

"But, I don't—"

"He has also spoken to Thomas Karsh, who has agreed to attend in exchange for returning to his former posting as a federal judge," the agent continued. "We expect you there, in full dress, to stand beside Our Dear Jamison. Is that understood?"

"Uh, yes, of course. When?"

"Tomorrow morning, 9 o'clock. We'll send a car at 7."

Covington nodded, feeling his knees giving out from under him. The agents filed out.

"They've denied your transfer request, as well," Richard said quietly. "Over at the DA's office."

Covington nodded again.

"I need to tell Jordan," he said, in a voice quite unlike his own, leaving the office as well.

———

She didn't fight him. Didn't react. Seemed to hear him. Asked the time and walked into her room. She'd taken the master bedroom, and he'd moved permanently to his office, his chair as comfortable as anything else for the few moments of sleep he managed to get. If there was anything positive to be said about the situation, it was that it did at least appear that she was eating a bit more. Her skin had begun to return to its original milky color.

He sat at his desk, the case file sitting in the corner. It was full to bursting, from all the evidence of the movement, her intake file, and interrogation notes. And, at the bottom, a stack of the letters. Absentmindedly, he pulled them out of the file, and scanned through a few. He had, at one point, chunks of them memorized. It hadn't been intentional, but he thought it would help him, when they finally found her. Another way to make her talk. He shoved the file aside, papers scattered across the floor, and pressed a hand over his eyes, willing the pictures in his mind to burn away.

The next morning, Alexander slowly drank his way through half a pot of coffee. He put on his dress uniform, and considered that he had no idea how he and Jordan were supposed to stand next to each other and pretend all was well and normal. He met her in the living room and saw her wearing a nice, professional, black dress, her hair tied in a bun at the back of her head. Under other circumstances, he would have told her she looked lovely. However, he merely held the door open for her and led her to the car that was waiting for them outside.

They rode in silence; the streets empty in the early morning hours. Covington looked out the window and saw what could only be described as a ghost town. More buildings were boarded up, less people were walking along the sidewalks, less people were sitting in the doorways of buildings, no neighborly conversations. The streets were still, and empty.

What was this? The quarantine? The protests? What had happened over the last few months? What had happened while he'd had his head in that file? The city was never this quiet, except during curfew, and even then, you could still hear...something. People in their homes, music from apartments, machines whirring, generators going, streetlights buzzing.

It felt unnatural.

275

Then they were turning on to Constitution Avenue, and an enormous crowd began to appear, spanning for blocks upon blocks. He felt Jordan's sharp intake of breath alongside him. He reached for her hand, but she quickly withdrew into her corner of the car.

The car wound its way along to the back of the building, and Secret Service officials formed a barricade around the Covingtons, sheltering them as they made their way through to the building. They were rushed inside, and through the marble halls.

"He'll be speaking at the Western entrance," an officer said, ushering them through. "Police have barricaded the steps, but given what you've told us, we can't ensure that they won't have access to weaponry. We've covered his platform with bulletproof glass."

"And us?"

"It's a high elevation point. We'll be close by too," the officer shrugged, "but you're here to support him, with all the risks that come with."

Covington swallowed.

Jamison was not as intimidating in person as Covington had expected. His dark brown hair had been slicked back, and his face looked full of energy. Even at 58, he still seemed so young, his smile radiating with a nervous, childish spirit.

"Alexander!" He greeted, with a bright grin, "So glad you're here, and this must be the lovely Jordan," he took her hand, and Covington could tell she was trying very hard not to jerk back from the touch.

"I believe you've met Thomas?" Jamison asked, gesturing to the man behind him. Covington nodded, and the two men exchanged a glance.

"Perfect. Here's how it's going to go. I'm going to introduce you, congratulate you, introduce Thomas, who will say a few words, and then I'll bring it home, and put this whole mess behind us. We'll end with the anthem, and you'll be back home before you know it." He smiled widely.

Covington could see a few flaws with this plan but was not going to say them aloud. Jamison, though he seemed friendly enough, was not the kind of man to have holes poked in his logic. So, Covington nodded, and gave him a weak smile.

"Excellent. I'm going to check in with the TV crews." Jamison said, "You three hold tight." The President hurried away, leaving Thomas, Alexander, and Jordan waiting in the hall.

"What are you going to say?" Jordan finally asked.

"That Melody was a traitor and deserved everything that came to her," Thomas said stiffly.

"Your own daughter?" Jordan asked, quietly.

"The moment she wrote those letters, she was no longer my daughter." Thomas didn't make eye contact with either of them but became very interested in a spot on the wall.

Covington could think of nothing to say to that, and clearly Jordan couldn't either, because she lapsed into silence, crossing her arms tightly in front of her.

The next hour was a blur, someone was tapping powder on Covington's face, adjusting the cap on his head, telling him where to stand when he reached the platform.

Then they were outside, and the crowd was deafening, a never-ending mass of covered faces.

Jamison held up a hand, as if to silence the crowd, but they continued to scream and chant and jeer. Covington saw Jamison's face twitch, his fingers tightening on the platform.

Alexander saw, towards the left of the crowd, a little boy

clinging to his father. The father was listening intently, but the boy was distracted. He was wearing a ski mask and black sweater, sitting on his father's shoulders, hands reaching out towards a pigeon that had flown through the crowd.

Towards the front, a group of younger people, teenagers, maybe, were all grouped together holding posters that bore the old FREE MELODY and WE WILL NOT BE SILENCED slogans.

Near the center of the crowd, two women were standing higher than the rest, presumably on a platform of some kind, holding each other tightly. They were not screaming, though one did have a megaphone in her copper–colored hand.

Jamison began to speak, though Covington was not paying attention. His eyes were drawn to the girls on the platform, and he could've sworn, though from this far away he had no way of knowing for sure, that the girl with the megaphone was staring back at him.

Thomas had finished his bit, to deafening boos from the crowd.

Jamison took the platform back.

"I know that Thomas's words sound harsh, but they are the truth. You, all of you, are fighting for the freedom of a girl who would have seen this country burn. That would have liked to see all that we have achieved these last fifty years go to waste, that would see you suffer for the sake of adolescent, misguided ideals." He spoke as if trying to console a crying toddler.

The girls on the platform looked at each other, a look so intense, it could have scalded anyone standing close by. One second, they were only staring, the next they were wrapped in each other's embrace. Then, a mess of fiery red hair was running away from the platform, a megaphone in her hand as well.

They both began to scream, and the girl still on the platform stuck her fist into the air,

"FREE MELODY!"

The crowd shouted back, repeating the words,

"FREE MELODY!"

It was like nothing Covington had ever heard before. Thousands of voices ringing through his ears, making him numb to everything else.

But, Jamison, as if had he expected this, merely smiled.

"Fine. If you want your precious Melody back, you can have her!" He yelled into the microphone.

Two Secret Service agents hauled a bag out from behind them, and, reaching up and over Jamison, tossed it over the balcony where they were standing.

Bones crunched and cracked. The mutilated, frozen body rolled down the steps, towards the front line of the police barricade, who moved away in revulsion.

Jordan held a hand to her face in horror, as the protesters crowded around to see.

A hush fell over the crowd as the message of who and what it was passed from front to back. Jamison stood proudly over them; a look of smug satisfaction plastered over his face.

Covington thought he had never heard a silence so loud.

And then the screaming began again.